I certainly wasn't disappointed.' Goodreads reviewer

'A uniq[illegible]ensely.
It reall[illegible]viewer

'What a powerful novel. I have read most of Cathy Glass's books and here she is writing under a new name Lisa Stone. I love the fact she has branched into crime thriller and I think she has done it really well.'

Goodreads reviewer

'I really enjoyed this. Interesting and captivating story line, great characters and easy to read – not the subject matter which is difficult, dark and pretty violent, but the style of writing. A gripping thriller.' Goodreads reviewer

'*The Darkness Within* is certainly a dark and gripping read and one that will win over new fans as well as old.'

Goodreads reviewer

'With areas that lead us to the dark depths of our own imagination, and parts so well described you could almost be in the same room, *The Darkness Within* is a struggle to leave unfinished.' Amazon reviewer

'Thank you Lisa Stone for making my long train journey feel like a ten minute ride! I will now look forward to your next book.' Amazon reviewer

'A great read. The author has a style of writing that makes the words just flow off the page and as the story develops it's a difficult book to put down as you want to know how it's all going to end.' Amazon reviewer

'Absolutely fantastic, I could not put it down. Cannot recommend this book highly enough. You will become addicted to this author.' Amazon reviewer

'An enjoyable chiller for the summer reading pile!'
Goodreads reviewer

'I loved the premise, it appealed to the horror/sci-fi loving side of me. Lisa understands human relationships and the ugly side of people very well, and this shone through in her work.' Amazon reviewer

'*Stalker* had me hooked from the beginning and I read it in one session!' Amazon reviewer

'*Stalker* got better and better, with a few surprises along the way. I'd highly recommend Lisa Stone.'
Amazon reviewer

'Had my heart pounding towards the end! Couldn't put it down.' Amazon reviewer

'*Stalker* is a completely and utterly gripping, engrossing read. What starts off as a case of voyeurism turns into something much darker and sinister, leading up to a fantastic ending. If you want a cracking good crime thriller, then I highly recommend this one.' Amazon reviewer

ABOUT THE AUTHOR

Lisa Stone lives in England and has three children. She has always been a writer from when she was at school, with her poems and articles featured in the school magazine. In her teens she began writing short stories, a few radio plays and novels. She finally made it into the bestseller charts with *Damaged* in 2007, which she wrote under the pseudonym Cathy Glass. Since then she has had twenty-seven non-fiction books published, many of which have become international bestsellers. Her first fiction novel, *The Darkness Within*, was published in 2017, followed by *Stalker* in 2018.

BOOKS BY LISA STONE:

The Darkness Within
Stalker

BOOKS BY CATHY GLASS:

Damaged
Hidden
Cut
The Saddest Girl in the World
Happy Kids
The Girl in the Mirror
I Miss Mummy
Mummy Told Me Not to Tell
My Dad's a Policeman (a Quick Reads novel)
Run, Mummy, Run
The Night the Angels Came
Happy Adults
A Baby's Cry
Happy Mealtimes for Kids
Another Forgotten Child
Please Don't Take My Baby
Will You Love Me?
About Writing and How to Publish
Daddy's Little Princess
The Child Bride
Saving Danny
Girl Alone
The Silent Cry
Can I Let You Go?

LISA STONE

THE DOCTOR

avon.

Published by AVON
A division of HarperCollins*Publishers* Ltd
1 London Bridge Street
London SE1 9GF

www.harpercollins.co.uk

A Paperback Original 2019

A catalogue copy of this book is available from the British Library.

ISBN: 978-0-00-832292-2

This novel is entirely a work of fiction.
The names, characters and incidents portrayed in it are
the work of the author's imagination. Any resemblance to
actual persons, living or dead, events or localities is
entirely coincidental.

Typeset in Bembo Std by Palimpsest Book Production Limited, Falkirk, Stirlingshire
Printed and bound in UK by CPI Group (UK) Ltd, Croydon CR0 4YY

This book is produced from independently certified FSC™ paper
to ensure responsible forest management.

For more information visit: **www.harpercollins.co.uk/green**

A big thank you to: my editor, Phoebe; my literary agent, Andrew; all the team at Avon, HarperCollins, and of course my readers. Your reviews and kind comments are very much appreciated.

We all want to live forever,
don't we?

Chapter One

It was pitch-black outside except for the small light coming from the outbuilding at the very end of their neighbours' garden. Emily could just make out the slither of light through the tall shrubs and trees that flanked their boundary fence. No moon or stars shone in the cloud-laden sky and no wind stirred the foliage. She liked their secluded garden, it had been one of the reasons she and Ben had bought the house, but sometimes it felt just a bit creepy. Especially at night.

'What do you think Dr Burman does in that outbuilding so late at night?' she asked Ben as she stood at their bedroom window, gazing out, before drawing the curtains. 'He's in there most nights, often until very late.'

'It's his man cave,' Ben replied. 'His escape. It can't be easy being a doctor all day, only to come home and have to look after your sick wife.'

'I suppose,' Emily said. 'But I do find him and his wife odd. We've been in this house over a year now and they just about manage to say hello. I've tried to be neighbourly, but she doesn't want to know.'

'He says a few words to me in passing,' Ben said, joining her at the window.

'I would have thought she'd be grateful for some company. I never see her go out or have any visitors.'

'Not everyone is sociable like you,' Ben said, kissing her cheek.

'And all those CCTV cameras at the front of their house,' Emily continued, reluctant to let the matter go. 'It's completely over the top for these houses. I mean, none of us is rich or famous.'

'Perhaps they're secret millionaires,' Ben laughed, then looked seriously at Emily. 'Em, are you sure you don't want to go back to work when your maternity leave ends? Is being at home really enough for you?'

'Yes, I'm sure,' she said, and turned to him with a smile. 'Thank you for giving me the chance. I want to stay with Robbie a while longer. I know money will be tight, but I really wouldn't be happy leaving him with a childminder all day until he's a bit older.'

'OK, I just wanted to make sure. I should be due a rise soon.' He kissed her cheek again. 'It's late, love, I'm going to hop into the shower now.'

As he left their bedroom, Emily turned again to the window and began to close the curtains. The light went off in Dr Burman's outbuilding, plunging their garden into complete darkness. Eleven-thirty. The same time as the night before. Why she should make a mental note of the time, she wasn't sure. It was something she found herself doing, as well as looking into their house and garden at any opportunity. It seemed important to keep watch. A gut feeling that it felt safer that way. Although had she told Ben, she was sure he would have laughed.

Chapter Two

BACK FROM THE DEAD!

A 15-year-old boy is to be frozen in the hope he can be brought back to life at a later date and cured of the disease that killed him.

The teenager, who cannot be named for legal reasons, is close to death from a rare genetic condition. Because he is a minor he needed the court's permission to have his body frozen using a process called cryonics.

He told the judge he had investigated cryonics and was convinced that it would give him the chance of life in years to come when a cure had been found. The judge agreed.

Following his death, his body will be taken from where he lives in England to the US, where it will be frozen and preserved at a cost of £40,000.

'Read it!' Dr Amit Burman snapped, throwing the newspaper onto his wife's lap. 'Perhaps you will believe me now a judge has ruled it's acceptable.'

Alisha picked up the newspaper, her fingers trembling, and read the article while he stood by waiting impatiently. She hated him when he was like this, all agitated. He scared her even more.

'No, I'm sorry,' she said, her voice slight. 'You know my feelings. I think it's unnatural, macabre, and against the laws of God and nature.'

'And where is your God now, you silly bitch?' Amit demanded, his eyes blazing. 'I don't see him saving your life. Only doctors and advances in medicine can do that, and research is not progressing fast enough.'

'But . . .' she began and had to stop as a coughing fit took hold. She picked up the glass of water she always kept within reach and took a few sips. Her hand shook.

'Don't you see there's nothing else the doctors can do for you?' Amit persisted, trying to lower his voice. 'You'd be making medical history. At the forefront of science. I'd do it if it was me.'

'This is not the answer,' she said quietly. 'And there is no proof it will work. I think that poor lad and his parents have had their hopes raised for nothing. It is immoral. All that money that could have been better spent. I would hate to think of being sealed in a metal drum rather than at peace in the earth. He won't even have a grave they can visit.'

'No! Because he won't be dead. You're not listening to

me!' He thumped the coffee table hard and her water slopped from its glass. 'He'll be in a state of suspended animation. Haven't you listened to a word I've said?'

'Amit,' she said, already recoiling from the blow that was sure to follow if she crossed him, 'I'm not doing it. I don't want to be frozen when I die and you can't make me.'

But the look in his eye as he raised his fist said that he could and would if necessary.

Chapter Three

'Welcome to the future. Welcome to ELECT – the gateway to everlasting life. I'm Owen, your guide for the day. You all have your information packs? Good. Sit back and make yourselves comfortable. I'll start by saying a bit about our organization, then we'll watch a short film of an operation in progress, followed by a tour of our facility.'

As Owen began his talk, Dr Amit Burman glanced around the room. There were twenty of them seated in rows of matching leather armchairs in this small lecture room. Of different ages, ethnicity, male and female, but united in the belief that they or a family member could be preserved after death and brought back to continue their life. Some were clearly already ill – one woman had a portable oxygen tank hissing quietly by her side, while others, like him, were planning ahead. Here was the proof that old age and terminal illness needn't be the end, that science would allow them to return and continue where they'd left off. Amit couldn't understand why there weren't more here. Twenty wasn't a huge number considering what was on offer.

He was taking notes, as were some of the others, although he thought he probably knew more than most – from being a doctor and all the research he'd done. He probably knew as much as Owen, he thought smugly, who was, after all, only their rep and tour guide.

Owen was winding up the introductory talk now and about to start the film. The room fell silent as he pressed the remote control to dim the lights, and moved away from the large wall-mounted screen. The film began with a smiling shot of the founder, welcoming them and explaining their mission statement. Then his voice continued on the voice-over as the film moved to the operating theatre.

Amit sat upright in his chair and concentrated hard. It was just like any high-tech operating theatre, and he was used to that. A dozen gowned-and-gloved staff: doctors, nurses, technicians, but with one significant difference – the patient was already technically dead. As the surgeon cut into the patient's artery to drain the blood, the camera moved to a discreet angle to protect the squeamish. But Amit didn't mind blood, not one bit. He saw it a lot in his job.

'The patient's blood is replaced by a chemical solution to stop ice crystals forming,' the commentary on the film continued. A mass of wires and tubes could be seen snaking from the patient to bottles, monitors and a computer. 'Then the body is gradually cooled down to minus 130 degrees Celsius before being submerged in the aluminium tank.' A shot of rows of aluminium tanks standing like soldiers in the storage facility, their motors running in the background and labelled with the dangerous chemical symbol. 'Inside the tanks, the temperature is minus 190 degrees Celsius. Colder than any place on earth and cold enough to stop the body from deteriorating. They are checked daily and will remain there until a cure is found when they will be brought back to life. Welcome to the future. Welcome to ELECT – Eternal Life Education Cryonics Trust.'

The film ended and the room remained very quiet as the enormity of what they'd seen stayed with them.

Owen slowly raised the lights and then returned to the front. The silence in the room continued until he spoke.

'Quite something, isn't it?' There were murmurs of agreement. 'I'm sure you have plenty of questions, so if you could raise your hands we'll take it in turns.'

'I'm sorry.' A middle-aged woman stood. 'You'll have to excuse me, this isn't for me. I won't waste your time further.'

'No problem. If you go to reception someone will see you out.'

Apologizing again, she hurried from the room, which left the group feeling united with the dissenter gone.

Hands waved in the air.

'Yes, sir,' Owen said, pointing to a man in the front row. 'Your question.'

'How do you check on them each day? Is there a window in the aluminium tank?'

'No, sir, we lift the lid of the tank. The liquid nitrogen needs topping up a little each day and this is done manually at the same time.'

The man nodded and Owen pointed to the next hand.

'Why are the patients suspended upside down in their tanks?' a young woman in her thirties asked.

'So that if there was an incident, the head would be the last to be affected. I would add that we haven't had an incident yet.'

He moved swiftly on, pointing to another person with their hand in the air.

'All this relies on electricity. What happens if there is a power cut?'

'We have our own emergency generating system. Also, the building is designed to withstand hurricanes and earthquakes.'

'Do you store family members?' a man asked.

'Yes, we have a husband and wife here already.'

Amit watched as an elderly lady raised her hand a little sheepishly.

'Yes, ma'am?'

'This may sound silly, but do you store pets?'

Idiot, Amit thought.

'Absolutely,' Owen said. 'It's not a silly question. We have two dogs and a cat. They are held in a separate room as their preservation tanks are that much smaller.'

'Is ELECT financially stable?' a middle-aged man asked. 'What you are doing here is obviously very long term. How can we be sure you will still be here in fifty or a hundred years' time?'

'We have insurance to cover bankruptcy but our organization is sound. You can view our accounts online.'

'Can loved ones visit the deceased here?'

'Yes, but we encourage them to visit their memorial stone instead. It's a more pleasant experience. All you can see here is a metal tank.'

'The film we've just watched said you also store body parts,' someone else asked. 'Why?'

'So that when we wake the patient we can replace any damaged or diseased organs.'

'I am right in saying that no one has ever been woken yet?' a man asked sceptically.

'That's correct,' Owen said, unfazed. 'No human at least. But we know the process works. Embryos have been frozen successfully for years using this method.'

Amit slowly raised his hand.

'Yes, sir, your question.'

'Do you always need the consent of the person to be preserved or do you accept the consent of their next of kin?'

'We always need the consent of the person,' Owen replied. 'The decision to be preserved is made in life, unlike organ donation that can be made by the next of kin after death.'

'And there is no way round it?' Amit asked. 'I mean, supposing the person is too ill to make the decision or not of sound mind?'

'Then it would be a matter for the court to decide.'

Amit was about to follow this up with another question when Owen's phone bleeped. 'Excuse me,' he said and read the message, then addressed the audience. 'That was to let me know a new patient is on their way. A fifteen-year-old boy from England. We have time for a quick tour, then the operating theatre will need to be prepared for his arrival. I'll answer any further questions as we go.'

Chapter Four

'Not again!' Amit shouted as he read the delivery card Alisha had left on the hall table. 'I told you a parcel was coming for me today! Couldn't you have answered the fucking door?'

'I'm sorry,' she said, anxiously watching him from the far end of the hall. 'I was upstairs and couldn't get down in time. They only ring once and then rush off and leave it with the neighbour.'

'That's the third time in two weeks, you silly cow, and that woman next door is fucking nosy.'

'I'm sorry,' Alisha said again. 'I'll serve your dinner so it's ready when you get back.'

Amit threw open the front door and went down their garden path, seething at her incompetence. He didn't ask much of his wife but got even less! Couldn't she do anything he asked?

Latching their garden gate behind him, he paused and breathed in the fresh air. He couldn't turn up next door in a rage. Others weren't as forgiving as Alisha.

At seven o'clock it was still light, but the air had an edge to it, a reminder that autumn wasn't far away. Amit liked the seasons, the changes, the cycle of nature, that spring came after winter with the promise of new life. It was a metaphor for his plans, he thought as he began along the pavement. Alisha had refused to sign up to ELECT, but that wasn't the end of it, oh no, not by a long way. He could – and would – succeed. Maybe not the first time; it would take trial and error, but he would practise until he got it right. Thanks to the internet, he could buy virtually everything he needed online, but it was worrying that his parcels kept being delivered next door.

He continued up the neighbours' drive. They didn't have a gate; their front garden and drive were open-plan. Ben Johnston and Emily King; they weren't married. He seemed OK and was content with 'good morning' and a few words, but she wanted to talk and kept inviting Alisha in for a coffee. He'd warned Alisha to stay away and he knew she wouldn't disobey him. He'd seen Emily King looking at their house, scrutinizing it as she walked by or drove past in her car. He doubted she suspected, he was too careful, and had given her no cause for suspicion. She'd do well to concentrate on her baby and housework. The elderly couple on the other side weren't a problem, but he couldn't ask them to take his packages, they were frail and took longer to answer their door than Alisha did.

Pressing the doorbell, he took a step back and waited. Their cat appeared from around the corner and meowed loudly, wanting to be let in. Amit detested cats or any domestic animal. As far as he was concerned, they served no useful purpose and just cost the owner money.

The door opened, the cat shot in, and even before he'd had a chance to say good evening, she was inviting him in.

'Come in while I fetch your parcel,' Emily said, smiling.

'Thank you, but I'll wait here.'

'You always say that,' she laughed and disappeared down the hall, leaving the door open. Why didn't she have his parcels ready in the hall? There was always this palaver and she knew he collected them on the day they were delivered.

Ben appeared. 'Hi, how are you?'

'Well, thank you.'

'Em won't be a minute. She puts your parcels upstairs for safekeeping. Robbie is crawling now and into everything.'

Amit assumed Robbie was their child and managed a polite smile.

'Here we go,' Emily said, reappearing and handing him the shoebox-sized package.

'Thank you,' he said stiffly. 'I'm sorry you've been troubled again.'

'No problem. How is Alisha?' she asked.

'As well as can be expected,' he said tightly.

'Please tell her I'd love to see her for coffee. If she isn't up to coming here, I could pop in with Robbie.'

'I'll tell her,' he said, with no intention of doing so.

Saying goodbye, he returned down their drive and the front door closed behind him.

The irritation he felt at Emily's bouncy, cheerful personality was quickly replaced by excitement. He knew what the package contained: another vital piece of equipment. As soon as he'd had dinner, he'd go to his workshop and continue.

Half an hour later, leaving Alisha at the sink washing the dishes, Amit let himself out the back door, briefcase in hand and the package under his arm, and went down their garden path. The sun was setting now, elongating the shadows of the house and trees across the lawn. He preferred this time to the harsh light of day, which seemed to highlight flaws and imperfections. At the end of the path, he unlocked the padlock on his workshop, switched on the light and, going in, bolted the door behind him. No one could see him now. Blackout blinds were permanently down at all the windows, and he'd covered the glass in opaque film. It was pure luck the house had come with this substantial outbuilding, built by the previous owner as a recording studio. Already soundproofed, well insulated and with electricity running from the house, it hadn't taken much for him to adapt it for its present purpose.

With a growing sense of pride and a little apprehension, Amit carefully took the bottle of anaesthetic from his briefcase. Opening one of the metal cabinets that stood against the wall, he placed the bottle on the top shelf with the other bottles of solutions. Drugs such as these were the only items he needed that couldn't be bought legitimately from the internet as they required a special licence. Doubtless he could have bought them illegally, but there would be no guarantee they were pure and hadn't been watered down or mixed with something to give the supplier more profit. The wrong or inferior drugs would be disastrous, and besides, no one at the hospital would notice the drugs were missing. As the anaesthetist, he was responsible for signing the drugs in and out of the operating room, and he took them one at a time.

Returning to the workbench, he slit open the package and took out the bag valve mask. It was in a sealed sterile package and was used for manually pumping air into a patient's lungs. It would be crucial that Alisha's brain received oxygen while he lowered her body temperature. He'd already bought a portable heart-lung-machine. He'd use the manual pump as he transported her body from the house down the garden to his lab and then hook her up to the machine.

Retrieving a pen from the bench, he flicked through his list of essential items and ticked off the bag valve mask. He placed it in the cabinet on the second shelf. The shelves were nearly full now: bottles, tubing, scissors, forceps, scalpels, speculums, retractors, wound dressings, and so on. Items he would need to operate. Not a standard operation of course. He'd do what ELECT were doing: drain the blood from the body and replace it with preservation fluid. Then he'd store Alisha in liquid nitrogen at minus 190°C until a cure for her condition could be found. He'd be at the forefront of medical science, making a name for himself, and finally his parents would be proud of him.

Taking his laptop from his briefcase, Amit set it on his bench and perched on the stool. He brought up the bookmarked web page and ordered an aluminium tank large enough to hold a body. He'd been surprised at just how easy it had been to find what he needed online, partly due to the trend in cryotherapy – a treatment where otherwise healthy people paid to stand in a tank at minus 90°C for two minutes. It was being used to treat minor conditions, including sports injuries and skin conditions, as well as supposedly generating a feeling of youthfulness and well-being.

Having entered his card details to pay for the tank, he arranged a delivery date, then went to another website and ordered half a dozen white mice. He'd only get one chance with Alisha, so he'd practise the procedure on small animals first, until he was confident he had everything right, just as any reputable scientist would.

His mobile phone rang, making him start. He took it from his pocket and saw the call was from the house. It would be Alisha. Reliant on him, she phoned if she needed him urgently. Irritated at being interrupted, he pressed to accept the call.

'What is it?' he demanded.

'I need your help quickly.'

He sighed. He had to go. 'I'm coming.'

Leaving everything as it was – he'd return later – he let himself out of his workshop.

The sun had set now and the lights were on in his and his neighbours' houses, including Ben and Emily's bedroom window. Emily was standing at the window looking out, watching him, as he'd seen her do before. His anger flared. Didn't the nosy cow have anything better to do! Standing there brazenly. She must know he could see her. Drawing his head in, he hurried down the path to the back door. She needed to be careful, if she knew what was good for her.

Chapter Five

While the surgeon, Mr Barry Lowe, worked on his patient's abdomen, Amit sat by her head and monitored her vital signs on the screen. Heart rate and rhythm, breathing, blood pressure, body temperature, oxygen level and body fluid balance were all normal. It was a relatively minor and straightforward procedure – an appendectomy – on an otherwise healthy thirty-year-old, so he didn't envisage any problems. In operations like this, once the patient was under there was little for him to do but monitor the green and blue lines that ran across the screen.

Being an anaesthetist was a thankless job, he thought now as he often had before. Anaesthetists were at the bottom end of medicine. A branch you went into when you didn't really want to be a doctor or didn't make the grade. He'd been forced into medicine by his pushy parents who saw it as the gold-standard career. That or being a lawyer, which had appealed even less. Having a doctor or lawyer in the family gave his parents respect in their community, and he hadn't had the guts to stand up to them. So with no calling to medicine or the law, and achieving poor grades at med school, he'd become an anaesthetist. Thankfully it involved very little contact with patients and required no bedside manner as they were unconscious, which suited him fine.

He watched Barry Lowe snip the infected appendix clear of the intestine and, with a sigh of satisfaction for a job well done, drop it into the stainless-steel bowl. He began closing the wound.

'How's your wife?' he asked Amit, glancing at him over his surgical glasses.

'As well as can be expected,' Amit replied stiffly. 'Thank you for asking.' Those he worked with were vaguely aware Alisha had a life-limiting illness, but he'd never told them the details. He kept himself to himself and used Alisha's illness as an excuse for not socializing with colleagues or attending hospital functions.

'Did you ever get in any agency help?' Barry Lowe asked, stitching the wound.

'It's not necessary,' Amit replied. 'She's still able to look after herself. I can manage.'

'Well, don't get burnt out, we need you here,' he said and put in the last stitch.

With the wound closed, Amit switched off the drugs that had kept the patient asleep and began the process of bringing her out of the anaesthetic. He turned down the nitrous oxide and turned up the oxygen. As expected, the patient's facial muscles began to twitch as she started to regain consciousness. Then she gagged and he removed the endotracheal tube from her throat.

The operation over, the team began to disperse. Barry Lowe removed his surgical gloves, dropped them in the bin and called goodbye as he left. The theatre nurses were clearing up, but, as usual, Amit stayed by the patient, monitoring her vital signs until she was responsive enough to speak.

'Can you hear me?' he asked her. 'Your operation is over.'

'Thank you,' came her groggy reply.

Satisfied, Amit flexed his shoulders. They were always stiff, even after a short operation. His patient was ready for the recovery room and one of the theatre nurses would take her through soon. They were occupied at present, facing away from him as they cleared up and swabbed down after the operation. Quietly and quickly, in a smooth, well-practised movement, he slid the unused bottle of anaesthetic from the trolley and tucked it into the pocket of his scrubs.

'Thank you for your assistance,' he said politely, moving away from the operating table. He always remembered to thank the theatre staff even if the surgeon forgot.

'Goodbye, Dr Burman,' the nurses returned.

The locker room was empty, good. Changing out of his scrubs, he transferred the bottle into his briefcase and headed for home where his true work awaited him.

Chapter Six

'Well? What do you think?' Emily asked Ben as soon as he came home from work. 'Have I been busy or what?' She led him to the patio doors.

'You have been busy,' Ben agreed. 'You've done a good job, Em. It must have taken you ages.'

'Most of the day. But it's saved us having to pay a gardener. I enjoyed it. Robbie was with me, playing in the leaves. Now he's toddling it's so much easier to do stuff as he can amuse himself.'

'Where is the little fellow?' Ben asked, looking around.

'In bed. He was exhausted. So am I. My arms are already aching from using the pruning shears. I've got muscles I didn't know I had.' She laughed. 'Obviously I couldn't trim the trees, they're too high, but the hedge looks neater.'

'It does. I hope Amit approves.'

'What's it got to do with him?' Emily asked. 'It's our hedge and on our side of the fence.'

'Whoa,' Ben said, raising his hands in defence. 'I just thought perhaps we should have mentioned it to him first. You really don't like that bloke, do you?'

'Even less so now,' she admitted. 'While I was up the ladder trimming the top of the hedge, I could see over and into the living room. Alisha was standing at their living room window watching me. I waved and signalled for her to come out, but she shook her head. She looked like a scared rabbit, Ben. I'm not kidding. I'm sure it wasn't that she didn't want to come out but more that she daren't. I think he could be abusing her.'

'Oh come on, Em, just because you don't like the guy doesn't mean he's a wife-beater.'

'Maybe not, but there was something in the way she stood there – like a trapped animal. I might have another go at asking her in. Anyway, glad you approve of my gardening. Let's eat. The spag bol is ready. Can you dish up while I try to get Tibs in? She hasn't been back all day.'

'Will do,' Ben said and kissed her cheek.

As Ben served dinner, Emily took the bag of cat treats from the cupboard. Opening the patio door, she called, 'Tibs! Tibs!' whilst shaking the bag. Usually by this time of day Tibs was home and wanting her dinner, but if not, then hearing the bag of treats brought her running from whichever garden she was in. 'Tibs, Tibby,' Emily called again, rattling the bag of treats, but there was no sign of her. 'I'll try again later,' she said at last. After closing the patio door, she took her place at the dining table. 'It's not like her. I wonder if she's got shut in somewhere. If she's not back by tomorrow, I'll knock on some of our neighbours' doors and ask them to check their sheds and garages.'

'I'm sure she's fine,' Ben said. 'It's a dry evening. She'll be off hunting.'

'Tibs! Tibby!' Emily called repeatedly at 9.30 p.m. She was outside now, standing on the patio and shaking the bag of treats. 'Tibs!' She paused and listened for any sound suggesting Tibs had heard and was starting her journey home. Sometimes when she strayed a long way she could hear her in the distance. The foliage stirring, her claws scraping as she clambered over wooden fences, going from garden to garden. Then, when she entered her own garden and saw Emily, she meowed loudly. But now the air remained still and eerily quiet, a clear November night, with a waxing moon rising in a cloudless sky.

Emily tried once more before she went to bed at 11 p.m. This time she put on her coat and went right down to the bottom of the garden, calling 'Tibs, Tibby!' The light in the outbuilding next door was on and with the hedge lower now she could see the top of the windows. As usual, the door was closed and the blinds were down, but even if they hadn't been it would have been impossible to see in for the film covering the glass. She had watched Amit stick it on about six months ago when he'd started using the building every evening and most weekends. What he did in there, she'd no idea, but if Tibs wasn't back in the morning, she'd ask him or his wife to check it and their garage for Tibs, although she doubted she was in there. Amit didn't hide the fact he hated cats. She'd heard him throwing stones at Tibs when she'd strayed into his garden – one of the reasons she didn't like the man. She'd read somewhere that people who were cruel to animals were invariably cruel to people too.

'Tibs! Tibs!' she called again. Giving the bag of treats a final good shake, she admitted defeat and returned indoors. All she could do now was leave the cat flap open and hope that Tibs found her way back during the night.

'We're going to find Tibs,' she told Robbie the following morning as she zipped him into his snowsuit. 'She hasn't come home. I think she's lost or got shut in somewhere.' The alternative – that she'd been run over – she pushed from her mind.

Robbie babbled baby talk and tried to say Tibs.

'Yes, that's right. Tibs. Good boy.'

Strapping him into his pushchair, she then tucked her phone, keys and the missing cat leaflets she'd printed into her coat pocket and left the house. It was mid-morning and she knew many of the houses would be empty, with their occupants at work. If there was no reply, she'd push one of the leaflets through their letter box. It had a picture of Tibs and gave her address, telephone number and asked them to check their shed, garage and any outbuilding in case she'd been shut in. It was of some consolation that Tibs had been microchipped and Emily's mobile phone number was engraved on a metal disc on her collar, so if someone found her dead or alive they would hopefully contact her. However, it was also possible, Emily thought, that Tibs had been lured into a home with food and hadn't wanted to leave. Cats were renowned for cupboard love. But when they let her out for a run, she'd return home.

'Tibs,' Robbie gurgled again.

Emily approached the task methodically and began with the house to the left of theirs. She knew the family would be at work, so she pushed one of the 'missing cat' leaflets through their letter box. She continued to the next house and worked her way up the street, crossed over at the end and began back down the other side. It was time-consuming, but those who were in were generally sympathetic. Some invited her in to check their garage or shed, others said they'd check as soon as she'd gone and hoped she found Tibs soon. The Burmans' house was the last and by now Robbie had grown restless, having had enough of sitting in his pushchair. 'Soon be home,' Emily reassured him and gave him a leaflet to hold.

It was only after she'd unlatched their gate and began up their path, giving her a clear view of the house, that she saw it.

'Bloody hell!' she said out loud. All the windows at the front of the Burmans' house were now covered with the same opaque film Amit had used on the windows of his outbuilding. He must have done it last night after she'd cut the hedges, for it hadn't been there yesterday. Although she'd cut the front hedge as well as the back, it still offered them privacy. The man was obsessed, she thought. Had he done the same to the windows at the back of the house? Surely not?

Robbie agitated again, squirming to get out.

'Last house,' she told him.

Glancing up at the CCTV, she pressed the bell on the entry system, then began folding one of the missing cat leaflets ready to push through their letter box. She doubted Alisha would answer the door; she hadn't for a long while. Robbie grumbled and struggled to get out, then to Emily's amazement, she heard a noise on the other side of the door and a key turn in the lock.

'Alisha, how nice to see you. How are you?' she asked, barely able to hide her surprise.

'I'm not bad, thank you.' She looked very thin and pale and had dark circles under her eyes, but she managed a small smile.

'I'm sorry to disturb you, but have you seen our cat, Tibs? She's been missing for twenty-four hours.'

'No, I haven't. But I'll ask Amit when he comes home tonight.'

'Thank you. Can you ask him to check your garage and that outbuilding in your garden in case she's got shut in?'

'Yes, of course.' She didn't immediately start to close the door as she had done before.

'Your husband has certainly gone to town on your windows,' Emily couldn't resist commenting. 'Is that because I trimmed the hedges?'

Alisha nodded, embarrassed. 'Amit worries about security with me in the house all day. We were broken into where we lived before.'

'Oh, I see. I'm sorry,' Emily said and felt slightly guilty. 'Has he done the back windows as well?'

'Yes, even the upstairs. I've told him we're safe here, it's a nice neighbourhood. But when he gets an idea into his head he won't listen to reason and there's no stopping him.' It was the most Alisha had ever said to her, Emily thought.

'I understand,' Emily said. Robbie began whinging. 'I've got to go now, but won't you come in for a coffee? I know I've asked you before, but I would really like it if you did.'

Alisha hesitated but didn't refuse outright. 'It's difficult. Amit wouldn't like it. He worries about me.'

'Does he have to know?' Emily asked. 'I mean, I'm not suggesting you lie, but couldn't you just pop round while he's at work? Or I could come to you?'

'No, it's better if I visit you,' Alisha said quietly. 'But I can't stay for long.'

'That's fine. Stay as long as you like. I'm free tomorrow afternoon.'

'OK. I'll try to come at one-thirty.'

'Great. See you then.'

And although Tibs hadn't been found yet, Emily went away feeling she had achieved something very positive indeed.

Chapter Seven

That night, Amit sat at the workbench in his lab and looked dejectedly at the dead rat; its pink eyes bulging and its mouth fixed open in a rigor mortis snarl. He couldn't understand why it and the mice had died. He'd only stopped its heart for fifteen minutes, during which time it had been submerged in ice. Animals and humans had survived much longer than that after accidentally falling into icy water; their hearts stopping as they entered a state of suspended animation and then restarting once resuscitated. In one case, a child had been brought back after being submerged in a freezing lake for two hours with no ill effect, so why couldn't he replicate that here?

He threw the rat into the bin with the others and dug his hands into the pockets of his white lab coat. He stared at the remaining two rats in the cage. Perhaps there was a genetic weakness in the rats and the mice he'd bought, for doubtless they'd been interbred. Yet the other animals he'd tried the procedure on had all gone the same way. He knew from a science journal that dogs in a lab had been brought back to life after three hours following this process, so what on earth was he doing wrong?

Resting his head in his hands, Amit studied his notes and calculations, then opened the cage door and took out one of the remaining rats. It squirmed and squeaked as if sensing its fate. He placed it on the bench beside the syringe that was ready with the solution and held it down firmly. He'd try a smaller dose this time – see if that made any difference. Then he suddenly stopped and looked up, deep in thought.

He'd been stopping their hearts artificially, but of course when a person or animal fell into icy water, their heart was still beating as they went under and suspended animation occurred. Patients who were going to be preserved for cryonics treatment were put on a heart-lung machine until they could be submerged in ice, so they, too, were technically alive. Was that the answer? Something so simple: the subject's heart had to still be beating. At what point the heart-lung machine was switched off, he didn't know. It wasn't a detail ELECT made public. But it was possible it wasn't switched off until the person was frozen, so they were frozen alive, although unconscious. Could that really be the solution? If he froze the rat while its heart was beating would that allow him to bring it back from the dead?

Amit temporarily returned the rat to its cage while he

took a bottle of anaesthetic from the top shelf of the cabinet and drew some into a syringe. It was the anaesthetic he used on his patients at the hospital and would keep the rat asleep while maintaining its vital signs. He would only need a drip or two as the rat's body was a fraction of the size of a human's. If this worked, he'd try the process on larger animals, just as scientists did in lab experiments, before he attempted it on a human.

After opening the cage, he picked up one of the rats – the other squeaked in protest at losing its mate – and set it on the workbench. Holding it firmly by the scruff of its neck, he injected the anaesthetic. Almost immediately, the rat's eyes closed and it relaxed, unconscious, on the bench. Taking his stethoscope, he listened to its heartbeat and then placed it into the ice bath and began monitoring its temperature. Normal body temperature for a rat was 37°C, the same as for humans. It quickly plummeted to 30°C, 24°C, and then down to 20°C. Circulatory arrest happened at 18°C and its heart stopped beating. The rat's temperature continued to drop to zero and further still. When it reached minus 90°C, following the procedure used at ELECT, Amit took a scalpel and made a small incision into the rat's jugular vein and drained off half its blood into a bottle. He then injected preservation fluid into the vein – the same solution used for preserving organs for transplant – and returned the rat to the ice bath.

He felt hot, clammy and anxious, for despite carrying out similar procedures before, if he failed now he'd made the adjustment he'd no idea what else he could do. Failure wasn't an option.

The rat's temperature continued to fall down to minus 130°C. It was at this point in the cryonics procedure the body was lowered into the tank of liquid nitrogen and stored at minus 195°C. But Amit waited five minutes and began to reverse the process, gradually raising the rat's temperature and then returning its blood. At 37°C he tentatively placed his stethoscope on the rat's chest and listened for any sign of a heartbeat. Nothing. Not the faintest murmur. He massaged the rat's chest, hoping to stimulate its heart, and listened again. Still nothing. It had gone the same way as all the others! Whatever was he doing wrong?

He stared at the lifeless body of the rat and was about to give up and throw it in the bin when he thought he saw one of its toes twitch. Returning his stethoscope to its chest, he listened hard, his breath coming fast and low. It wasn't his imagination! He could hear the very faintest murmur of a heartbeat. He massaged the rat's chest again and listened. Yes, there it was, stronger now. The irregular beats joining to form a steady rhythm. Then the rat gasped its first breath. He'd done it! He'd really done it. He could barely contain his excitement.

But scientists never rely on one positive result, he reminded himself, so he would repeat it on the last rat and then on larger animals. How proud his father would be if he knew his son was about to create immortality.

Chapter Eight

'Come in,' Emily welcomed Alisha the following afternoon as she opened her front door. 'So pleased you came. I wondered if you would.'

'Thank you, but I can't stay for long,' Alisha said straight away, slightly out of breath from walking from next door.

'Come through into the living room. We're in here.'

'We?' Alisha asked, stopping still in the hall.

'Yes. Robbie and me,' Emily laughed. 'Don't look so worried.'

'Oh, I see,' Alisha replied and cautiously followed her into the living room. Emily noticed how tense she was, as if attending an interview rather than a neighbour's for coffee.

'Do sit down. Make yourself at home,' Emily encouraged. 'What would you like to drink?'

'Just a glass of water please.'

'Sure?'

'Yes. Thank you.'

Emily left Alisha in the living room perched on the edge of the sofa and went into the kitchen to pour two glasses of water. Robbie toddled after her. Returning, she set the glasses on the occasional table within reach. 'So how are you?' she asked.

'Not too bad, I manage.'

'You know if you ever need anything to let me know. I'm on extended maternity leave.'

'That's kind, but Amit sees to everything I need.'

'OK,' Emily said. She took a sip of her water and wondered what to say next. The poor woman seemed so ill at ease. 'Good boy,' Emily told Robbie who was playing with his toys, then smiled at Alisha. An awkward silence fell, and then Emily asked, 'You don't have children?'

Alisha shook her head.

Another silence before Emily asked, 'Are you sure you wouldn't like a hot drink?'

'No, thank you. Did you ever find your cat?'

'No. But she's microchipped and my mobile number is on her collar, so I'm still hopeful someone will spot her and contact me.'

Alisha nodded.

'I miss her,' Emily said. 'She's like one of the family. We had her before we had Robbie.'

Alisha gave another small nod. 'I'd like a pet, but Amit won't have one.'

'Oh? Why is that?' Emily asked, seizing the chance to make conversation.

'He doesn't like them. Says they carry germs. My immune system is weak, so I have to be careful.'

'I see. Although I think if pets are well looked after they don't carry many germs, do they?'

'I don't know, but Amit won't change his mind.' As Alisha took a sip of her water, Emily saw her hand tremble.

'So Amit looks after you and treats you well, then?' she asked.

'Yes.'

'What does he do in that shed every evening? He's often still in there when I go to bed.'

'Research,' she replied without hesitation.

'Research on what?'

'The disease I have. It's a rare genetic condition and hardly any research has gone into finding a cure. We lost our only son to it five years ago.'

'Oh, I'm sorry. I'd no idea.'

'We don't really talk about it. It's too upsetting, especially now I'm going the same way.'

'I am sorry,' Emily said again and felt even more uncomfortable. 'Do you have friends and family who can help and support you?'

'A few.'

Robbie came over and tried to engage Alisha by placing a toy on her lap. She removed it straight away and set it on the floor. Then stood. 'Thank you for the drink, but I must go now.'

'Really, already? You've only just arrived.'

'I can't be away from home for long.'

Was it Robbie's presence, after losing her own son? Emily wondered as she saw Alisha to the door. But if that was the reason for her sudden departure, why come at all? She had known she had a child.

'If it's difficult for you to go out, perhaps I could come to you next time?' Emily offered as she said goodbye. But Alisha was already heading down the path, eager to get home.

Chapter Nine

'Fifteen minutes, that was all,' Emily told Ben as they sat at the dinner table that evening. Robbie was in his highchair.

'You made a good impression then,' Ben laughed.

'I wondered if it was Robbie, you know, reminding her of the son she lost, but I don't think so. She seemed on edge from the start and when I suggested I went over there next time, she blanked me.'

'I don't think she wants to be your best friend, Em,' Ben said dryly. 'At least you tried. Would you like to hear my news now?'

'Yes, of course. I'm sorry, I've been talking non-stop since you walked in. I've been a bit short of conversation today.'

'I've got the promotion – marketing manager for the whole of the South East. It comes with a decent pay rise.'

'Well done!' Emily cried, delighted. 'That's fantastic. I'm so proud of you.' Leaning across the table, she planted a big kiss on his cheek. Robbie chuckled.

'It'll mean more travelling, but I'll keep it to the minimum. I don't intend to leave you and Robbie alone any more than I have to.'

'We'll be fine, don't you worry. I'm just glad the company has recognized your worth.'

'I thought we could celebrate at the weekend. Go out for a meal somewhere nice, if your parents are free to babysit.'

'Great. I'll phone them just as soon as we've finished dinner. All we need now is for Tibs to return and my week will be complete.'

Ben's smile faded. 'Em, you realize Tibs might not come back. I mean, if she's been run over. She's been gone some time now.'

'I know, but at present I'm staying with the hope she's in someone else's house.'

He nodded and wiped Robbie's mouth. 'Where would you like to go to eat? You decide.'

'There's the new Italian on the high street, or The Steak House – that's always reliable. Or we could drive out to The Horse & Carriage . . .'

Twenty minutes later, Emily had decided on L'Escargot, a French restaurant they'd been to once, prior to having Robbie, and had been wanting an excuse to return. Having cleared away the dishes, she went through to the living room to phone her parents to see if they were free to babysit at the weekend, while Ben took Robbie upstairs to get him ready for bed. Her parents' answerphone was on, as it often was now they'd both retired and were out enjoying themselves. Emily left a message. They'd return her call either this evening or, if they were back late, first thing in the morning. She could rely on them; they loved babysitting Robbie, their only grandchild.

As she replaced the handset, she heard the letter box snap shut. Seven-thirty, too late for regular post. It was probably a circular. Leaving the living room, she crossed the hall from where she could hear Robbie chuckling loudly in the bathroom as Ben changed him. There was a brown envelope lying face down on the mat. She picked it up. It held something – something firm, more than just paper. Turning it over, she read the writing on the front. *Ms King, I found this in the road. I think it belongs to you.* Signed, *Dr Amit Burman.*

The formality was weird and why not knock and give it to her in person? Emily assumed it was a small item of Robbie's. He was always jettisoning his belongings from the pushchair as she wheeled him along the pavement – small toys, socks, mittens and boots in winter. Sometimes she spotted them straight away, other times she found them on their next trip or a neighbour returned them, and sometimes they just disappeared. She supposed it was good of Dr Burman, although it didn't feel like a sock or toy of Robbie's. Opening the envelope, she saw straight away what it was. Her stomach churned; she felt sick with fear. Not something of Robbie's, but Tibs' red felt collar. Her mouth went dry and her heart raced. No mistake, there was her mobile number engraved on the metal tab and the bell was missing. Tibs had lost the bell a while back and Emily had never got around to replacing the collar.

'Ben!' she cried, running upstairs. 'Ben!'

Hearing the panic in her voice, he came onto the landing with Robbie in his arms half-dressed. 'What is it?'

'Look! Burman has just pushed this through the letter box.' She held out the collar and envelope for him to see, her voice unsteady and her hand shaking. 'What does it mean and why didn't he knock?'

'Perhaps he didn't want to disturb us. It must have come off Tibs. Cat collars are designed to come off if the cat gets caught so they don't choke.'

'I know, but it says he found it in the road. Does that mean . . . ?'

'I'm sorry, Em, love, but it was decent of him to return it.'

'But we'd have seen her body. Perhaps she slipped it and is still alive, but why hasn't she come home? I need to know where and when he found it. I'm going to see him now.' She tore downstairs.

Ignoring her coat in the hall and wearing her slippers, Emily rushed out the front door and down the drive, still clutching Tibs' collar and the envelope. A damp November mist had descended, thickening the darkness. The alarm box just below the eaves of the Burmans' house flashed like a warning beacon. Throwing open their front gate, Emily slowed her pace and walked to their front door. It was very dark here, the light from the street lamp mostly blocked by the large evergreen trees and shrubs at the front.

She pressed the buzzer and waited, the cold and damp seeping into her. The downstairs lights were off and only one shone from an upstairs window, faint behind closed curtains and the opaque film now covering all the glass. She pressed the buzzer again. Someone must be in. Alisha never went out and Amit's car was on the drive. She glanced up at the CCTV camera trained on the front door and shivered. She should have grabbed her coat.

A light went on in the hall, a door chain rattled and a key turned in the lock. Amit Burman opened the door, the top button on his shirt undone and his tie loosened at the neck. She felt a familiar stab of unease, something in his expression, although she couldn't say what.

'I'm sorry to trouble you,' she began, trying to meet his gaze. 'You pushed this through our letter box just now.' She held up the envelope and collar.

'I did. It is yours?'

'Yes, but where did you find it?'

'In the road outside my house.'

'But you didn't see Tibs, our cat?'

'Clearly not, or I would have told you.' His eyes narrowed to a patronizing smile. It was then Emily realized what she found so unsettling in his expression. His eyes were completely different colours. The iris in one eye was brown while the other was green. 'The correct term is heterochromia,' he said. 'My vision is normal.'

'I'm sorry,' she stammered, embarrassed and trying not to stare.

'It's not a problem. We're all different, aren't we? You told my wife your cat was missing, so I thought you'd want its collar back. She's resting. She's exhausted from visiting you.' He held her gaze, his green eye seeming to bore into her. 'Of course, she would tell me of her visit. We have no secrets. I'm only concerned for her health and well-being.' The tone in his voice made it feel like a threat. 'Is that everything?'

'When did you find Tibs' collar?' Emily asked.

'About an hour ago, when I came home from work. Now, if that's all, I must go. I have to see to my wife.'

'Yes, of course.'

Emily supposed she should have thanked him, but the door had already closed. She walked back down his path, looking left and right and into the foliage for any sign of Tibs. Then in the gutter. She must be dead. If she'd been alive and had slipped her collar outside the Burmans' house, then she was close enough to find her way home. The most likely explanation for her collar being in the road was that she'd been run over, perhaps separating from her collar in the accident. If someone in the street had found Tibs' body there was a chance they may call, as her number was on the leaflets she'd pushed through letter boxes. Otherwise she might never know, for she doubted anyone would bother to take a dead cat to have its microchip read. If there was still no sign of Tibs by the weekend, she'd have to accept she was dead.

Chapter Ten

'I disagree,' Amit said forcefully. 'The process of cryonics has already been shown to work on animals in laboratories. They have survived three hours using existing medical technology. Even longer periods if the preservation solution is continuously circulated.'

Mr Barry Lowe was staring at him, as was the student doctor.

'You seem well-informed,' Lowe said. 'But three hours isn't a hundred years. It's a fantasy playing on people's fears of death. Humans have been searching for immortality since they became intelligent enough to realize that one day they would die. It used to be just religion that offered immortality, but now this pseudoscience has got in on the act.' He paused to concentrate on what he was doing – a hernia operation. The discussion had begun after he'd asked if anyone had seen the documentary on television the night before on cryonics and had quickly become heated.

'You can't put religion and cryonics in the same category,' Amit retaliated. 'And it doesn't matter if it's three hours or a thousand years. At minus 190 Celsius there is no cell degeneration.'

'And you can be sure of that?' Lowe asked sceptically, glancing up at him. 'There is no proof whatsoever. Those frozen bodies could be mush when they are thawed.'

'Also, cell degeneration will have already occurred,' the student doctor put in. 'My cousin is a doctor at Saint Claire's where that fifteen-year-old boy died. It was over an hour before he was put on ice.'

'That's appalling!' Amit cried passionately, unable to hide his feelings any longer. 'It's a breach of our code of ethics.'

'That's a bit strong,' Lowe said. 'The boy was dead.'

'Temporarily, and his wishes were that he should be frozen. The system failed him.'

'Why the wait?' Lowe now asked the student as he began to close the wound.

'My cousin said the instructions were not to touch him as it needed someone trained from ELECT who knew what to do.'

'Who knew how to stabilize him,' Amit clarified.

'His mother phoned a member of ELECT,' the student continued. 'But he got stuck in traffic.'

Lowe laughed cynically. 'The traffic always gets you in the end!'

'I assumed the boy was put on a heart-lung machine during that time?' Amit said.

'No. The staff didn't realize he should be. He was dead and his organs weren't going to be used for transplant.'

Amit shook his head. 'Appalling. What a waste. When I . . .' he stopped. 'It's crucial the patient is kept on a heart-lung machine until intravenous lines can be put in and protective medications administered.'

'You know a lot about it,' Lowe said. 'Is bringing people back from the dead a hobby of yours?'

The theatre staff laughed.

Amit fought to retain control. Ignorant lot. What did they know? But he had expected better of Lowe, a surgeon. He'd be laughing on the other side of his face one day when he showed them what could be achieved. Just you wait and see, he thought.

Chapter Eleven

'Let go of me!' Alisha cried in pain as Amit's fingers dug into her arm. 'You're hurting me.' He was half pushing, half dragging her out of the living room and through the hall. 'What are you doing? I haven't done anything wrong. Where are you taking me?'

'The cloakroom,' he snarled.

'No! I don't like being shut in there. I'll be good. Please. No.' The room didn't have a window and Amit had changed the lock so it could be locked from the outside. Alisha knew from experience what it meant to be shut in there – sometimes for hours at a time. She struggled and tried to free her arm, but his grip tightened. 'Please,' she begged.

'If you're good and stay very quiet, I'll let you out after he's gone.'

'Who? No, don't, please. I can go upstairs and be quiet if you want.'

He dragged her the last few paces and pushed her in. Slamming the door shut, he locked it.

'Amit! Let me out. Please, I promise I won't look.' She banged on the door.

'Shut up now or I'll leave you in there all night.'

Alisha bit into her bottom lip and tried not to cry.

Perspiration stood out on Amit's forehead as he hurried to the back door, let himself out and then rushed down the sideway. He unpadlocked the gate. The lorry was just parking outside, half an hour fucking early! If it had arrived when it was supposed to, he'd have had Alisha sedated and out of the way in plenty of time. He had taken the day off work to receive the delivery and a couple of minutes ago the driver had texted to say he'd be with him shortly. There was no way he could risk Alisha seeing – the size and shape would raise her suspicions. He hoped the nosy cow next door wasn't watching. He needed to get the cylinder down the sideway and into his lab as quickly as possible.

'Delivery for Dr Burman,' the lorry driver called from the pavement, reading from his e-Pod.

'That's me, but you're early.'

'Do you want me to come back later then, mate?'

For a second Amit thought he meant it and was about to say yes.

'Where's it going?' the driver asked. 'It's big.'

'The building at the very rear of my garden. It will fit down the sideway.'

'I've heard that before; I'd better take a look.'

Amit led the way down the path.

'It'll be a tight squeeze, but I'll give it a go,' the driver said. 'What's plan B?'

'Through the house,' Amit said. 'But it will fit down here. I know, I measured it.'

'With the packaging?'

Amit felt his stomach sink. He should have thought of that. How stupid! He'd taken the dimensions of the cylinder from the website and had checked them against the width of the sideway. He could have kicked himself.

'If it won't fit down here, it will have to go through the house and out through the patio doors,' he said. But with Alisha not sedated that ran the risk of the driver hearing her if she began screaming and shouting again.

Amit followed the driver out to the front and then watched nervously as he climbed into the back of the lorry. He reappeared a few moments later with his precious package balanced on a hand truck. It was huge and, clad in padding, overhung the edges of the truck, but at a glance it could pass as a very large hot-water cylinder, Amit thought. His heart raced as the driver slowly lowered the tailgate and then pushed the hand truck off, then paused and waved up at the neighbour's house. Amit followed his gaze. The bloody woman next door was holding her son up at the window to look!

'All kids like big lorries,' the driver said amicably as he pushed the truck up the drive.

Amit hurried down the sideway, which thankfully was

on the opposite side of the house to Emily, and out of her view. He watched and waited, his breath coming fast and shallow as the driver began inching the package in through the side gate. Pressing the cladding in to ease it through, it just fitted.

'Thank God,' Amit said, relieved once it was clear, and hurried ahead to the outbuilding. The driver followed.

'You want it in there?' he asked, surprised.

'No. Leave it outside.' Amit pointed to a spot to the left of the door.

'You sure, mate? It's not so heavy, but it is bulky. I can put it inside if you like.'

'No. It's fine there.'

The driver manoeuvred the cylinder from the trolley and stood it where Amit pointed, then passed him his e-Pod to sign for the delivery.

Glancing anxiously at his neighbours' houses, Amit quickly saw him out and padlocked the side gate behind him. He returned down the garden path to his lab and unlocked the padlock there, then took out the two sheets of hardboard he'd previously cut to size to use as ramps. He'd had it all planned days ago. He placed them either side of the step and then, encircling the cylinder with his arms, he began walking it forward. Small measured steps, as if dancing with a partner, up one side of his makeshift ramp, over the top, down the other and into the security of his lab.

Relieved, he quickly closed the door. He'd done it. The most important item he needed to continue had been safely delivered.

Chapter Twelve

Inside the house, Alisha sat on the floor in the cloakroom, cold and sick with fear, willing Amit to return and release her, but at the same time dreading having to face him. His behaviour was becoming more and more alarming with each passing week, frighteningly so now. She no longer recognized the man she'd married. But had she ever really known him, even back then? She doubted it. She'd had to trust him and, as far as she'd known, they'd had no secrets, but now most of his life excluded her. She was sorry she'd failed to give him healthy children, but did she really deserve the punishment he meted out? The abuse – verbal and physical. It was frightening. She spent most of her time terrified of him. And the grim determination on his face when he'd locked her in here said he would stop at nothing to make her do as he wanted.

She rubbed her wrist and looked at her upper arm. Bruises were already forming under the skin. She bruised easily now, just as their son, Daniel, had done as the disease progressed. His tissue breaking down, blood capillaries rupturing, his skin sloughing off. Even when she bathed him and was so gentle, he still bled.

It was a cruel disease and she could understand why Amit had become obsessed with finding a cure, just as other parents of children with rare genetic conditions had. Michaela and Augusto Odone had produced Lorenzo's Oil. She'd seen the film of the same name. Years of research and then a breakthrough. Perhaps Amit might find a cure, but there was no excuse for treating her as he did. He was so unpredictable and violent.

She knew he had a right to blame her for the compromises he'd had to make now she'd fallen ill too. Once she died he would be free to marry a healthy woman who could give him normal children, for she doubted he would find a cure in time to save her. She thought he doubted it too. Hence all that nonsense about freezing her until a cure had been found. What a macabre thought! She'd been shocked that he'd even considered it. It made her skin creep. She couldn't imagine anything worse – replacing her blood with preserving fluid and then suspended upside down in a cylinder when she should be at peace in the earth. It was the stuff of nightmares. Yet many had signed up to it and had paid huge amounts to be stored. Thankfully, Amit had finally taken no for an answer and had put away the literature and stopped talking about it.

But his behaviour was even worse now. Sometimes injecting her to sedate her or locking her in. But why? Why was she in here and for how long? It was the third time he'd shut her in the cloakroom. She wished she had someone to confide in. Estranged from her parents, she knew they wouldn't sympathize. Not after everything that had happened between them and Amit. She could hear her mother's admonishing voice: *you've made your bed, so you'll have to lie in it.*

It had crossed her mind that maybe Emily next door would be a good confidante. She wondered if she might even suspect that Amit didn't always treat her right. She seemed perceptive and, being at home with her child during the day, had perhaps seen things the other neighbours hadn't. And the way Emily kept inviting her into her house, and when she'd finally accepted, she'd asked if Amit looked after her and treated her well. A pity she hadn't had the courage to admit that Amit treated her badly and she was petrified of him, for she doubted Emily would invite her again, not after staying such a short time and leaving so abruptly. Her behaviour had been rude, but she couldn't tell Emily the real reason she had only stayed fifteen minutes. Pity. It would have been reassuring, comforting, to have her knowing, even looking out for her.

Chapter Thirteen

'What do you make of this?' Emily asked Ben as they settled in front of the television to watch the evening news. She clicked on the video clip, passed her phone to him and waited while he watched it.

Ben laughed. 'Goodness knows. But I hope he didn't see you take it. It won't help neighbourly relations.' He handed back her phone.

'He was too busy with what he was doing to see me,' Emily said. 'I heard the lorry at the front while I was changing Robbie. He was all excited when I showed him. When the driver took that thing off the lorry and wheeled it down their sideway, I couldn't resist going into our bedroom for a better view. Why would you want that in your shed?'

'No idea. It looks like a water cylinder. Perhaps he likes a bath down there,' Ben joked.

'It's the right size and shape to hold a body.' Emily shuddered.

'Perhaps he's going to do you in,' Ben teased.

'Or his wife,' Emily said. 'Seriously though. Don't you think it's odd?'

'I guess. But each to his own.'

They fell silent as the main news came on. They always tried to watch the news in the evening once Robbie was in bed. There was the usual depressingly familiar update on war-torn Syria, rape allegations against another prominent figure, doom and gloom about the world economy and the persistently high levels of city pollution. After the UK and international news, the channel went through to regional news, where a female reporter was standing beside a taped-off area in Coleshaw Woods.

'A shocking and grisly discovery was made here early this morning by a man walking his dog,' the report began. 'A grave containing more than fifty animals including cats and dogs was unearthed when the man's dog began digging. The owner called the police and they and the RSPCA – Royal Society for the Prevention of Cruelty to Animals – have taken away the carcasses for examination. One line of enquiry is that this could be part of a gruesome satanic ritual, as all the animal bodies appear to have been drained of their blood.'

'Oh no!' Emily cried, shocked and disgusted, her hand flying to her mouth.

'There are some nutters around,' Ben said.

The man whose dog had dug up the animals was

now interviewed. 'It's left me completely shocked,' he said. 'I took a different route through the woods this morning, a part that not many use in winter, and suddenly Rex began digging frantically in that spot.' He pointed to the area behind them. 'He dug up a few mice first and I thought they might have died naturally, but then he dug up part of a rabbit, a cat and a dog and I realized it was a graveyard.' He said again that the incident had left him badly shaken; he was an animal lover and would hate the thought of his pet ending up like this. The reporter said that other possible reasons for the animals being there were that they had come from a laboratory or a veterinary practice that had dumped the animals rather than pay for the correct disposal, which was illegal.

Emily felt sick. 'You don't think Tibs could be among them?'

'I doubt it,' Ben said. 'Coleshaw Woods is over half an hour's drive from here. It'll be as the reporter said – a lab or vet avoiding the costs of disposing of them properly. Gruesome all the same.'

The camera went to another local news item and Emily took her iPad from the coffee table. As Ben continued watching the news, she began searching online to see if there were any more details about the animals found in Coleshaw Woods. There was nothing beyond what the news report had said. A shame there wasn't a telephone number for those worried about their pets to phone, she thought, similar to the helpline number given out for relatives after a major disaster. She closed the tablet and sat with it on her lap, half watching the news. Ben was probably right, but it didn't stop her worrying. Bad enough that Tibs hadn't returned and they'd had to accept she was probably dead, but far worse if she'd met her end sacrificed as part of a sadistic cult ritual.

She went cold. Who knew what Tibs might have suffered in her final hours. The news item had said the animals had been drained of blood. How? Why? Had they been alive? She tried to push these thoughts from her mind, but they returned. Again and again. There were some really evil people out there.

That night, Emily dreamt she heard Tibs meowing, crying out for them as she was held down and gruesomely slaughtered. She woke in a cold sweat. Coleshaw Woods was half an hour's drive away as Ben had said, trying to reassure her, but that wasn't far, not really.

The following morning as soon as Emily was up and Ben had left for work, she checked online to see if any more details had been added to the news story. The local *Gazette* had covered the story, but it was now old news so it had been pushed off the first page. There were no further details.

She'd arranged to meet a friend, Hannah, for lunch. She lived locally, had a similar-aged child and had also seen the news item. It wasn't long before they were discussing it and Emily confided she feared Tibs might be among the dead animals.

'I think it's unlikely,' Hannah said. 'I mean, how would Tibs have got all the way over there?'

'Unless someone grabbed her close to home – from our street?'

'I think they've come from a lab, probably been bred there or bought for experimenting on. Poor things,' Hannah sighed. Emily knew she was trying to reassure her, but it didn't help any more than Ben's words had.

'Tibs was microchipped,' Emily said. 'I've been wondering if any of those animals were.'

'It didn't say on the news, but if they've come from a lab they won't be.'

'But if they haven't, they could be people's pets,' Emily persisted. 'Dogs run off and you can't watch cats the whole time.'

'It's obviously worrying you, so if you think there's a chance Tibs might be among them, why not phone and ask if any were microchipped?'

'Yes, but who would I phone?'

'The RSPCA, I guess, or our local police station. If it's not them, then they should know who's dealing with it.'

Robbie was asleep in the pushchair by the time Emily arrived home and she quietly parked him in the hall. It was virtually impossible to have a phone conversation when he was awake, so she grabbed the opportunity to make the call now. Closing the living room door so she wouldn't disturb him, she used her mobile to google the number for the RSPCA.

The customer services number went through to a recorded message that offered various options including animal emergencies, but none of them were relevant for what she needed to ask, and included the suggestion of looking at their website. She cut the call, googled the number of the local police station and pressed to call. Another answerphone message that began by saying if it was an emergency to hang up and dial 999, if not stay on the line. She waited and was then presented with more options, the last of which was to hold to speak to someone in person.

Five minutes later, her call was answered and she explained she was phoning about the animal bodies found in Coleshaw Woods. The officer said he was unfamiliar with the case but would find out who she needed to speak to. He came back on the line with another number for her to phone. She thanked him, tried the new number, but an answerphone clicked in inviting her to leave a message. At the same time, Robbie woke; frustrated, she knew she'd have to try again later.

The rest of the day disappeared in keeping Robbie amused, housework and then preparing dinner. Ben was late home, tired, and had to catch an early train in the morning. They watched the news, although there was nothing more about the animals in Coleshaw Woods and Emily didn't mention it again.

The following morning she kissed Ben goodbye and saw him off at the door in her dressing gown, grateful that she didn't have to leave for work on a cold frosty morning. It was only when Robbie had his lunchtime nap that Emily was able to use the phone again uninterrupted. She called the number she'd been given by the officer the day before and this time it didn't go through to answerphone but call waiting. She was third in the queue. Her initial enthusiasm for trying to find out if Tibs could be among the animals in Coleshaw Woods was waning and she wondered if she was wasting police time – phoning about a missing cat when they would have many other more important crimes to solve. When it was finally her turn, she began with an apology. 'I'm sorry, this is probably nothing, but my cat is missing. I saw the news report about the animals found in Coleshaw Woods and was given this number to phone.'

'Yes, your name, please,' the officer said with resignation.

'Emily King.'

'And your address and telephone number? We're keeping details of all those who've phoned in.'

'So others have contacted you with missing pets?'

'Yes, hundreds,' he sighed. 'From all over the country.'

She gave him her contact details.

'And a description of your cat, please, although I should say we won't be able to match owners to their pets.'

'So they are definitely pets?' Emily asked.

'It seems likely.'

'They haven't come from a lab?'

'No. Would you like to leave a description of your cat?' he asked a little impatiently.

'Yes. Sorry. She was four years old, a brown tabby,

spayed. She used to wear a collar with my mobile phone number on, but that was returned to me.'

'So why do you think your cat might be among those in Coleshaw Woods?'

'She's vanished without trace. Were any of the cats microchipped? Tibs was.'

'We believe some were, yes.'

Her heart missed a beat. 'Have you contacted the owners?'

'No. The microchips were cut out from the animals.'

'What?' she gasped. 'Cut out? Why?'

'Presumably to stop identification.'

'Oh my God. That's horrible.' She thought she was going to be sick. 'So I'll never know if Tibs was one of them?'

'It's unlikely.'

She took a deep breath. 'How long had they been dead?'

'Varying lengths of time, but some quite recent. I've noted your details and someone will be in touch if we have any news. But, as I said, it's unlikely we will be able to match the animals to their owners.'

'Has anyone else had their pet's collar returned to them?' Emily asked.

'Not as far as I know.'

'So perhaps Tibs isn't among them.'

'I'm sorry, ma'am, it's impossible for me to say.' And with a polite goodbye he ended the call.

Emily told herself that Tibs wasn't one of the cats dumped in Coleshaw Woods, for the alternative – that she had died as part of a sadistic ritual and her microchip had been cut out – was too awful to contemplate. No, Tibs was dead, probably run over when her collar had become detached, as Ben had said.

That night, she put Tibs' food bowl and bed in a bag in the garage where they stored items they no longer needed but couldn't bear to get rid of.

Chapter Fourteen

Generally, Emily was enjoying her extended maternity leave, she thought, although it was essential to get out of the house with Robbie each day, otherwise he grew fractious and she developed cabin fever. Even now winter was setting in, she wrapped him up warm and they went out. The fresh air, exercise and change of scenery did them both good. Sometimes she met up with friends, other times, if the weather was fine, she took Robbie to the local playground, where he chuckled loudly as she pushed him in the baby swings and enjoyed playing on the apparatus for very young children.

Christmas was only three weeks away and Emily was also visiting the shops in the high street more to buy gifts. She was looking forward to Christmas but with a little trepidation as this would be the first time she was hosting Christmas dinner for both sets of parents. She wanted it to be perfect: the table laid with the festive linen tablecloth she'd bought, silver pine place mats, matching table centre-piece, turkey with all the trimmings. It was a huge operation and she had numerous lists of what to buy and when. She and Ben were also throwing a drinks party for their friends the Saturday before Christmas – home-made canapés, sweet mince pies and mulled wine. It would be their best Christmas ever!

Returning from the high street with yet more shopping, the pushchair was loaded with bags. They'd been to the park first and Robbie was exhausted and reasonably happy to sit in his pushchair rather than wanting to walk, which took forever. Emily turned into their road and glanced at the houses they passed. Like theirs, most of the houses in the street were decorated ready for Christmas, many with a Christmas tree in their front room window, festooned with baubles and fairy lights. Some had really gone to town – even over the top – with model reindeer, Santas on sleighs and illuminated snow scenes in their front gardens. Sometimes, less was more, Emily thought as she continued looking at the houses.

It had come as no surprise that the Burmans' house wasn't showing any signs of the festive season. It was possible they didn't celebrate Christmas, Emily acknow-ledged, although it seemed more likely they just didn't want to. She doubted Dr Burman had any Christmas spirit in him – definitely a bah-humbug type of person. Dour and sour. And, of course, Alisha, being ill, couldn't make the effort by herself. Emily hadn't seen Alisha since her fifteen-minute visit and had only caught glimpses of the doctor going in and out of his house and shed. She thought Alisha might have been a very different person without him, but then again she was ill and he seemed to take care of her, so she shouldn't really criticize.

As she passed their house, she automatically glanced over as she had the others in the street. But the glimpse between the trees and high evergreen shrubs showed the same gloomy front with blacked-out windows. It was a sad-looking house, even more so now many of their neighbours' houses were gaily decorated. The sadness inside seemed to seep out, bleed through the walls, Emily thought and hurried by. She was pleased to turn into their drive with its warmth of fairy lights draped under the eaves and sparkling through the glass panel of their front door. She switched the lights on when she got up in the morning and they stayed on until she and Ben went to bed. Having gone to all the trouble of putting them up, she wanted to make the most of them. Their house looked welcoming and, with a frisson of excitement, she took her keys from her coat pocket and unlocked the front door. Closer to Christmas – so they would still be fresh on the big day – she was going to buy a Christmas planter with seasonal flowers and set it just to the right of the front door. The finishing touch.

Her key in the lock, she suddenly stopped, senses alert. She thought she'd heard a child cry from next door – from the Burmans' house? She must have been mistaken. They didn't have any children, nor had she ever seen any visitors. Perhaps it was the television or radio, although she'd never heard any noise come from their house before. The windows were always closed, even in summer, and they never used their garden. She pushed open her front door and was about to go in but stopped.

There it was again. It sounded like an older child, not a baby, a girl, and it had definitely come from the Burmans' house. It didn't sound like a radio or television. Could they have visitors? It would be a first, as far as she was aware. But why was the child crying? Was she upset? It was a distressing cry, no words spoken, a shriek, animal-like and intense. It made her blood run cold. What should she do?

Emily stood still for a moment, torn between ignoring the crying child and continuing indoors, or going next door and asking if everything was all right. Dr Burman wasn't home, his car wasn't on the drive where he kept it, and there were no other cars there suggesting visitors. She knew what Ben would have said – mind your own business and go indoors. Her head agreed with him, while her heart told her something wasn't right. A child in distress in a house where there were no children and the woman was unwell. Since she'd had a child of her own, Emily was more sensitive to the cries of children, especially if they were upset. It was as if something had been switched on when her milk had come in – a primeval need to protect children that was too strong to ignore.

Closing her front door, she dropped her keys into her coat pocket and wheeled the pushchair to their boundary fence. Robbie, wanting to be home, protested. 'We won't be long, little man,' she said, her voice tight.

From her side of the fence, she looked down the Burmans' sideway and up at their house – to where the cries seemed to have come from. It was quiet now, but a small fan-like window on the upper floor was slightly open, which was unusual. Emily didn't know which room the window was in as all the houses in the street were different. As she looked, the cry came again, followed by Alisha's voice, high-pitched and distressed, 'Oh my God! I'm trying to help you!'

Emily stayed where she was, her unease building. What was going on? Who was Alisha talking to and why was the child upset? Surely, she wasn't a guest? It had gone quiet again now and it crossed her mind to call up – 'Is everything all right?' – but the child screamed and the decision was made.

Quickly turning the pushchair round, Emily hurried back down her drive then up the Burmans', trying to convince herself there was a rational explanation for what she'd heard. But what rational explanation there could be escaped her. Better to look a fool than ignore a tragedy, she told herself. If she'd known the Burmans better, she could have made a more informed decision. Now she acted on instinct. She pressed the bell on their entry system as the camera focused on the porch watched her. Robbie struggled to get out. 'We won't be long,' she reassured him again.

She waited. Perhaps no one would answer. Then what would she do? Return home and try to forget it? Impossible. Things heard cannot be unheard, and she knew she'd worry about this until she found out that Alisha and the child were all right. Perhaps she should call the police? And say what? That she'd heard a child crying next door, but the woman who lived there didn't have a child and was ill? Wouldn't they suggest she might have a visitor? Perhaps she should go home, but the desperation she'd heard in Alisha's voice told her to stay.

The door suddenly opened and Alisha stood before her, distraught. 'Thank goodness. I need your help. Come in.'

'Is something wrong?' Emily asked.

'Yes. Come quickly. You must help me, but never tell anyone what you see.'

Emily stopped, fear gripping her. 'Why not? What's going on?'

'Come quickly. You'll see. This way.'

Emily pushed the stroller into the hall as Alisha began upstairs. She glanced at Robbie, wondering if it was safe to leave him alone in the hall, but the child above cried out again, even more distressed.

'Please come now,' Alisha nearly begged.

Glancing at Robbie, Emily ran up the stairs behind Alisha and then followed her into a room at the side of the house. It was a bathroom, adapted for disabled use. Alisha was going to a bundle on the floor, something wrapped in a towel and wedged between the side of the bath and the hand basin. The cry came again from the bundle, like a trapped animal, and Emily realized it was a child. But not like any child she'd seen. She remained where she stood as Alisha knelt beside her. No child should ever look like that.

Chapter Fifteen

'Please help,' Alisha said. 'She won't hurt you.'

Emily pulled herself together, crossed the bathroom and knelt beside Alisha.

'If you take that side,' Alisha said, 'we can hopefully move her onto her side and be able to slide her out.' Emily did as Alisha directed and together they released the child from where she'd become trapped. She moaned.

'It's OK,' Alisha soothed, stroking her forehead. 'We're going to sit you up now.'

Emily tried to concentrate on what she was doing and not look at the child's deformities. Together, they eased her into a sitting position. One claw-like hand tightened on Emily's arm and she tensed. *There is nothing to be frightened of*, she told herself. She's a child.

Alisha quickly drew the girl's bathrobe around her. She whimpered again. 'It's all right, you're not hurt,' she reassured her. Then to Emily, 'I need to get her into that wheelchair. That's what I was trying to do when the hoist broke. I can't lift her alone.'

Alisha pulled the wheelchair closer and Emily helped draw the child upright and then into the wheelchair.

'Thank goodness,' Alisha sighed and carefully set the child's feet on the footplate. It was clear the child's wasted legs would never be able to carry her weight even though she was thin. Her small blue eyes were set too far apart in her enormously swollen forehead, giving the poor child a bulbous appearance as though she were top-heavy.

'Naughty Daddy,' Alisha said as she made the child comfortable. 'I told him the hoist needed looking at.'

'Daddy?' Emily repeated numbly.

'Yes, this is our daughter, Eva.'

'Your daughter. But . . .'

'I know. Don't tell anyone, please.'

Downstairs in the hall, Robbie began to cry. 'I need to go,' Emily said.

'Don't go until I've had a chance to explain,' Alisha pleaded. 'See to Robbie but stay until I come down. I won't be long, just a few minutes while I settle Eva in her room. Take Robbie in the living room. Please wait.'

Emily hesitated.

'Please, I won't be long.'

She saw the fear in her eyes. 'All right. Do you need any help here?'

'No, thank you. Wait for me in the living room.'

'Mummy!' Robbie called again from the hall and Emily

went downstairs. Releasing him from the harness, she picked him up and held him close.

Alisha had said to wait in the living room. With her heart thumping and her thoughts racing, Emily pushed open the door directly in front that she guessed could be the living room. It was. She carried Robbie in and then sat on the sofa with him on her lap. The house was hot and she undid their coats. She looked around as her heartbeat began to settle. It was an ordinary enough living room with a large black leather sofa, two matching armchairs, a television, bookshelves and a hearth rug. Strangely normal and at odds with whatever else was going on in the house. Through the patio window, she could see the outbuilding where Dr Burman spent so much of his time. Although it was a closer view than the one she had from her bedroom window, it was no more distinctive, as the opaque film covering the glass gave everything outside a hazy look.

Robbie agitated to be off her lap and she put him down so he could toddle around. There were no children's toys in the room, nothing to say there was a child living here at all. Whatever was going on? Alisha had called the child Eva. How old was she? Emily guessed about six or seven, although it was difficult to tell with her disabilities. How had they kept her a secret for so long, and why? She had so many questions, comments and criticisms. The situation was unreal and she wasn't sure she should stay.

She could hear Alisha moving around upstairs. A child had been living here all this time and she'd had no idea.

A secret child hidden away. It was unsettling and worrying. It reminded her of cases that came to light every so often and were reported by the press, when a child or sometimes an adult had been held hostage for years. When interviewed, neighbours always said the same thing: that the couple were quiet, polite and kept themselves to themselves. Wasn't that exactly what she would have said about the Burmans? Kept themselves to themselves. Their house and their lives cloaked in secrecy. What other secrets did they have? Ben had been dismissive of her concerns, sometimes making fun of her, but she'd been vindicated, proven right. She'd said Amit Burman was odd and had something to hide, and he certainly did – his daughter!

Emily had just decided that it would be better to leave now, when she heard footsteps on the stairs.

'Thank you for waiting,' Alisha said, coming into the living room. 'And thank you for your help. Eva is fine, nothing broken, but I couldn't have managed without you.' She sat in one of the armchairs and threw Robbie a small smile. She seemed more relaxed now. 'I am annoyed with Amit. I told him that hoist in the bathroom needed fixing, but he was too busy in his lab last night.'

'So, Eva *is* your daughter?' Emily said, still struggling to believe it.

'Yes. She has the same genetic condition that I have and that killed my son. The difference is Eva was born with it. The damage was being done while she was in the womb. My son never looked like that, but I love Eva as I loved my son and always try to do my best for her.'

Emily held her gaze. 'I am sorry. I'd no idea. I mean, I knew you were ill and you'd lost another child, but I'd no idea Eva was living here.'

'That was our intention. No one knows. Our son spent all his life in and out of hospital. There was nothing they could do to save him. We don't want the same for Eva. We had to move from our last house because someone passing saw her at the window. News spread that we had a monster in the house. That's what they used to call her – our pet monster.'

'That's dreadful,' Emily gasped.

'Yes, yobs would gather outside and throw stones at the windows and push things through our letter box. You understand now why we have all this security?'.

'Yes, I do. I can't have helped by cutting the hedge.'

'No. But you weren't to know.'

'Don't you have any help? Surely the social services can offer something? Shouldn't they know?'

'They offered help a long time ago when Eva was born, but we refused. They will keep wanting to take her into hospital, like they did our son, and it doesn't do any good. The doctors can't help. Eva stays upstairs; the main bedroom has been converted for her use. She is comfortable and has everything she needs. It has become more difficult looking after her since I became ill, but I manage.'

'Do you?' Emily asked sceptically. 'Supposing I hadn't been here today. What would you have done?'

'Phoned Amit at work. He would be annoyed, but he always comes eventually. I was about to when I saw on the CCTV it was you at the door. I thought I could trust you. I can, can't I?' She looked worried.

'You mean trust me not to tell anyone?' Emily asked. Alisha nodded. 'I suppose so, but don't you ever take her out?'

'No. She doesn't need to go out. She has everything she wants upstairs.'

'But don't *you* need to go out?' Emily persisted, feeling Alisha was a prisoner in her own home. She glanced at Robbie, who had his face pressed to the patio window.

'I can't leave Eva alone. She was the reason I could only visit you for fifteen minutes. You were so insistent, I felt it was easier to accept your invitation so you wouldn't keep asking me.'

'Sorry, I was just trying to be friendly. I'd no idea . . .' Her voice fell away.

Alisha raised a small smile. 'It's fine. I would have liked for us to be friends, but Amit said you'd tell if you found out.'

Emily shrugged. 'I would probably have told Ben. We share most things.'

'Please don't tell him. I don't want to have to move again and if Amit found out he'd be very angry. He spends every night working in his lab, trying to find a cure, not just for me, but Eva too and others with the same condition. I doubt he will, time is running out, but it has become his obsession. His way of coping.'

Just for a moment Emily felt a pang of guilt that she had judged him so harshly. There were clearly worse obsessions than trying to save your wife and child. She also felt she couldn't just walk away without offering something. 'I understand why you don't go out, so perhaps Robbie and I could come here again to visit you?'

'Oh I don't know,' Alisha said, concerned. 'I mean, I'd like that but . . .' She looked at Robbie. 'Wouldn't he say something to his father?'

'No, he only has single words at present – mummy, daddy, car, that type of thing. I could pop in when it suits you. No one would know. But only if you want me to.'

'Yes, I'd like that. I really would. I get so lonely, but you must promise never to tell anyone.' Fear appeared in her eyes again.

'I promise,' Emily said.

'Early afternoon is good for me,' Alisha said, visibly brightening. 'After I've given Eva her lunch, and I know Amit will be in the operating theatre all afternoon.'

'Great. Pick your day.'

'How about this Friday? At two o'clock.'

'Suits me. Do you have a mobile?'

'No. Only the house phone.'

'I'll give you my mobile number just in case you need me again in an emergency.'

'Thank you.' Alisha found a pen and sheet of paper and wrote it down. 'I'll keep it somewhere safe.' She smiled.

'See you Friday then.'

'I'll look forward to it.'

Chapter Sixteen

That night, Emily stood at her bedroom window gazing into the clear still air. As usual, the light was on in Amit Burman's lab, although nothing could be seen but the faint glow around the very edge of the opaque film and blinds. Ben was downstairs finishing off a report for work and she'd come up for an early night. She was tired. Exhausted. She'd worn herself out thinking about what she'd seen and learnt at Alisha's that afternoon. How she would have liked to have confided in Ben. Share the burden of this, as she normally shared most things with him. Her thoughts were in chaos. She needed some perspective on what she'd found out, but to do so would break her promise to Alisha, and she couldn't risk the consequences of doing that. If she told Ben, he could let it slip to Amit. They often exchanged a few words when they saw each other going in or out of the house. Ben was as honest as they came and wasn't good at keeping secrets or telling lies. But the fact that she was the only one apart from the Burmans who knew they had a child was a huge responsibility. At the time Alisha had explained the reasons for keeping Eva secret it had seemed rational, but now Emily wasn't so sure.

Supposing something dreadful happened in that house and she hadn't told anyone? Wouldn't she be partly responsible and to blame? Parents under huge pressure, such as the Burmans were, must sometimes snap and the result could be devastating. The strain must be enormous and Alisha had admitted Amit was obsessed with finding a cure, although it was obvious that Eva could never be cured. Might there come a time when he realized this and it all became too much and he lost it? Theirs wouldn't be the first family to be found slaughtered in their beds after a parent had suffered a breakdown and run berserk. Perhaps he was already at breaking point, Emily thought, and she was the only one who knew Eva was there. It was a confidence she wished she didn't have.

Her mobile phone, already on her bedside cabinet for the night, began to vibrate behind her. She turned from the window. Their bedside clock showed it was after ten o'clock. It wouldn't be her parents or friends phoning at this time. Nuisance call? She picked up the phone and saw the call was coming from a local landline number, although not one the phone recognized as a contact. Something stopped her from letting it go through to voicemail and she pressed to accept the call. 'Hello?'

'Emily?' a small female voice asked tentatively. It was vaguely familiar but so slight it was impossible to place.

'Yes. Who is it?'

'Alisha. I am so worried.'

'Oh Alisha. What's the matter?' Concern immediately kicked in, but why was she phoning when Amit was home?

'I'm in trouble, Emily. I've just realized that your visit today will all be recorded on our CCTV. If Amit sees it, he will be furious. I don't know what to do. You must never come here again. It was wrong of me to ask you for help. I don't know what to do.'

'Calm down,' Emily said and returned to the window. The light was still on in the outbuilding. 'Amit is in his shed, isn't he?'

'Yes, for now, but supposing he looks at the recording? He does sometimes. If he checks it, he'll see you've been here.'

'Can you delete part of the recording? We haven't got CCTV, but I'm guessing you can.'

'I think so, but I don't know how.' Emily heard the panic and desperation in her voice.

'There must be a control box somewhere. How do you control it?' Emily asked, watching the outbuilding for any sign that Amit might be leaving it.

'There's a box under the television. Amit views the recordings on our TV. I've seen him do it.'

'And he hasn't viewed it yet today?'

'No.'

'So delete the bit where I arrive and leave.'

'Yes, but how?' Alisha's hysteria grew.

'Calm down. It can't be that difficult. Are you in the living room now?'

'Yes.'

'Have you got the remote control there?'

'Yes. It's on the table.'

'Look at it now while Amit is in the lab. I'm in my bedroom. I can see him from here if he leaves.'

Alisha fell silent and Emily concentrated on the outbuilding. 'I've found the channel it's on,' Alisha said at last.

'Good. Can you see a main menu?'

A short pause then, 'Yes.'

'Click on the menu,' Emily said. 'I'm guessing there will be something that says device.'

Silence again. Emily hoped Ben wouldn't choose this moment to come up. She'd have difficulty explaining what she was doing.

'Got it,' Alisha said.

'Right, move the recording to the bit just before I arrive.'

'How?' Alisha's panic rose again.

'Try to stay calm. There must be a way of rewinding it. Some little arrows maybe, pointing backwards?'

Another silence. 'Yes. Here they are. Shall I click on it?'

'Yes.'

A second later. 'It's rewinding.'

'Good.' Emily watched the outbuilding, her mouth dry and her pulse racing. Alisha's fear and anxiety were contagious.

A minute later, 'I'm back to where you arrive.'

'OK, now press delete and keep deleting until just after I've gone.'

'Yes, I'm doing it.'

Emily waited. She could hear Alisha's breath coming fast and shallow.

'Done it.'

'Good. If Amit finds out, just act dumb and say you don't know anything about it. He'll think it's malfunctioning.'

'I think I must be dumb,' Alisha said.

'No. You just panicked. Are you OK now?'

'Yes.'

At that moment, the light went off in the outbuilding and the door opened. 'Alisha, Amit's leaving now. Is the television back to normal viewing?'

'Yes.'

'Try to relax and stay calm. Do what you would usually do. I'll see you Friday. You can switch off the CCTV before I arrive and then put it back on after I've gone, but we'll speak again before then.'

'Yes. Thank you.' The line went dead.

Emily stayed by the window and watched Amit Burman as he carefully padlocked the door of the outbuilding and then began up the path towards the house. Alisha's fear of being discovered had unsettled Emily. She had been panic-stricken. Genuinely afraid. Emily had heard it in her voice. Why, if Amit really was looking after her, as Alisha had claimed? She had doubts now.

Emily drew the curtains and then saved Alisha's house phone number to the list of contacts in her mobile, just in case it should ever be needed.

Chapter Seventeen

'It's off, I've switched it off!' Alisha declared, having phoned Emily's mobile at 1.55 p.m. on Friday. Emily heard her sense of achievement and the excitement in her voice.

'Great. Well done. I'll be round in five minutes. Just putting Robbie into his coat.'

'See you soon.'

Alisha was waiting behind her front door and ready to open it as soon as Emily and Robbie approached. She was smiling, wearing a lovely dress and had styled her hair.

'You look nice,' Emily said, helping Robbie over the doorstep.

'Thank you. I thought I should make an effort. You always look very fashionable. It's so long since I had a visitor.' Alisha quickly closed the door. 'You and Robbie can sit in the living room while I make us some tea.

Oh, but I need to take your coats first,' she flustered. 'Sorry, I forgot.'

'Don't worry,' Emily said and slipped off her coat, touched by just how much their visit meant to Alisha. It nearly hadn't happened. The day before, she'd had to spend ages on the phone persuading Alisha that the sky wouldn't fall in if she switched off the CCTV for a while.

Emily handed their coats to Alisha, who hung them in the under-stairs cupboard.

'Please go through to the living room and make yourself comfortable,' she said a little formally. 'I found some of Eva's toys from when she was younger for Robbie to play with.'

'Great,' Emily said. Taking hold of Robbie's hand, she steered him into the living room while Alisha went into the kitchen to make tea.

Laid out on the rug by the hearth was a collection of brightly coloured early years activity toys. They were similar to the ones Robbie had at home with buttons and knobs that could be turned and pressed to make different sounds, music, numbers, words and letters. Robbie toddled over to investigate as Emily sat on the sofa and looked down the garden. While her own garden was very bare in winter – a sea of lifeless twigs and brown earth – this garden was largely evergreen, with a screen of shrubs all around the edges forming a tall hedge. The one she'd cut between their gardens was shorter than those on the other two sides and she felt another stab of guilt. But she hadn't known then that they were there to stop prying eyes from seeing Eva.

'Please help yourself,' Alisha said, returning with a tray set with tea and a plate of pastry savouries.

'Wow. You've been busy,' Emily enthused, impressed. 'These look delicious.'

'It was nice to cook something different. Eva's food is very simple and Amit often eats at work.'

Emily took a couple of the pastries and put them on the plate Alisha gave to her, together with tea in a white bone china cup and saucer.

'What about Robbie?' Alisha asked. 'Does he want anything?'

'He's all right for now, he's just had lunch.' Emily settled back, took a sip of her tea and a bite of one of the pastries. 'Very nice,' she said. Alisha smiled, pleased. 'So, you worked out how to switch off the cameras, well done. And you know how to switch them on again?' she asked.

'Yes. It's simple when you know how. I'd never had a reason to learn how to use it before.'

'You seemed very worried that Amit might find out.'

'He . . .' She stopped.

'Yes?' Emily prompted.

'Amit has a lot on his mind and he can sometimes become angry over little things, but everything is all right, really. It was nice of you to help me.'

Emily gave a half-hearted nod. 'No worries.' Perhaps with time Alisha would confide in her. 'What exactly does Amit do in that outbuilding?' she asked as she had before. 'I know you said it was research to try to find a cure for your illness, but how?'

'I don't know the details,' Alisha replied, avoiding Emily's gaze. 'And I don't ask questions.'

'You're very good. I'm sure I'd ask,' Emily returned with a small irreverent laugh.

'But you're different to me,' Alisha said, and looked sad. 'You're more confident and do as you wish. You feel you can speak your mind.'

'Too much sometimes,' Emily said. 'So tell me to shut up when you've had enough.'

'I wouldn't do that,' Alisha said seriously. 'I am pleased you came. But I honestly don't know what Amit does in his lab and I wouldn't question him.'

'Ben is jealous. He calls it a man cave. He wants one,' Emily laughed.

'I'm sure Ben would much rather spend his time with you and Robbie in the evenings and weekends than in a building at the bottom of the garden.'

Emily saw Alisha's hurt and disappointment. 'Yes, I suppose he would, really,' she said quietly and took another sip of her tea. 'I've accepted Tibs isn't coming back,' she said, changing the subject.

'I am sorry. Will you have another cat?'

'Maybe in the future, although Ben would like a dog.'

'It's such a pity she didn't come home. When I found her collar, I was hopeful it had just come off and she would return.'

Emily set her cup in her saucer and stared at her. 'You found the collar? I thought Amit found it?'

'No, I found it just outside our back door. Amit returned it to you.'

'It wasn't in the road, then?'

'No. Didn't Amit explain?'

'Yes, but I'm sure he said he'd found it in the road.'

'You must have misunderstood. It was outside our back door. I was putting out some rubbish and found it by the bin.'

'I see,' Emily said thoughtfully. 'I don't suppose it matters.'

'No,' Alisha agreed.

But it did matter.

'Why would Amit lie about where and who found Tibs' collar?' Emily asked Ben that evening. She had told him she'd seen Alisha briefly when she'd taken a parcel there.

'I don't suppose he lied on purpose,' Ben said with a small sigh. 'It was probably just a mistake. The bloke got home knackered from work and his wife started going on about the cat collar and that he had to return it. So he quickly scribbles a note and pushes it through our letter box, then you rush round and cross-examine him. He says he found it in the road, which is the most likely place if a cat has been run over. It was a mistake, that's all. No evil intent.'

'But Alisha never goes out as far as the road. How could he make that mistake?' Emily persisted.

'What are you talking about, Em?' Ben said testily.

'She came here once, didn't she? Of course she goes out sometimes. Just not very far as she's ill.'

She looked at him and realized how ridiculous it must sound if you didn't know the full story – that Alisha couldn't go out, not so much because of her illness but because she had a severely disabled daughter whom she couldn't leave. There was no doubt in Emily's mind that Alisha's version of events was true and, for whatever reason, Amit Burman had lied, but she knew she needed to let it go. She was starting to sound obsessive, and Ben's comment about Amit arriving home from work knackered and his wife going on at him about the cat collar was surely a dig at her.

'Sorry, I won't mention it again.' She kissed his cheek. 'Tell me about your day at work.'

Chapter Eighteen

It mattered, Alisha also thought that evening, and it had worried her since Emily had left. It had plagued and dominated her thoughts. She'd done her best to hide her surprise and concern when Emily had told her what Amit had said about Tibs' collar, but after Emily had gone she'd found it impossible to think of anything else. She felt unsettled, anxious and couldn't understand why Amit had lied to Emily. Without doubt he had known he wasn't the one who'd found the cat collar, and she'd told him exactly where she'd found it. So why had he told Emily he'd found it in the road? Had he forgotten what she'd said? Unlikely. He rarely forgot anything and he'd taken the collar round straight away; there hadn't been time to forget. 'I'll return it,' he'd said, snatching it from her and placing it in an envelope.

Alisha liked Emily a lot, she acknowledged. She seemed

a genuine sort of person who could be relied upon, and she trusted her not to tell anyone – even Ben – about Eva. She was pleased they were becoming friends; indeed, Emily was the only friend she had now. Amit had seen to that, telling her old friends she was too ill to meet them or come to the phone, so eventually they'd stopped calling. But now she had Emily, and it felt safe having her telephone number and knowing she was just next door. She'd enjoyed Emily and Robbie's visit and now she was confident in working the CCTV and could switch it off and on they could visit any time and Amit would never know. She'd already made a date for their next visit. Yes, she liked Emily and wanted to do right by her.

Alisha was suddenly jolted into the present by something she'd just thought. The CCTV. Now she was competent at using it why didn't she rewind it to the day she'd found the collar? It might give a clue as to how it had got there, even to where Tibs was, then she could tell Emily. She'd be so pleased to know, even if it was bad news. Emily had said it was the not knowing what had happened to Tibs that was the worst. There was a camera pointing down the sideway that covered the back door. Amit was in his lab for the evening and wouldn't reappear for hours.

Alisha picked up the remote control for the television and pressed for the CCTV channel. Recordings were kept for three months before being automatically wiped clean. She began rewinding, quickly covering the previous weeks. Day followed night and night day in a tedious routine of nothing. If she ever needed proof of how humdrum her life was then she had it here. Amit went to work in the morning, returned home in the evening and went to his lab. Occasionally, she saw herself answering the front door if one of Amit's deliveries needed signing for. She also saw herself in the sideway putting rubbish out, but other than that she was always indoors looking after Eva. But just a minute, hadn't she found the collar on the day the bins were emptied? She was almost certain. Amit put the bins out on Wednesday evening ready for collection on Thursday.

She nudged the tape back, now pausing at Wednesdays only, and saw Amit leaving for work in the mornings, then returning home in the evenings and putting out the bins. Then abruptly one evening his routine changed. She slowed the tape to play, sat forward and concentrated hard on the screen. It was pitch-dark at 7.28 p.m. and the cameras relied on infrared. He could be seen going out of their back door, but instead of putting out the bins, he disappeared down the garden, presumably to his lab. There was no camera covering the lab.

Alisha waited, then moved the recording forward again. Finally, at 11.30 p.m., he reappeared down the sideway, having finished in his lab for the night. But now he was carrying two large heavy-duty rubbish sacks. He was struggling, they looked very heavy, and he couldn't get a good grip on the bag in his right hand as he seemed to be carrying something else. From the angle of the camera she couldn't tell what. He stopped at the bins, set the two sacks on the ground, lifted the lid on the general rubbish bin and threw in whatever he'd been holding, not realizing he'd dropped something. He then picked up the rubbish sacks but, instead of putting those into the bin, continued down the sideway. A few seconds later she saw him on the camera at the front. What was he going to do? He glanced up at their neighbours' houses, presumably checking he wasn't being watched, before opening the boot of his car and heaving in the sacks. He closed the door, quickly got into the car and drove off.

Alisha stopped the recording and stared at the screen, her thoughts racing and her mouth dry. She remembered now. It was one of the nights Amit had gone out very late and returned in the early hours. It had happened a few times and although they no longer slept in the same bedroom – she'd slept in Eva's room for years – she'd been woken when he'd returned and had put out the bins. She never questioned his movements – he wouldn't have told her anyway. But why had he taken those rubbish sacks away instead of putting them in the bin to be collected with the other rubbish? What was in them that needed to be got rid of separately? Fear gripped her.

She rewound the tape again to where Amit could be seen approaching the bins carrying the sacks. They were bulging, but the bulges gave no clue as to what was inside. And what had he been carrying apart from the sacks? She still couldn't tell. She watched carefully as he set down the sacks and then lifted the lid with one hand and raised the other to throw in whatever else he'd been carrying, one of which slipped from his grasp. She pressed the remote to freeze the frame, zoomed in and stared in horror.

Collars, he'd been holding animal collars. Four, five, possibly more, she couldn't be sure. That's what he'd thrown in the bin, and as he'd done so one had dropped. He hadn't noticed in the dark, but it was clear on the infrared camera.

Animal collars. She felt sick. She zoomed in closer to the one on the floor. A red felt cat collar, no bell but a telephone number engraved on the metal tab. The number was too small to read, but she didn't need to read it to know it was Emily's number. The collar Amit had dropped belonged to Tibs. The collar she'd found, exactly as she remembered it.

Chapter Nineteen

It was an unlikely friendship, Emily thought as she helped Robbie into his coat. They were visiting regularly now and in any other situation their friendship probably wouldn't have flourished. She and Alisha had very different personalities. Emily would have described herself as gregarious, a leader, impulsive maybe, but someone who met life's challenges head-on and didn't shy away from conflict. Alisha, on the other hand, was unassuming, self-effacing and, while kind, relied heavily on others – her husband and increasingly on Emily. Emily hoped Alisha appreciated that at some point in the future she would be returning to work and these daytime visits would stop.

As usual, Alisha was waiting for them and the door opened as they approached.

'Alisha, I've been thinking,' Emily said as soon as they were in. 'There's something we need to talk about.'

'What?' Alisha gasped, immediately concerned. 'What is it? You look serious.'

'Relax. It's OK. Nothing bad. Don't look so guilty.' Emily began taking off Robbie's coat. 'I've been thinking that it doesn't feel right us sitting in the living room while Eva is alone upstairs. I know you said you can't bring her down because of the wheelchair, but couldn't we go up there with her?'

'Oh, I see, is that what you wanted to say?' Alisha asked, clearly relieved.

'Yes. Why? What on earth did you think I was going to say?'

'Nothing. It's just me. Let me take your coats,' she fussed. 'Yes, we could go up to Eva's room. I didn't think you'd want to. I saw your expression that time you helped me with Eva.'

'I know, I'm sorry. It was a shock seeing her for the first time. I'd like to, really.'

Alisha managed a small smile. She didn't smile often enough, Emily thought. 'All right. I usually sit upstairs with Eva during the day. The living room is hardly used. I'll make us some tea and then we'll all go up together.'

Taking Robbie's hand, Emily went with Alisha into her gleaming white kitchen. Spotless, fastidiously tidy and with the contents of the cupboards organized and labelled to the point of it being clinical. It had come as little surprise to Emily to learn that Alisha had been a nurse before she'd stopped work to look after her first child. Emily watched as Alisha moved around the kitchen, opening and closing the cupboard doors, laying the tray with cups and saucers, side plates and freshly baked savouries and a napkin each.

'So I really can't persuade you to come to my little Christmas drinks party tomorrow night, even for a short while?' Emily asked. Alisha didn't reply and seemed preoccupied.

'Sorry,' she said after a moment. 'What did you say?'

'My little do tomorrow evening. Could you come for just an hour?'

'Oh, no. That's impossible. I can't leave Eva.' Which is what she'd said the last time she'd asked her. Emily didn't understand why Amit couldn't stay with Eva for an hour or so instead of being in his shed but she didn't say.

Alisha picked up the kettle and began to pour the boiling water into the tea pot, but as she did, Emily saw her hand tremble.

'Are you OK?' she asked, going to her.

'Yes. Just a bit tired. I have good days and bad days.'

'Should we come back another time?'

'Oh no, stay. Please stay. I want you to.'

'If you're sure, but let me help.'

'I can manage, really. Please don't worry. I'm fine.' She picked up the tray and Emily followed her out of the kitchen, holding Robbie's hand as they went upstairs.

'We're going to play with Eva,' Emily told him positively. But she had concerns as to how he would react. It had been a shock for her to see Eva the first time. She hoped

Robbie wouldn't scream or shy away. How embarrassing that would be.

It was as though Alisha read her thoughts. 'I'm sure Robbie will be fine with Eva,' she said as they arrived on the landing. 'I used to work in a burns unit and I found children were a lot more accepting of facial disfigurement than adults. Can you open that door please, my hands are full.'

'Yes, of course.' Emily opened the door and then stood aside to let Alisha go in first. She gave Robbie's hand a reassuring squeeze as they followed her in.

It was a big room, more like a studio flat than a bedroom. Light and airy with gaily patterned wallpaper, collages and murals, and mobiles hanging from the ceiling. There was a living area at one end, with a small sofa, table, shelves and a television, all at wheelchair height. Two single beds were at the other end, one with a hoist. Alisha had told her she slept here, too. A door with a pretty rose ceramic tile-marked bathroom led off the far side, yet although this room was on the second floor and at the back of the house, the windows were covered with opaque film just like the others.

Emily looked at Eva sitting in her wheelchair facing away from them and watching a cartoon film on the television.

Alisha set the tray on the table, went over to her daughter and gently removed her headphones. 'Hello, lovely. Look we have visitors.' She turned the chair slightly so Eva could see.

'Hi,' Emily said, taking a few steps towards her. 'Do

you remember me? I helped your mother once after you'd fallen.'

Eva smiled, her facial disfigurement absorbed into the grin.

'She remembers,' Alisha said.

'This is Robbie,' Emily said gently.

Eva turned her wheelchair so she was fully facing Robbie. Emily saw a flash of uncertainty cross his face before he let go of her hand and went to one of the toys on the floor near her.

'He likes your toys,' Emily told Eva.

'Yes,' Eva agreed.

'She understands?' Emily asked, surprised.

'Yes. About the same as the average eight-year-old, but sometimes she has difficulty expressing herself.'

Emily felt guilty. She'd assumed that because Eva was extremely disabled, she'd have learning difficulties, too. It was a prejudgement of which she wasn't proud.

Alisha poured the tea and then handed out the savouries, including one for Eva, which she put on a tray that fitted across the wheelchair. Emily sat Robbie beside her at the end of the sofa and gave him a pastry and his plastic beaker containing water. It was a smaller version of the one Eva was drinking from.

It felt much better all of them sitting together, Emily thought, and she was pleased she'd suggested it. As Alisha had said, Robbie seemed to be fine with Eva – treating her just like any other child. Indeed, now Emily was here with Eva, she was finding she was able to see beyond her physical deformity to the person. And the more Emily talked to her, the more she was able to make eye contact instead of fixating on her disfigurement.

Robbie finished his snack and, picking up one of Eva's toys, went over to show her.

'I think you have a new friend,' Emily said.

'I like Robbie,' Eva replied.

'He likes you too,' Alisha said.

Emily saw that Alisha was finally starting to relax. She'd seemed so tense and on edge when they'd first arrived that Emily had thought something was seriously wrong. It was probably stress. The stress of looking after Eva while coping with her own ill health must be overwhelming at times.

'Alisha, if you ever want me to sit with Eva so you can go out for a while, you only have to say,' Emily offered.

Alisha looked shocked. 'Oh no, thank you, but I don't go out.'

'I know you don't. But you could. Why not? On a day when you're feeling well enough. It would do you good.'

'But where would I go?' she asked, astonished.

'Anywhere you like. Shopping? For a walk? Just for a change of scenery.'

'That's kind of you, but I'm OK really . . . and Amit wouldn't like it.'

Emily stopped herself from saying that Amit need never know. 'Think about it,' she said. 'The offer stands until I have to return to work.'

Alisha nodded, but Emily doubted she would ask her.

A moment later, the doorbell rang, making Alisha start.

'It'll be a parcel for Amit,' she said. Immediately standing, she crossed the room. 'I must hurry. I daren't miss it.'

Emily threw Eva a reassuring smile, for she too was looking concerned. 'Mummy's gone to get the parcel, she won't be long.'

'She has to hurry,' Eva said slowly, her words hampered by the shape of her mouth. 'Daddy gets angry if they go next door.'

'Does he?' Emily said. 'How does he show he's angry?'

'He shouts,' Eva said, her eyes sad like Alisha's were sometimes.

'At Mummy?' Emily asked.

'Yes. I hear him.'

'Does he shout at you?'

'He stays away from me. I love Mummy but not Daddy.'

Emily was taken aback by the child's forthrightness and was about to ask her why she didn't love her father, and if he ever hit her or her mother, when Alisha returned.

'Got to the door in time,' she said, relieved and out of breath.

Emily nodded and then, after a moment, asked, 'How does Amit get on with Eva?'

'He doesn't have anything to do with her,' she said, her voice flat. 'He is ashamed of her as he was our son.'

Emily looked at Eva, wondering if she should hear this.

'She knows,' Alisha said. 'I can't protect her from everything. Amit has rejected her and blames me for making her as she is by carrying the faulty gene.'

'That's awful,' Emily sympathized.

Alisha gave a small nod. 'Yet I understand why he is angry and spends so much of his time trying to find a cure. He can't bear to be with us, and while a cure won't help us, he will make a name for himself.'

'That's so sad. I'd have thought he would want to spend as much time with you both as possible while he has the chance.'

'We're used to it.' Alisha shrugged despondently. 'It could be worse.'

Emily wasn't sure how, but she let it go. Alisha had tears in her eyes.

'Daddy's parcel?' Eva asked, looking at her mother.

'Yes. Another one!' Alisha exclaimed, raising a smile.

'Whatever was in that huge one that arrived a few weeks ago?' Emily asked, finishing her tea.

'When was that? There are so many, I don't remember.'

'You wouldn't forget that one. It was massive. Big enough to hold a body.' She laughed, but Alisha looked serious. 'I was in Robbie's bedroom and heard the lorry park outside. I held him up to the window to see. He loves lorries.'

'I don't remember that,' Alisha said, frowning.

'Amit was home and took care of the delivery.'

'Was he?' She wrung her hands in her lap.

'You don't remember? I think I still have the picture.' Emily took out her phone.

'You took a photo?' Alisha asked, amazed.

'Yes, I take photos of everything.' She laughed. 'I live my life through Snapchat.' She found the video clip. 'Here it is. The date and time is just above the recording.' Holding her phone so Alisha could see, Emily touched the arrow to play the short recording. The same one she'd shown to Ben, of Amit at the bottom of the garden manoeuvring the cylinder-like object into his shed.

'I must have been seeing to Eva,' Alisha said as the clip ended. 'But I really don't understand why you would want to photograph it.'

'I photograph everything,' Emily said again. 'A lot of people with smartphones do. Rather than text, we send snapshots of where we are and what we're doing. There are apps and websites that allow you to share photos with your family and friends instantly. So, if I'm in a restaurant, for example, I will send a picture of my meal before I start eating. Or if I'm shopping for something new to wear, I'll send photos of me trying on different outfits and ask my friends for their opinions. It's like having them there.' How difficult it was trying to explain the instant connectivity she enjoyed to someone who didn't even own a basic mobile phone.

'Look at all these,' Emily continued, scrolling through some of the hundreds of photos and video clips she'd taken: everyday scenes and settings. 'It must seem strange to you, but it's what my friends and I do. So when I saw Amit with that massive container, I automatically reached for my phone.'

'Who did you share it with? Your friends?' Alisha asked, immediately growing anxious.

'No. Only Ben.'

'You didn't tell him about Eva?'

'No, of course not.'

'What did Ben say when you showed him?' Alisha asked.

'Nothing really. I can delete it if you like.'

'Yes, I think that would be best, and please don't take any more of Amit. He'd be so angry if he saw you.'

Chapter Twenty

It was still daylight when Emily left that afternoon, but the cold winter evening was quickly closing in. From Eva's window, Alisha could see frost already settling outside. Amit would be in the operating theatre for another hour. Checking Eva was all right and didn't need anything, she hurried as fast as she could downstairs, slipped on her coat and shoes and, leaving the CCTV off, let herself out the back door.

She'd recognized the date and time on the video clip Emily had shown her. It was the day Amit had forced her into the downstairs cloakroom and locked her in. When he'd released her, he'd given her no explanation – she hadn't expected one, and she'd never have asked. But why hadn't he wanted her to see that delivery? She'd taken in plenty of others. What did he want with that tall cylinder that Emily had joked was big enough to hold a body?

What exactly was he doing in that lab? She was hoping there'd be a gap at the edge of the blinds big enough to see in. Normally she never ventured down the garden, but something was telling her she needed to now, to try to find out more. It must be something to do with his research into finding a cure, for what else could it be?

The lab was locked as always, and Alisha tried to peer in through the glass at the side of the blind in the main window. But the opaque film went right up to the very edge, so it was impossible to see anything inside. She tried the other windows, with the same result. Amit had certainly done a good job of stopping anyone from seeing in. Was it really to keep out the prying gaze of neighbours as he claimed, or to stop her seeing in too? He'd used the opaque film on the windows of the house so that Eva couldn't be seen from outside as had happened at their last house. He'd stuck it on this outbuilding about the same time he'd started calling it a lab and researching. Then the packages had started arriving.

Coming away from the windows, Alisha examined the padlock on the door. She'd no idea where Amit kept the key – with him, she assumed. She took a few steps down the side of the building; there were no windows here, but she trod on something soft. Looking down, she gave a small cry. Partially covered by fallen leaves was a dead mouse. She shivered. She didn't like mice, dead or alive. It was something about their beady eyes and pink furless tails. Perhaps Amit had put poison down; that's why it had died here. It couldn't have been dead for long though, there was no sign of decomposition and it appeared to be well preserved. Repelled yet fascinated, she nudged it with the tip of her shoe and grimaced. It was so well preserved, it looked as though it might get up and run off at any moment. Creepy. Stepping over the mouse, she began up the path towards the house. Amit would remove it.

Preserved. That term, why did it resonate with her? And the size and shape of the object Amit had had delivered reminded her of something, although she couldn't say what. She'd thought so when Emily had shown her the video clip of the delivery but hadn't said anything. Perhaps it resembled something she'd seen in a picture or on television? Big enough to hold a body, Emily had quipped, finding it amusing. But what did she know? Her life was perfect, with a partner who doted on her, a healthy child, and a career. Someone like Emily couldn't possibly understand her life, although she pretended to. She shouldn't have taken that photo. It was intrusive. Perhaps Amit was right to distrust her. Yet . . .

Arriving at the back door, Alisha paused before going in. She raised her right hand as if to lift the lid on the bin, then decided otherwise and continued indoors. Sometimes it was better to ignore things and pretend you hadn't seen them for your own good. She and Eva needed Amit and would never survive without him.

Chapter Twenty-One

In the week before Christmas, the flu epidemic peaked and many National Health Service hospitals in England were stretched to the limit. Targets for routine operations were being missed as elderly patients were admitted, treated and then bed-blocked as they lived alone and there was no care plan in place for them to return home. The tabloid press ran regular front-page horror stories of the elderly being left on trolleys in hospital corridors for hours until a bed became available. One even died there. Shocking and unacceptable for a supposedly caring society, but perfect for what Amit had in mind.

Advising work that he, too, had succumbed to the flu virus – he'd never have been allowed the time off otherwise – he shut himself in his lab with his laptop and set about finding the hardest-hit hospitals. He needed one that was already struggling, failing to meet its targets and now found itself in crisis as the flu struck. It wasn't difficult. The online news was full of appalling statistics. St James' would do perfectly. He downloaded the visitor's guide to the hospital to his phone, locked up his lab and went indoors.

In his bedroom, he changed into his hospital scrubs, packed an overnight bag, including casual clothes, and then put on his overcoat. On the way out, he shouted to Alisha that he would be away a few nights on a conference and didn't know exactly when he'd be back. She didn't reply. She was in Eva's room, presumably seeing to the child who needed so much attention and gave nothing in return. Well, not for much longer.

Amit dropped his overnight bag on the back seat of his car and then settling into the driver's seat tapped the postcode for St James' Hospital into the satnav. It was fifty-three miles away. Ideal for his purpose. Not so close that he might be recognized on the ward, but not so far as to require an overnight stop on the return journey, which would be a problem.

He accelerated off the drive in a surge of adrenalin. He felt good. He'd made huge progress and was now on par with ELECT – at the forefront of the revolution to preserve life indefinitely. At some point in the future, his work would be recognized and he would go down in history alongside pioneers like Alexander Fleming and Louis Pasteur. Men at the cutting edge of medical science who'd pushed the barriers further than their contemporaries believed possible. True, what he was about to do was illegal, but needs must, and he couldn't find any moral objection to his plan. Just the opposite, in fact. He was going to save an old person from the indignity of dying catheterized in a hospital bed or alone at home.

He switched on the radio to classical music and relaxed into the drive. This was the next and final stage in the testing. He'd perfected the procedure on animals, but now he needed to trial it on a human before he was ready for Alisha. He needed someone who wouldn't be missed. What better than an old person without any relatives. Then the only decision was whether to deal with Eva before or after Alisha. Clearly, it would be a waste of his time and resources to preserve the child. She was beyond hope, always had been, and he felt nothing towards her but bitter resentment. The ancient Amazonian tribes had the right idea when they left sick and deformed babies to die in the forest. But he'd deal with Eva when the time came. There was no rush, as no one knew she was there except him and Alisha.

Arriving as planned at 2.30 p.m., Amit parked in a side road close to St James' Hospital. With mounting anticipation and pushing aside any fear he may fail or, worse, be caught, he removed his coat and clipped his identity badge to the pocket of his scrubs. He needed to stay focused and positive, his plan required bravado. There was no room for doubt or hesitation. He was relying on the security guard and hospital staff being too busy with the flu epidemic to notice his ID was from a different hospital. They looked very similar from a distance. And with nearly half of St James' staff being agency, there'd be little continuity, so he doubted another new face in their midst would stand out.

Amit wiped the perspiration from his forehead. Then, summoning the confidence of a man in hospital scrubs who has every right to be there, and with his heart drumming loudly, he went in the main entrance and through reception. The security guard nodded respectfully at him and he returned a tight smile. It was very busy, as he knew it would be, especially at this time. In addition to those attending outpatients appointments, it was half an hour after the start of visiting time and he knew from the hospital where he worked this was when most people visited. They generally left around 4 p.m., then there was a lull until the evening visitors began to arrive around 5.30 p.m. He needed to be out by 4 p.m.

His palms sweating, Amit checked the map of the hospital he'd downloaded to his phone and continued to the staircase, then up to the second floor. Elizabeth Ward, St Anne's and King Edward were situated here and were top of his list. These were general medical wards where patients would be recovering from a number of different illnesses, including transfers from Accident and Emergency. But, more crucially, they were now having to act as holding stations for the elderly until they could be discharged home.

Elizabeth Ward first, he decided, and getting in was the first hurdle. His swipe card wouldn't work in another hospital, so he waited a little way up the corridor until a group of visitors buzzed to be admitted and he followed them in. Easy.

The layout of this ward and the other wards he planned to visit was standard, with a central corridor and six-bed wards leading off. Forty-two beds in all. The nurses' station was in the centre and it was empty. All the nurses were occupied, tending to patients or answering relatives' questions. He could tell from the nurses' expressions as he passed them in the corridor just how stressed and overworked they were. Other than an acknowledging nod or hello they didn't bother with him – a doctor in blue scrubs and wearing an ID badge.

He was sweating freely now – why were hospital wards always so fucking hot? The temperature and humidity in the operating theatre where he spent most of his time was carefully regulated. Taking a tissue from his pocket, he mopped his brow. Then, assuming the air of a doctor checking on his patients, he wandered in and out of the wards. They were full to capacity. There wasn't a single empty bed, and since he'd arrived a new patient had been wheeled in on a gurney. There were plenty of elderly patients, but most of them had visitors. He took another tour, then returned to the first of the two possible candidates who appeared to meet his criteria: old and infirm and who didn't have any visitors. Heavily wrinkled and nearly bald, she was propped up on a mound of pillows and staring into space. Amit set his expression to professional doctorly concern and unhooked the observation chart from the end of her bed.

'How are you today, Elsie?' he asked, reading her name from the chart.

'Not too bad,' she croaked, her voice hoarse and her lips dry.

'Are you drinking enough?' He nudged the beaker on her bedside cabinet closer.

'Yes, Doctor.'

'No visitors, then?' he asked nonchalantly while studying her chart.

'My son will be here later when he's finished work.'

That ruled her out. 'Good,' he said. 'Well, make sure you drink plenty.'

He returned the chart to the end of her bed, went into the main corridor and gulped in air. Now for the other possible. Using the same tactics, he approached Miss Kerry, but she told him she was expecting her brother to visit shortly. Having exhausted both possibilities on this ward, Amit left.

He would try the male ward next, King Edward. He went further along the corridor. A visitor was coming out and held the door open for him to go in. 'Thank you,' he said politely.

He would employ the same modus operandi. A couple of tours of the wards as if he was looking for a patient he needed to check on, then approach those without visitors. Again, the staff were far too busy to notice him. There were five patients here without visitors, but three of them were too young to be of any use to him. He went to the first of the other two.

'Hello, Mr Ridley,' he said, unclipping his chart from the end of the bed. 'How are you?'

'Not too bad.'

'No visitors today?'

'My wife's coming later.'

'Very good.'

As he left, a nurse came in wheeling a blood pressure monitor but gave him no more than a cursory glance. He nodded as she passed and went to the next six-bed ward and to Mr Smith, but as he unclipped the chart, a visitor arrived.

'Wrong Mr Smith,' he said, returning the chart to the bed, and quickly left.

Disappointed, but aware he'd have been lucky finding what he wanted straight away, he continued to the other women's ward, St Anne's. This time he had to buzz to be let in, but, as he expected, they were too busy to worry about who they were admitting and released the door without question. Chaos greeted him. A woman, presumably with dementia, was shouting nonsense at the top of her voice, call bells were bleeping, two patients lay on trolleys waiting to be admitted, and the red-faced charge nurse at the nurses' station was agitatedly telling someone on the phone that it was impossible, they were completely full and she couldn't magic a bed out of thin air.

'Mrs Lynda Jones was supposed to have gone today, but her social worker cancelled,' she said as he passed. That was good news.

Keeping his head down, Amit went in search of Mrs

Jones and found her in bed 27. No visitors present, and when he read her chart, he saw she'd had a stroke that had affected her mobility and speech and left her very confused. Perfect. Fingers crossed.

His adrenalin kicked in.

'Hello, Mrs Jones,' he said, enunciating every word. She turned her scrawny head to look at him. 'How are you?'

She frowned, puzzled.

'Are you looking forward to going home?'

A long pause, a sigh and then her mouth twisted to form the words, not unlike the way Eva's did. 'They won't let me.'

'Why is that?' he asked.

She frowned again but didn't offer any reason.

'She can't understand much, poor dear,' the woman in the next bed called over.

'Thank you,' Amit said and partially drew the curtain. Nosy bitch.

He returned to Mrs Jones.

'Is there no one at home to look after you?' he asked, his mouth close to her ear. He could smell hospital soap on old flesh. Disgusting.

Another pause, then, after much effort, her damaged brain slowly made the connection. 'I want to be with Harry.'

Amit's heart sank. 'Who is Harry?'

'My husband,' she uttered.

He was about to return the chart to the end of the bed and leave when she began to speak again, slow and faltering, but her words were pure joy.

'He died last year. I want to be with him.' Her eyes filled.

Amit returned to her side. 'I am sorry. Don't you have any other relatives who can look after you?'

Her mouth worked silently before her brain engaged. 'No. Only a nephew and he doesn't want me.'

Amit smiled. 'I'm sure he could be persuaded. What's his name?'

She looked confused, her face lopsided from the stroke. 'Bert.'

'And his surname?'

'Bert.'

'Bert what?' Stupid woman. Sweat was running off him. He daren't stay for much longer. 'What's Bert's surname? Do you know?'

She stared at him without a clue.

'Saunders,' he said, using the first name that came to mind. 'Bert Saunders, your nephew, will be coming to collect you tomorrow. Can you remember that?'

She looked back vacantly. He doubted she would remember, but it didn't matter; she was so confused, she wouldn't know what was going on and protest.

He returned her chart to the end of the bed, then, keeping his back to the woman in the next bed, left. He congratulated himself; he'd done well, made better progress than he'd expected. The next part of his plan relied on timing, panache and a pinch of good luck. If he failed, he'd have to start all over again at another hospital and he didn't have the time for that.

Chapter Twenty-Two

Seven o'clock in the evening was the best time to phone, Amit decided. In most NHS hospitals that was when the night shift took over from the day staff. Showered and out of his scrubs, he sat on the edge of the bed in the anonymous motel room and watched the minutes tick by on his phone. The name Bert Saunders and his contact details were written on a piece of paper by his side, for he mustn't hesitate or falter. He knew hospital discharge procedure, and as long as he delivered what they needed to hear with enough confidence, his plan should work. He eased his collar from his neck; he was perspiring again and he'd only just showered.

He had allowed two minutes for the hospital switchboard to connect him, so at 6.58 p.m. he keyed in the number for St James' Hospital. All calls to NHS hospitals were routed through a main hospital number and members of the public couldn't phone a ward direct. As far as St James' Hospital was concerned, he was a relative. The line was busy and it was 7.03 p.m. before the call was connected and a tired voice said, 'St James' General Hospital.'

'Can you put me through to St Anne's Ward, please? I need to make arrangements to collect a relative being discharged tomorrow.' It was more information than she needed, but he'd found before in other matters that if you gave more information than was required it stopped the person from thinking up their own questions or even following procedure. Stating his intentions also bolstered his confidence.

'Putting you through to the ward now,' the call handler said without hesitation.

Amit took a deep breath and tried to calm his racing heart. There was a click on the line, a short silence and then the phone on the ward began ringing. It rang and rang. Amit could picture the scene at the other end. The handover meeting on the ward, where exhausted day staff passed information on patients to the night shift while call buzzers bleeped and relatives tried to find a nurse.

At 7.06 p.m. the phone was finally answered tersely by a male nurse. 'St Anne's Ward.'

'Good evening. My name is Mr Bert Saunders. I'm sorry I didn't return your call earlier. I've been in meetings most of the day. Just to confirm I will be able to collect my aunt, Mrs Lynda Jones, tomorrow afternoon at three o'clock. I've spoken to her social worker. Can you make sure she is ready please, with any medication she needs?'

'Yes, I'll make a note on the system. Thank you for letting us know.'

Saying goodbye, Amit cut the call and smiled. He knew from working in hospitals, and human nature being what it was, that the nurse would assume the missing information – the phone call, relative's name and details of discharge – hadn't been entered because of an oversight and would quickly correct the mistake. He'd seen similar happen before, omissions and errors corrected before management noticed.

Thankfully, Mrs Jones was frail and confused, so Amit doubted she'd raise any queries about who was taking her home, but if she did he'd have to think on his feet and deal with any problems as they arose. Once she was in the car, he'd sedate her – the syringe and sedative he needed were in his bag – then she'd look like any old woman asleep in a car. He should be home around five o'clock when it would be dark. He'd park the car in his garage, tell Alisha he needed his dinner straight away so she was kept occupied, then wrap the old woman in a large bin bag and take her to the lab. If anyone did see him, they'd think he was shifting a sack of rubbish, similar to when he'd disposed of the animals. Once inside his lab he would be safe; no one could see or hear a thing. He planned to have dinner first before he began the procedure – he could never concentrate on an empty stomach. No need to bring her round from the sedation, he'd put her straight into the ice bath, then, following the same technique he'd perfected on the animals, he'd drain her blood, replace it with preservation fluid, then lower her temperature to minus 130°C, when he'd place her in the cylinder of liquid nitrogen and store her overnight at minus 190°C. It would be the first time he'd used the cylinder and he felt a stab of excitement.

Assuming he revived her successfully the following day – and there was no reason why he shouldn't – he'd be ready for Alisha. He thought Christmas Day would be good. There'd be no deliveries or callers and neighbours – namely Emily King – would be too ensconced with their families to notice what was going on next door. It would be the ultimate Christmas present, he thought with a wry smile as he prepared to leave his hotel room for something to eat. Life everlasting, and although Mrs Jones wouldn't appreciate what he'd achieved, the world of medical science would.

Chapter Twenty-Three

Despite downing a bottle of wine with his dinner, Amit didn't sleep well and it left him in a bad mood. The hotel was close to a main road and although the windows were double-glazed he'd heard the steady hum of traffic most of the night. Also, guests had arrived noisily along his corridor at 1 a.m. People were so thoughtless. His house was quiet; Alisha knew not to disturb him when she saw to Eva in the night.

He made a coffee and drank it while he showered, and then dressed in the brown corduroy trousers, open-neck shirt and jersey he'd packed. It was 9 a.m. He had nearly six hours to kill before he could go to St James' Hospital to collect his subject – as he now considered Mrs Jones to be. The time yawned before him. It was such a waste when he had so much to do, but to have arranged to collect her any earlier would have been too risky. The doctors did their rounds in the morning and the day shift of nurses would be bright and fresh. Much better to wait until the afternoon and go at peak visiting time as he had before. Breakfast first.

Making sure he hadn't left anything in his room, Amit went down to reception and checked out, complaining about the noise as he did. The young receptionist stared unabashed at his different-coloured irises and said she'd make a note of his complaint but didn't offer a refund. Ignorant bitch. On the way out, he allowed the front door to slam shut to emphasize his point about noise. Breakfast should put him in a better mood.

He found his car was covered with a thick layer of frost and he had to sit for some moments with the engine running waiting for the windscreen to clear. He left the hotel's car park and then joined the main road, heading in the direction of Lewis city. He'd look out for a roadside café with plenty of lorries and white vans suggesting a good breakfast at a reasonable price, and found one after a few miles.

He parked and went in; the air was heavy with the smell of fried food. Delicious. He was starving. Helping himself to a copy of the free local newspaper, he chose a table away from the window and ordered a full English breakfast with a mug of coffee. Later, he'd phone Alisha and tell her he would be home for dinner that evening. There was no point in phoning her now, she'd be washing and dressing that useless child.

As he ate, he flipped through the newspaper and spotted

an advertisement for the History of Surgery Museum, which had fascinated him as a medical student. That would keep him occupied until it was time to go to St James'. Now he had a plan for the morning, and with his appetite satiated, he felt much better. He drained the last of his coffee, paid the bill and returned to his car.

He had visited the museum regularly as a student, and often alone. His fellow students had been once or twice out of curiosity but not regularly. They found his obsession with the gruesome exhibits odd, but they were an unimaginative lot who could see no further than passing their exams.

The building was virtually unchanged from his last visit. A detached atmospheric Victorian house adapted in the 1950s for its present use. He went in and paid. They weren't busy, the curator told him, as most of the students from the local universities – their most regular attenders – had gone home for Christmas. Amit thanked him, took his ticket and entered the first room.

The dank smell of furniture polish wafted from the wood of the display cabinets, nostalgically reminding him of his previous visits. Going to the first cabinet, he began poring over the exhibits, reading the printed captions beneath each item, as he had before. The surgical tools dating back to the 1700s were like instruments of torture and used before anaesthetic had been discovered. He thought now, as he had before, it was a wonder any of the patients survived. How they must have screamed! If they didn't die from the shock or the pain of being operated on while conscious, then many of them died soon after from infection, a caption said.

Amputation knives that looked like machetes, he remembered them well, with a caption explaining that the surgeon cut through the skin and muscle first, then used a saw for severing the bone. He moved on to an artificial leech used for bloodletting with a rotating blade attached to a cup that caught the patient's blood. Amazing that they used to think bloodletting would cure an illness!

Next was a cervical dilator used to stretch a woman's cervix during labour. Serrated and going to a sharp point, it often did more harm than good. Circumcision knives that looked like giant scissors with a wire noose for slicing off the foreskin. He grimaced. Tonsil guillotines, haemorrhoid forceps, hernia tools, a skull saw. Mostly rusty now and some with what could have been dried blood and tissue still on them. Sepia photographs of operations in progress added to his imagination. Fascinating.

Absorbed in the barbaric world of primitive surgery, Amit wandered from room to room and wondered how current medical practices would be looked on in two hundred years. It would probably seem as crude as this – except for his work, of course. That was ahead of time.

Three hours quickly passed, during which time he only saw two other visitors. Suddenly he found it was 1.15 p.m. and he needed to be leaving. Thanking the curator, he said goodbye and returned to his car. He programmed the satnav and began in the direction of St James' Hospital.

He stopped briefly to pick up a coffee from a layby café, which he drank while parked, and also took the opportunity to phone Alisha. The line was engaged, which was very odd. Alisha didn't use the phone; she didn't know anyone to call. He tried again with the same result. Perhaps the line was faulty? Puzzled and annoyed, he finished his coffee and pressed his landline number again. This time it was answered immediately with a small, 'Hello?'

'Who were you talking to just now?' he demanded.

'No one,' Alisha replied.

'The phone has been engaged for at least the last ten minutes.'

'I must have knocked it off its base while cleaning.'

He heard the quiver in her voice and knew she was lying. It would be easy to check later.

'The conference finished early, so I'll be home tonight for dinner.'

'There isn't much, we're running low.'

'Cook what you have,' he snapped, irritated. 'I'll do an online shop tonight.'

'Or I could do it if you showed me how.'

He took a breath, his fingers clenching in anger. She'd never suggested that before. 'You don't know the first thing about computers or the internet,' he said, his voice tight.

'No. But I could learn.'

'Rubbish,' he said and ended the call.

Of course she couldn't be allowed to learn how to use the internet, for the same reasons he'd never let her have a phone, laptop or tablet. If she had access to the outside world, who knew who she might talk to and what she might find out. Not long now and then he wouldn't have to worry any more. She wouldn't be accessing anything for a very long time.

At 2.50 p.m., Amit parked his car in one of the bays close to the main entrance of St James' Hospital reserved for collecting and dropping off patients. Despite the cold, he was perspiring again. This was the critical phase of his plan. Success or failure loomed, and he couldn't afford to fail. He wiped his brow with a tissue and slipped on his jacket. He took the collapsible wheelchair he'd hired for a week from the boot of the car and began towards the main doors of the hospital, keeping his head down and away from the CCTV.

Inside, the security guard was nowhere to be seen and he continued towards the lift. Suddenly, he froze. A woman was coming towards him, waving. Did she know him? Shit! His stomach clenched. Sometimes patients recognized their surgeon in the street but not normally their anaesthetist. But no. Thank goodness. False alarm. It wasn't him. She was approaching the man to his right.

Amit allowed himself to breathe again. *Stay calm*, he told himself. *Don't lose your nerve. It's unlikely anyone will recognize you here.*

Pushing the wheelchair to the lift, he rose to the second floor. No scrubs or ID badge now to protect him. Just Bert Saunders collecting his elderly aunt. It relied on him acting confidently and delivering what he had to say with authority. He'd practised it enough in front of the mirror.

Steeling himself for what lay ahead, Amit pressed the security buzzer for the ward and a few seconds later the door released. He drew himself to his full height and pushed the wheelchair confidently down the corridor, past the nurses' station, which was empty, and towards the side ward where Mrs Jones lay. He peered in but didn't enter. Good. She was out of bed, dressed and sitting in her bedside chair, ready to go home. While it may have made sense to have gone in and said a few words to prepare her for leaving, he couldn't take the risk that the woman in the next bed wouldn't see him. 'Aunty' was unlikely to remember him in his scrubs from the day before, but that woman might.

Satisfied she was ready to go, he went in search of a nurse. 'I'm here to collect my aunt, Mrs Lynda Jones,' he said evenly, glancing at his watch as if he was short of time. 'Is her medication ready?' He knew that patients who'd been discharged were often kept waiting on the ward for their medicines to arrive from the pharmacy.

'I'll just check,' she said. He went with her to the nurses' station and waited while she logged on to the computer. 'I'm sorry,' she said at last. 'Her meds aren't here yet. They shouldn't be long.'

'We'll collect them on our way out,' he said. 'Would you phone the pharmacy and tell them we're on our way, please?'

She nodded and he left her making the call as he

began back towards the side ward. He knew the procedure, although he had no intention of wasting time by collecting her medication. She wouldn't need tablets where she was going.

The next part was make or break. He pushed the wheelchair onto the ward and up to Mrs Jones' chair, quickly drawing the curtains around her bed. They were hidden from view.

'Hello, Aunty,' he whispered, close to her ear. 'It's your nephew, Bert. We're going home.'

She tried to turn her head to look at him, but he moved out of her line of vision. She didn't appear to have a coat but was wearing a thick cardigan. That would have to do.

'Time to go,' he said. 'Can you stand by yourself?'

She shook her head. Stemming his revulsion at having to touch her, he slid one arm under her knees and the other around her back, scooped her up and dumped her into the wheelchair. She was light, there was nothing of her, but, Jesus, that smell. She gave a small startled cry like a strangled cat and her mouth worked as if trying to say something, but nothing came out.

'Soon have you home,' he said.

Positioning himself behind the wheelchair, he steered it to the end of the bed, parted the curtains just wide enough for them to get out and was quickly out of the side ward. Down the main corridor, past the nurses' station. The nurse he'd spoken to was still on the phone. He kept his gaze ahead and focused on the exit.

Suddenly, footsteps sounded behind them. He kept going. They quickened. Then a man's voice. 'Stop! Wait!'

Amit's breath caught in his throat, but he continued to the doors and pressed the button to exit. It was a few moments before the doors opened and in that time the footsteps caught up with him. He felt a tap on his shoulder and froze. Dear God, surely he wouldn't be caught now? He was nearly out.

'You left her bag, mate.'

Amit turned and looked at the youth.

'I'm visiting my mum in the bed opposite and she spotted her bag under her bed.' He handed Amit the bag.

'Thank you,' he said, his voice shaking.

'You're welcome. Mum says to give Mrs Jones her best wishes. She's sorry she didn't have a chance to say goodbye.'

'I will,' Amit called, and the doors closed behind him.

Chapter Twenty-Four

Fists knuckle-white, Amit gripped the handlebars of the wheelchair and pushed it towards the lift. How stupid of him not to have checked under the bed for her bag. A silly mistake like that could have cost him everything, but thankfully it hadn't. He'd soon be outside, he told himself, and his plans would continue.

The old woman kept trying to turn her head to see who was pushing the wheelchair, but the weakness in her neck muscles from the stroke wouldn't allow her to.

'It's your nephew, Bert,' he told her in his most conciliatory tone, for he didn't want a scene here in the hospital.

The lift seemed to take ages to arrive, although it was probably no more than a minute or so. A couple came in just behind him and he pushed the wheelchair to the rear wall. He felt their eyes on him as the lift descended, perhaps wondering why the old woman was so agitated and kept craning her neck, trying to see behind her. When the lift stopped, he waited until they were well clear before dragging the wheelchair out.

Head down, away from the CCTV, he felt perspiration trickle down his back as he began towards the exit. Past the security guard, the old woman uttered something, then they were outside.

'I'm cold,' she said clearly, and shivered.

'Soon have you in the warm,' he replied loudly for the benefit of anyone who'd overheard.

The parking bay where he'd left the car was too close to the main entrance to inject her there. Those going in and out might see, especially if she made a fuss. He positioned the wheelchair by the car and, opening the rear door, carefully lifted her in. Her face was close to his for a few seconds and he smelt her fetid breath as she tried to say something. He quickly deposited her on the seat, fastened her seat belt and closed the door. He breathed in the cool fresh air, mopped his brow, and then stowed the wheelchair in the boot.

As he slid into the driver's seat, she mumbled something.

'What?' he demanded, glancing at her in the rear-view mirror.

Her mouth worked. 'You're not Bert.'

'Really? And you're sure of that?' He laughed cruelly and, starting the engine, reversed out of the bay.

'Not Bert. Where's Harry?' she cried.

'Shut up, you silly old bitch!'

Amit accelerated as fast as the one-way system leading out of the hospital would allow.

She kept chuntering, 'You're not Bert.' Perhaps the cold had stimulated her, for she seemed more alert now than she had in hospital. He pressed the central-locking system in case she tried to escape and continued out of the hospital grounds and then into the quiet side street he'd parked in on his previous visit.

Cutting the engine, he opened the bag he had ready on the passenger seat and took out a leather pouch. He removed a syringe and one of the two phials of anaesthetic. Keeping his hands low behind the seat back so she couldn't see what he was doing, he drew the solution into the syringe. How much he would need to give her was a guesstimate. He didn't have access to her medical records as he did with patients who were being operated on. Doses were based on weight, age and medical history. To be on the safe side – he didn't want her waking halfway through the journey when he might not be able to easily stop to top it up – he'd give her the maximum. That should see her home and into his lab.

Concealing the filled syringe in the palm of his hand, Amit got out of the car and, opening the rear door, slid in beside her. She looked at him with a mixture of confusion and alarm. Checking there was no one passing, he quickly pulled up her sleeve and plunged the needle into her scrawny arm. She screamed and tried to pull away, but she was no match for him. Gripping her arm, he emptied in the rest of the phial. Within seconds, her body relaxed, her eyes closed and her head lolled to one side. Perfect. He smiled.

He reached over to the front seat and returned the syringe to the leather pouch for disposing of later, then propped the old woman upright and adjusted the headrest to support her head. With her eyes closed and her jaw hanging open, she looked like any old woman asleep in the car.

He sat back for a moment and forced himself to breathe normally. He'd done it. He'd actually done it! His bold, audacious plan had been executed successfully. All that planning, attention to detail, together with plain bravado, had paid off. Congratulating himself, he returned to the driver's seat, started the engine, and headed for home. Life was getting better and better.

Chapter Twenty-Five

'Sorry I had to dash away from the phone,' Emily said as soon as Alisha answered. 'Robbie was trying to climb up the Christmas tree.'

Alisha chuckled. 'He's into everything.'

'Tell me about it!'

'Eva misses Robbie,' Alisha said. 'She was so disappointed I had to cancel your visit. I tried to explain it was because her father's conference ended early and he was on his way home, but she wasn't impressed. Just as well Amit doesn't have anything to do with Eva or she could drop me in it.'

'Tell her we'll get together in the new year when everything is back to normal. You have a good Christmas.'

'And you. And, Emily . . .' Alisha paused, 'I really am sorry you never got Tibs back.'

'I know, you said. That's kind of you, but we've come

to terms with it. I guess you saw that update on the local news yesterday.'

'No. What was that?'

'You remember the dead animals that were found in Coleshaw Woods and had been drained of blood? The police thought they'd been used in some satanic ritual?'

'Yes,' Alisha said hesitantly. 'You phoned to see if any of them had been microchipped?'

'That's right. But they couldn't tell. They're now saying they think it was the work of an illegal taxidermist. You know, those people who stuff animals.'

'Really?' Alisha's voice was slight. 'Why do they think that?'

'Apparently all the bodies had traces of a preserving fluid in them similar to one used by taxidermists. The RSPCA spokesperson said it's usually rare animals like tigers that are poached and imported illegally to be stuffed. Collectors pay huge sums. But they warned pet owners to keep their pets in at night until they catch the person or persons responsible.'

'You don't think that could have happened to Tibs?' Alisha asked after a moment.

'I hope not. But the chances are we'll never know. Anyway, it's nearly Christmas, so have a good one, and we'll get together in the new year.'

'Yes, thanks, and you.' Alisha returned the phone to its cradle.

Preserving fluid. That word again. Alisha's gaze went to the building at the bottom of their garden, Amit's lab. The mouse she'd found there had been well preserved, and now the animals in Coleshaw Woods had been shown to have preserving fluid in them. With a familiar stab of fear, she reluctantly drew her thoughts to the CCTV recording she'd watched when Amit had thrown animal collars in the bin and had dropped Tibs'. It was the same night he'd left very late carrying the heavy sacks of what looked like rubbish. Was this all connected? Did she really want to know? And that large cylinder-shaped object Amit had taken delivery of the afternoon he'd shut her in the cloak-room, and Emily had captured on her phone. The size and shape of the object under its packaging had seemed familiar, but from where exactly?

There was over an hour before Amit would arrive home and Eva was upstairs watching television. Alisha went quickly into the study. It was Amit's domain now and while it wasn't locked she'd had no reason to go in it – until now. Crammed full of books, medical journals and research papers, they were everywhere, and not in any order. On the top shelf she spotted her old nursing books, untouched for years and largely out of date. But she didn't think it was a book she was looking for.

She began going through the magazines, brochures and flyers, advertising seminars, conferences, drug trials and new medicines. Read and then haphazardly thrown onto the piles in the order they'd arrived. She didn't know exactly what she was looking for – hopefully confirmation that her suspicions were completely unfounded and Amit wasn't experimenting on animals to find a cure for her condition.

She moved to the filing cabinet and tried the drawers, but they were locked. When had he started locking them? On top of the cabinet was a pile of invoices. She took them down and flicked through, but they were old – goods he'd had delivered over a year ago, including online grocery shopping. She returned them to the top of the cabinet and picked up a miscellaneous pile of journals and glossy leaflets. Again they weren't in any apparent order. A little way in, she found a page torn from a newspaper. An article headed 'Back From The Dead!'. She remembered Amit had shown her the article some time ago. She began to read it, the same horror and revulsion filling her now as it had then. A fifteen-year-old boy suffering from an incurable genetic condition was to be frozen in the hope he could be brought back to life at a later date and cured. Amit had wanted her to do the same and had become angry when she'd refused. He'd ridiculed her and sneered when she'd said it was going against the law of God and nature. So why had he bothered to cut out and keep this article? She returned it carefully to the pile.

Next was a glossy brochure with a photograph on the front showing a small group of men and women in white lab coats standing outside a building bearing the name ELECT. Eternal Life Education Cryonics Trust. The caption beneath said they were the team that ran ELECT, a cryonics organization, dedicated to preserving life.

Alisha slowly opened the booklet and stopped. Her stomach contracted and her hand trembled. The photograph she was now looking at had been taken inside a laboratory and showed rows of aluminium cylinders. The wording below explained bodies were preserved in these tanks at minus 190°C. She stared in horror. There was no mistake. The cylinder that had been delivered and was now in Amit's lab was exactly the same size and shape as these.

Chapter Twenty-Six

Mouth gaping open, the old woman was snoring heavily and it was getting on Amit's nerves. 'Shut up, will you!' he shouted as he drove, and turned up the radio to drown out the noise. He was driving steadily in the middle lane of the motorway, just below the speed limit. While he wanted to get to his lab as soon as possible, he certainly didn't want to draw the attention of a passing patrol car by speeding.

Other than the racket the old woman was making, life was good, he thought, and he was still feeling very pleased with himself. All had gone well in removing her from the hospital, and the mounting excitement he now felt at what lay ahead was orgasmic in its intensity. Not only would he be making medical history, but soon he would be one step ahead of ELECT and the other scientists working on cryonics. While freezing animals and bringing them back to life had been accomplished a number of times in laboratories, doing the same with a human would be a first! The old woman didn't know it, but she too was making an important contribution to medical science – as would Alisha.

He could picture it now, the world's media gathered outside his lab with their cameras and microphones at the ready. He'd only be able to let a few into his lab – the main broadcasters – for there wasn't much room. BBC, CNN, Fox News and *South China Morning Post* he decided. In front of a live audience of millions, he'd raise Alisha from the cylinder of liquid nitrogen, transfuse her blood back into her veins and gradually warm her body until she regained consciousness. Instant fame and acclamation! It was important, he'd decided, to have the world's media present so there could be no doubt that what he'd accomplished was genuine and recorded. To have used his own video recording could have led to claims of fraud, as it was so easy to manipulate and falsify videos and photographs online. But with a selection of journalists watching, there could be no doubt he had brought someone back to life and created immortality.

He glanced in the rear-view mirror at the old woman. Her head was lolling to one side and she was looking a bit pale. Unfortunately he couldn't monitor her vital signs as he could in the operating room. He turned down the music until he could hear her snoring, more lightly now, then turned it up again. 'Not too far now,' he said, more for his own benefit than hers.

Yes, he was feeling very pleased with himself and was sure he'd covered every eventuality, even his own demise. If he suddenly dropped dead or was run over before he'd woken Alisha, his work wouldn't go to waste. He'd recorded an ICE message on his phone: In Case of Emergency. ELECT were to be contacted and he'd included their phone number. They knew what to do. He'd given them instructions in a sealed envelope – his last wishes – when he'd signed up and paid to become a member and have his body preserved. It wasn't unusual – most of their members had last wishes. ELECT also knew he'd left everything to them in his will. Yes, he'd covered every eventuality.

Amit glanced again in the rear-view mirror. The old woman was now slumped forward so her chin was resting on her chest. Drat. That wasn't good. She could reduce her airflow in that position. With her neck muscles already weak from the stroke, she might cut off her trachea completely. He turned down the music and shouted, 'Sit up, you silly bitch!' Patients retained some hearing and could follow simple instructions under anaesthetic. 'Sit up!' he shouted again, then stamped on the brake as the red lights of the car in front came on. 'Mrs Jones! Get your fucking head up!'

She didn't; nor did she stir or give any sign she'd heard him. Fuck! He couldn't leave her like that. There was another half an hour to home. He'd have to pull onto the hard shoulder and prop up her head. But, on second thoughts, it would probably be best to lie her flat on the back seat for the rest of the journey so her airway could more easily stay open.

He indicated left, waited for a gap in the traffic, then pulled to the inside lane and onto the hard shoulder. Coming to a halt, he switched on the hazard warning lights and opened his door. The rush of traffic was deafening as cars, vans and lorries zoomed by in a relentless procession of fumes and wind rush. He knew that stopping on the hard shoulder was the most dangerous place on a motorway, so he needed to be quick.

A few strides took him round the back of the car and he opened the offside rear door. He released her seat belt, caught her before she fell forward and laid her flat on the seat, slightly bending her knees so she fitted in. If he anchored her with all three seat belts, she shouldn't roll off if he suddenly had to break. Reaching right over to the seat belt that was furthest away, he extended it to its full length and wrapped it under her arms and around her chest. She'd stopped snoring now, which was a relief. He fastened the buckle, moved to the next belt and, pulling it out, wrapped it around her middle. He paused, his gaze going to her chest, and waited. Nothing happened. He waited again. Her chest wasn't moving, or if it was it was very slight. He put his cheek to her mouth but couldn't feel her breath. Oh shit! This couldn't be happening. He grabbed her wrist and felt for a pulse. Nothing. Panic took hold. In the hospital he had oxygen and a defibrillator, but now there was just him.

'You stupid, stupid cow!' he yelled and slapped her face

hard. Her head jolted. 'Calm down,' he told himself. 'You need to do CPR.'

Stemming his revulsion, he placed his mouth over hers, gave two rescue breaths and gagged. Then, straddling her torso, he interlocked his fingers and used the heel of his hand to begin chest compressions. Press, release, press, release. It was years since he'd had to do this. There was no need in the theatre. Two compressions a second, so one hundred and twenty a minute, then two more rescue breaths and continue the compressions. He worked frantically, pressing down, releasing, down, releasing, putting all his weight behind it. Desperately forcing the blood around her body, willing her back to life by kick-starting the heart. He heard her ribs crack as he worked. He knew it could happen giving CPR, especially to the old whose bones were brittle. He paused and searched for a pulse. Nothing. Two more rescue breaths and he continued the compressions, more forcefully and desperate now.

'You silly fucking cow! Breathe!' he shouted and struck her chest. Blood oozed from the corner of her mouth. He stared at her in horror, wiped the sweat from his forehead, then roughly pulled up her eyelids. As he feared, the pupils were fixed and dilated. She was dead! There was no bringing her back. The silly bitch had died. It had all been for nothing.

Amit sat at the end of the back seat staring at her, unable to believe what had happened. All that work and planning – to end like this. But why had she died? Too much anaesthetic? Shock? It was possible. Or would she have died anyway, whatever he'd done and wherever she'd been? Perhaps her time had come, although he didn't sign up to that.

Half an hour and they would have been home! Now what? What was he supposed to do? *Calm down*, he told himself again, *and try to think what to do for the best.* He couldn't stay here on the hard shoulder of the motorway for much longer. The car might get hit by one of the lorries steaming by or be spotted by a passing patrol car. But what was he going to do with her? He couldn't dump her here, it was too open, someone would see. *Get off the motorway first and then decide*, he told himself. Yes, that would be the next best step.

Hot and clammy despite the cold, he slammed the rear door shut and returned to the driver's seat. He still couldn't believe it. All his plans and hard work destroyed, just like that. But he needed to concentrate. He had a dead body in the back of the car.

The traffic was relentless. Starting the car, he indicated and began along the hard shoulder, gradually picking up speed as he looked for a gap in the traffic. Lorries lumbered by far too close. 'Bastards!' he muttered, his fists clenched. So much traffic, unwilling to let him in. Finally a car flashed its headlights and pulled back to allow him room. 'Thank you,' he said and gave the driver a courtesy wave.

Relieved, Amit checked the rear-view mirror but couldn't see the old woman, which was good. Lying flat on the back seat, those passing wouldn't be able to see her either. He'd get off the motorway at the next exit and then take the quieter B roads home. But what was he supposed to do with her once he arrived? How would he dispose of her body? He could smuggle her into his lab as planned, but what then? Bury her in the garden? Hardly. All that digging to make a hole deep and wide enough to hold a body – someone was sure to see. Alisha, or that bitch next door looking out of her bedroom window. No, he couldn't risk burying her in the garden.

His original plan had been that after he'd brought the old woman back to life he'd drop her off somewhere and let whoever found her deal with her. She'd have been even more confused and wouldn't have had a clue where she'd been or what had happened to her. She certainly wouldn't have known who he was. If the police had launched an appeal to try to identify her and circulated her photograph, and *if* a member of staff at St James' Hospital had recognized her, that was where the trail would have ended. He'd covered his tracks well, and the police wouldn't have wasted much of their valuable time and resources on a confused old woman who hadn't long for this world.

But all that had changed now, and had he known he was going to have to dispose of a body, he could have prepared for it. An acid bath would have reduced her to nothing, but he hadn't bought acid, for never in all his planning had he imagined she would die like this!

He glanced in the rear-view mirror at the traffic behind and his breath caught in his throat. A police car was in the middle lane, three cars back. A routine patrol, he told himself, nothing to worry about, but he instinctively eased his foot off the accelerator as others were doing. A sign appeared to his left, showing the next exit, not far now.

He took a deep breath, tried to calm himself and checked in his mirror again for the patrol car. It was creeping slowly up the middle lane, two cars back now. Nothing to worry about. They wouldn't be able to see in any more than anyone else in a car would, and even if they did, it was just an old woman stretched out on the back seat asleep. The police would go by and continue on their way.

Don't act suspiciously and you'll be fine. There's no reason for them to stop you, he told himself. *They'll be looking for someone breaking the speed limit or driving an uninsured or stolen vehicle.* Keeping his gaze straight ahead and with both hands gripping the wheel, he continued at the same speed.

After a few moments, he surreptitiously glanced in his wing mirror again and saw the police car was only one car behind now. He continued steadily at sixty miles per hour. Out of the corner of his eye, he saw it draw parallel, but he kept looking to the front. It would pass soon and appear again in his line of vision. He waited as the three lanes of traffic continued to move together, no one daring to overtake the patrol car.

Suddenly he started as a car horn sounded to his right. Not the patrol car? Surely not? Not tooting at him? Perhaps it was tooting at the vehicle in front? His driving was perfect, he was doing nothing wrong, but he daren't risk looking over to his right.

The car horn sounded again. No doubt this time. The patrol car gave a single wail of its siren, trying to attract someone's attention. Not his. Please, not his. An icy chill ran up his spine. Another toot of the patrol car's horn. He had to look now, he couldn't ignore it any longer. He glanced to his right and met the gaze of the officer in the passenger seat, motioning at him.

Amit's first thought was to put his foot hard down on the accelerator and try to outrun them, but that was ridiculous. There was nowhere to go; the motorway was full of traffic all moving at the same speed. Another wail of the siren and he looked to his right again, perspiration running down his neck and back. The officer was signalling, a circular motion, and he realized he was telling him to lower his window. With his hand shaking and bile rising in his throat, Amit lowered his car window. The officer did the same. Amit braced himself for being told to pull over.

'Your hazard warning lights are on!' the officer shouted over the traffic noise. It took a moment for him to appreciate what he was saying, then logic returned.

'Thank you!' Amit shouted and switched off the hazard warning lights he'd left on from when he'd parked on the hard shoulder. Relief flooded through him.

The officer raised his window and the patrol car continued alongside for a short while and then, with its siren wailing, disappeared into the distance.

It was some time before Amit's heartbeat began to settle.

Had they not been called to an emergency, he was sure they'd been about to pull him over. He needed to get rid of the old woman as soon as possible. He might not be so lucky next time.

The exit appeared and he pulled off the motorway. It was dusk now; he was driving on dipped headlights. Another fifteen minutes and night would fall, and under cover of darkness he would dispose of her body. But where? He still had the same problem. Having left the motorway for the country route home, he was driving past farmers' fields and rough grassland, but he didn't have a shovel, so parking and digging a grave out here would be impossible. He also ruled out just dumping her in a ditch as she'd be found too quickly. The longer she lay undiscovered and rotting, the better.

The flooded quarry – of course! He should have thought of it sooner. On the far side of Coleshaw Woods was a very deep quarry. He'd seen it when he'd dumped the dead animals. It was used by anglers during the day but completely deserted after dark. Perfect for disposing of the old woman, and with hindsight he probably should have dumped the animals there too. He'd been surprised at the interest they'd created; the RSPCA had put out two statements, but they were well off the mark. They were looking for an illegal taxidermist, not a respected anaesthetist. If he'd filled the sacks with bricks and thrown them off the bridge into the deepest part of the quarry they'd never have been found, and nor would the old woman.

Chapter Twenty-Seven

Alisha stared at the telephone in its rest as if it were red hot and would burn her if she touched it. If she was going to make the call, she needed to do so now. Amit was due home soon, and if she waited until another day she was sure she'd lose her nerve. It had to be done now, at this very moment.

Summoning all her courage, she picked up the handset and, with the brochure open on her lap, keyed in the number for ELECT.

It was answered on the second ring by a woman with an American accent. 'Hi, you're through to ELECT – Eternal Life Education Cryonics Trust. I'm Tammy. How can I help you today?'

Alisha knew what she needed to say, but the words failed to materialize. 'I'm not sure.'

'Would you like me to send you some information on our organization and the work we do here?'

'No,' Alisha stammered. 'I've read your brochure. I have some questions.'

'I'm sure you do,' Tammy said warmly, trying to be helpful. 'Most of our members had plenty of questions before they joined us. I'm here to answer your questions and help in any way I can.'

Alisha took another deep breath. 'Do you need the permission of the person who is going to be frozen?' she blurted.

'Yes. Absolutely. Although we prefer to call it cryonic preservation rather than frozen. The patient isn't frozen as such but is in a state of suspended animation.'

'So you need permission, even if they're a family member?'

'Yes, except in the case of a minor, when the court's permission is needed.'

'So a husband couldn't give permission for his wife to be frozen – I mean, preserved?'

'No, we'd still need her authority. Think of it as part of the person's will. Their last wishes.'

'And there is no way round that?' Alisha could feel her pulse racing.

'No. We need the patient's authority. Although it helps if their family are aware, to make sure they are properly looked after until one of our team arrives to stabilize them.'

'What do you mean by looked after?' she asked, listening for any sound that might suggest Amit was returning.

'If a person dies in hospital, then they should be kept

on life support until one of our team arrives. Sometimes the doctors and nurses on duty aren't aware of this and the next of kin has to tell them.'

'And if they die at home?' Alisha asked, unable to keep the tremor from her voice.

'Then we ask the next of kin to keep the body as cold as possible to stop cells deteriorating until we arrive.'

'Then what happens?'

'Our team member places them on life support, injects a stabilizing fluid into their veins and then puts them in an ice bath ready for their journey to us.'

'When do they go into the tank?'

'The tank?'

'The big cylinders like the ones in your brochure.'

'Oh yes, the aluminium containers. They are the final stage. That's where the patient is kept until medical science progresses enough to wake them and cure their condition.'

Alisha braced herself to ask the next question. 'Can anyone carry out this process at home or does it have to be in your laboratory?'

'It's always done here as it requires a lot of expertise and high-grade equipment.'

'Even if the person was a doctor?'

'It's possible that in the future members might be able to cryonically preserve their loved ones at home, but not yet.'

'Has anyone been brought back to life after going through this process?'

'Not a person. But animals have, and preserving organs

for transplant uses the same process. That has been going for many years. It's only a matter of time before a human is returned to life. Personally, I think that probably someone already has.'

'What makes you say that?' Alisha asked, her stomach contracting with fear.

'It's a very short step between bringing back animals and humans, in science terms, but the implication for religion is enormous. It will take a lot of courage to announce it to the world and risk . . .'

But Alisha had heard enough. Saying a quick goodbye, she hung up and tried not to be sick.

Only a matter of time, she'd said, perhaps someone already has. How long did she have? Months, weeks, days? How close was Amit to taking that final step? She had no idea and didn't know how to find out. She should really leave now and get to a safe place where he couldn't touch her. But that was impossible with Eva. Even if she managed to leave the house with her, where would she go? She needed help.

Chapter Twenty-Eight

Amit's car bounced slowly along the rough single-track lane, the old woman's body secured in the back by the seat belts. It was pitch-dark now, no street lamps here, just the car's headlights and a pale crescent moon that gave no light at all. Coleshaw Woods lay dense and deserted to his left and right. No dog walkers or bird spotters out at this time. Just him and the dead woman.

Gripping the steering wheel, he peered through the windscreen and continued in the direction of the flooded quarry. After half a mile, the lane opened into a small gravelled parking area. His car's headlights illuminated the warning sign on the far side just in front of the wooden footbridge:

DANGER
DEEP WATER.

He continued across the car park, the tyres crunching over the gravel, and stopped a little way in front of the sign. He cut the engine but left the headlamps on. He'd need them so he could see what he was doing. He got out and the cold night air bit into him. His hands tingled from gripping the wheel and he rubbed them on his trousers to stimulate circulation. Opening the rear door, he reached in and released the seat belts. She smelt even worse now. He'd have to give the back seat a good clean to get rid of any bodily fluids that had leaked out.

Taking hold of the old woman's lifeless body by the feet, he dragged her out of the car. Her head hit the ground with a dull thud and air escaped from her lungs, making him start. He needed to weigh her down before he threw her into the water and he'd have to improvise. He checked her clothes for pockets; her cardigan and trousers had them, which was good. He began scooping up handfuls of gravel and stuffing them into her pockets. They were soon full, but it wasn't enough. He needed something heavy to make sure she sank and stayed at the very bottom of the quarry for good.

He looked around. There was nothing in sight. An owl hooted eerily from the depths of the woods and a twig crackled as though it might have been stepped on. The sooner he was out of here the better. He didn't think he had anything heavy in his car, but on opening the boot, he saw the metal jack he carried with him in case of a puncture. It was certainly heavy enough, but how to attach it to her? He didn't have any rope. His gaze went to the litter bin by the footbridge illuminated by the car's headlights. It gave him an idea.

Amit went over and, gingerly lifting the lid, removed the black plastic bin liner. It reeked of dead fish, but the bag would serve his purpose. Tipping out the contents, he returned to the old woman and placed the jack at the very bottom of the bin liner. He then began pushing her body into the bag, head first and bending her knees to fit her in. Small and shrunken with age, she just fitted. He knotted the end firmly with the attached ties and lifted it to test its weight. Yes, he was sure it was heavy enough now with the combined weight of her body, the jack and the gravel. He glanced towards the woods. The air was still, just the faintest sound of water lapping from the quarry behind him.

He decided not to drag the bag to the bridge for fear of it ripping, so with a massive effort, he hauled it up and onto his shoulder. Jesus, it was heavy now with the jack and gravel. As he walked, he heard some of the gravel spill out of her pockets and into the sack, but it didn't matter, the bag was sealed.

The car's headlights showed him the way – up the wooden steps and onto the footbridge, his dark, distorted shadow a few steps in front. He continued to the middle of the bridge, his footsteps echoing on the wooden planks. Leaning over the handrail, he looked into the dark water below. He was sure this was the deepest part.

Heaving the bag from his shoulder, he rested it on the

handrail first and then pushed it over. He heard it splash, saw it float for a moment as if hesitating and then gradually disappear in a pool of ripples. Satisfied she was gone for good, he began back across the bridge, relieved yet angry. Yes, he'd got rid of her, but all that fucking trouble for nothing! He was back where he started. Next time, he'd find someone younger, healthier and more robust, who wouldn't die until it was time and he said so.

Chapter Twenty-Nine

Act normal, Alisha told herself. *Behave as you would normally in the evening. Do what you usually do.*

Amit said he wanted dinner, so she'd prepared it ready for his return. She checked the kitchen and then the living room. Everything seemed as it should. Seven o'clock; her insides were knotted into a tight ball. He could arrive home any time.

With a final glance around downstairs, Alisha went up to Eva's room. She felt a familiar pang of guilt for having left her alone. 'All right, love?' she asked, going over and kissing her forehead.

'Yes, thank you, Mummy,' Eva said and continued playing on the games console, the sound on low.

Alisha drew up a chair and sat beside her. The poor child. She was always content – it broke Alisha's heart. She never complained or grew angry and frustrated at the life she'd been dealt. She accepted her lot and was grateful for anything she was given. But what stung most was that despite her father rejecting her and hiding her away, she still called him Daddy.

It wasn't right to keep her shut up, Alisha could see that now. Although she'd gone along with it after what had happened at their last house where they'd been terrorized and their lives put in danger by the mob that had gathered outside, things had changed. Amit couldn't be trusted. He was working to his own agenda, obsessed with finding a cure and bringing them back to life. She was sure it was a type of madness.

She wrung her hands in her lap as she looked at Eva absorbed in the game. She needed to get them both out of here, somewhere safe, for whatever time they had left. But how? She couldn't possibly get Eva and her wheelchair down the stairs, and even if she could, they had nowhere to go. She was as much a prisoner here as Eva was. The only person she trusted was Emily. If she confided her suspicions about Amit, would she help them? It was their only hope. Once Amit was back and in his lab for the evening, she'd phone Emily, tell her everything she'd found out, including that she knew what had happened to Tibs, and ask for her help.

'Mummy, will you play?' Eva asked.

'Yes, love, of course.' But at that moment she heard Amit's car pull onto the drive. 'I have to go. I'll be back later.'

Alisha hurried downstairs as fast as she could, her legs

unsteady and praying her face wouldn't betray her thoughts. She'd give Amit his dinner as he'd asked and then, once he was in his lab, she'd phone Emily. She needed to be strong, stay focused, for Eva's sake. But supposing Emily wasn't in or couldn't talk to her? She pushed the thought from her mind.

As she reached the bottom step, the front door opened and Amit walked in. She gasped when she saw him.

'What have you been doing?' she blurted, unable to hide her shock. He looked at her, confused. 'There's blood on your jersey and your shoes are covered in mud.'

He followed her line of vision. 'I came across a road traffic accident on the way home and stopped to help. I'll shower and change.' Taking off his shoes, he then went upstairs.

Plausible, yes, so plausible, Alisha thought, but then he always was. Able to justify everything. Even now, with what she'd found out, it was impossible to know for sure if he was lying.

Going into the kitchen, she finished preparing his dinner and set it on a tray. She wasn't hungry, and Eva had eaten earlier.

Amit appeared in the kitchen carrying his stained clothes and thrust them at her. 'I'll be in the study,' he said, taking the tray.

'I'll be with Eva,' Alisha said, as she would normally, and watched him go. Sometimes he went to his study before going to the lab, but he was never in there for long.

Upstairs, she found that Eva was still absorbed in the video game. She could spend hours playing the same game, sometimes days. Alisha went over to the window, slightly parted the curtains and sat on the bedside chair, looking out. As soon as she saw the light go on in Amit's lab, she'd telephone Emily and ask for her help. Sometimes she sat here in summer gazing out, wishing she could take Eva into the garden. Let her feel the warm sun on her face, see the flowers in bloom and listen to the sound of the birds singing, but Amit had forbidden it for fear someone might see. Eva's life and hers had become this room, but if she kept her resolve all that would change soon.

As Alisha waited, tense and afraid, she ran through what she was going to say to Emily. She'd start by apologizing – I'm sorry I haven't been honest with you. Then she'd tell her she'd seen Amit drop Tibs' cat collar when he'd thrown other animal collars into their bin and that she believed he had killed animals as part of his experiments. And that as ludicrous as it sounded, he was planning on freezing her, storing her in the cylinder Emily had seen delivered, then bringing her back to life, and probably Eva too. Crazy as it was, she had to make Emily believe her. It was their only hope; their lives were in danger, she was sure.

No light came on in Amit's lab, but he must have finished his dinner by now. What was taking him so long in the study tonight? Alisha glanced at the wall clock. He was usually in the lab by now. Perhaps after a night away he was catching up on emails, or possibly he was opening his letters or looking for some paperwork. She'd made sure she'd left everything as she'd found it in the study. He wouldn't be doing an online grocery shop. He'd been far too preoccupied when he'd come in to be bothered with that, and why had he really arrived home with blood on his clothes and mud on his shoes? She doubted it was from coming across a car accident, but she daren't go there. Surely he would go to his lab before long? She would need to start getting Eva ready for bed soon. She nervously picked at her fingers and watched and waited some more.

At eight-thirty, Alisha reluctantly began Eva's bedtime routine. If Amit came upstairs to find no water running and Eva's light still on, it would arouse his suspicions. She kept to the same routine every night.

By the time she'd finished and was putting Eva to bed, it was nine o'clock, and there was still no light on in his lab. She hadn't heard any movement downstairs so assumed Amit was still in the study. What was he doing?

She read Eva a bedtime story, dimmed the lights and returned to the bedside chair. She held Eva's hand while her daughter fell asleep, as she did most evenings, although tonight, instead of gazing at Eva, she watched through the gap in the curtains. Often she went to bed soon after Eva as she had no reason to stay up, but now as Eva slept she sat by the window and maintained her vigil.

At ten o'clock, Alisha was forced to admit Amit probably wasn't going to his lab tonight. It was the first night he'd missed in months. She knew something had dramatically changed and she feared it was for the worse.

Chapter Thirty

Downstairs, Amit sat in front of his laptop, concentrating hard. He was feeling more positive now. There was no point in going to his lab tonight – there was nothing for him to do without a subject – but the frustration and disappointment of the day was receding. He had eaten and, by chance, while he'd been online researching, a pop-up advertisement had given him a brilliant idea on how to obtain his next subject. He was now looking at a website offering brides from overseas. Not that he wanted a bride, but as the advertisement said, these women were young and healthy; they were also plentiful, easily available and unlikely to be missed. Even if they were missed, he thought, their families were too poor to buy a plane ticket and come looking for them.

Women by mail order, the website said; they made it so easy. You registered your details, got chatting online to those you fancied, chose one and then paid to bring her here. Like fishing in a goldfish pond, he smiled smugly. It was a wonder the idea hadn't occurred to him before, rather than going to all that trouble of finding an old woman, only to have her die. These women were robust and wouldn't die – well, not until he was ready.

There were thousands to choose from; exporting women seemed to be a national pastime in some countries. You could choose the age range and he'd selected the youngest group, 18–25, so they wouldn't be worldly-wise and start asking too many questions. He was already messaging four now. They were so naïve and trusting and desperate to marry a Westerner. He wasn't messaging as himself, of course, but as a twenty-eight-year-old handsome doctor whose photograph he'd stolen from Facebook. He vaguely wondered how many of these gullible desperate women disappeared abroad, never to be heard of again, for he doubted his bride-to-be would be the only one to meet an unnatural end.

The website said these brides typically had happy dispositions, were thoughtful, loyal, full of smiles and fun. Good, he thought, although he doubted his would be very happy when she found out what he had in store for her: that instead of walking up the church aisle, she was going into a tank of liquid nitrogen at minus 190°C. Probably best not go into too much detail beforehand, he thought and smiled to himself.

After an hour, Amit had made his choice, Kyla, but then, annoyingly, he had to spend another hour 'getting to know each other', which was completely unnecessary as far as he was concerned, but expected by her. Thankfully, because of the eight-hour time difference, Kyla then had to get ready for work – as a cleaner in a hotel, a job she hated – so he was saved from further irritating messaging. Before signing off he reassured her she wouldn't have to work for much longer. He said he already loved and missed her, and he'd look into flights so they could arrange her first visit to England. She was so gullible. Her excitement was palpable and she closed with rows of kisses. Her first visit would, of course, be her last.

A job well done, Amit thought, pleased with himself, but before he set about finding a flight, he should deal with the day's emails. With a sigh, he opened the inbox and deleted the junk mail first, then filed the newsletter from The Royal College of Anaesthetists in his saved box before opening the next email. It was a standard notice from his energy provider that a direct debit would shortly be taken from his current account for gas and electricity. As usual in winter it was extremely high. Their idiot child had poor circulation in addition to everything else and needed to be kept warm. She cost him a fortune! But not for much longer.

The second bill was for the house phone, but what the fuck was going on! It had more than trebled since the last quarterly bill and he hardly used it, making most of his calls on his mobile. The landline was there in case Alisha needed to contact him while he was at work as he didn't allow her a mobile. But as far as he could remember, she'd phoned him once in the last three months and the call certainly hadn't been long enough to treble his bill. Then he remembered the line had been engaged when he'd tried to phone her from his car while away.

He clicked on the link to view the invoice online, but that didn't give any more information. He had to download a full itemized bill where all the calls were listed with their date, time, number and duration. He stared at it, incredulous. It was obvious why the bill was so high – dozens of calls to a mobile number, some lasting thirty minutes or more. It must be a mistake. It wasn't his mobile number that had been phoned and Alisha didn't know anyone else to call apart from him. Eva certainly couldn't use a phone and he hadn't made those calls. He checked the top of the page where the account holder's name, address and telephone number were shown to see if they were his details, and they were. The rest of the bill – the charges for the call package and internet – was correct. Tomorrow he would complain to the company that a mistake had been made, but first he'd find out who the number belonged to. It would give credence to his claim that as he didn't know the person, the calls weren't his.

Picking up his mobile from the desk, he paused and set it down again. Better to make the call from the landline – the number showing on his bill. With the invoice still open on his laptop, Amit picked up the handset and entered the mobile phone number shown. It was getting late, so there was a chance the person might not answer and his call would go through to voicemail. In which case he'd leave a message, explaining who he was, why he was calling and that he would phone again tomorrow.

But it was answered by a woman, her voice intense and familiar. 'Alisha, what's the matter? Is everything all right?'

Amit stared straight ahead, his eyes narrowing in disbelief. His fists slowly clenched in anger.

'Alisha? Are you there?' she asked again.

Without speaking, he returned the handset to its cradle and continued to stare across the room.

It was their neighbour Emily, and she'd recognized his number. Alisha must have been telephoning her behind his back while he had been at work! His anger flared. What else had she been doing, goaded on by that bitch next door? He hadn't a clue, but one thing was certain: before the night was over he'd find out.

Chapter Thirty-One

Next door, Emily stared at the screen of her mobile phone, unsure what to do for the best. She was sure Alisha wouldn't have phoned just for a chat at this time. It was after ten o'clock. She hadn't before and, indeed, had told her she went to bed soon after Eva. She'd only phone this late if there was an emergency and she needed help with Eva.

Emily was about to press to return the call but stopped. Why had Alisha hung up if she needed help? Perhaps Amit had just returned home? That could explain it. She glanced at Ben sprawled on the sofa watching television. 'I'm going to check on Robbie,' she said, and stood.

'Shall I go?' he offered.

'No. It's fine.' Feeling guilty for deceiving him, Emily left the room, went upstairs and crept into Robbie's room at the front of the house. She quietly crossed to the window and parted the curtains just enough to see next door's drive. Amit's car was there – he rarely used his garage – so he was home. But as she looked, she saw a thick layer of frost sparkling on the windscreen in the light of the street lamp. He hadn't just arrived home then but had been in for a while. It didn't make sense. If Alisha needed help with Eva while Amit was there, she would have asked him and she'd never have dared to phone her while he was there anyway. Unless it wasn't Eva who needed help but Alisha?

Was this a cry for help? Emily wondered. She'd had suspicions about Amit for a long time and was sure Alisha was scared of him. She'd seen the look in her eyes and the way her body tensed whenever his name was mentioned. Not being allowed friends, and having to turn off the CCTV when she visited so Amit wouldn't find out, was controlling and abusive. Yet, to some extent, Emily had understood when Alisha had explained why she stayed – that, ill herself, with a severely disabled child and no confidence or support network, she knew she'd never cope alone. Emily had said support was available but had then let the matter go, as it was clear Alisha was becoming anxious and would never leave. Perhaps she'd found the courage.

Quietly closing the curtains and with her mobile still in her hand, Emily left Robbie's room and went into her and Ben's bedroom. She looked out of the window. The light wasn't on in Amit's lab, so he must be in the house. Stranger still, then, that Alisha had dared to phone her. But what to do? If she returned Alisha's call, Amit might answer or at least overhear. What excuse could she give for having their number and phoning so late? If only Alisha had a mobile phone, she could have texted her to find out what was the matter. She'd offered to help her buy a pay-as-you-go that couldn't be traced, but Alisha had refused, saying Amit would be furious if he found out, and anyway she hadn't the money. That a married woman in this day and age couldn't lay her hands on £30 for a basic mobile phone Emily had found appalling. She had decided to buy Alisha one in the new year and give it to her as a late Christmas present. She could hide it in Eva's room; Amit never went in there.

But what was she going to do about tonight's call? What excuse did she have for phoning Alisha or going round there to check on her? She couldn't think of one, and what would she tell Ben?

'Is Robbie OK?' Ben called up from the foot of the stairs.

'Yes, I'll be down shortly.'

She wished she could have confided in him and told him about her visits and Eva. But it was too risky in case he accidentally let something slip to Amit when they exchanged pleasantries on their way in or out, and she'd promised Alisha she wouldn't ever tell.

She waited another five minutes in case Alisha phoned again, and then returned downstairs. She had to assume it wasn't an emergency or Alisha would have called back.

Chapter Thirty-Two

Alisha sat in the chair in the semi-darkness, staring across the room as Eva slept in her bed a short distance away. The night light was on as usual – Eva was frightened of the dark – and by its small light Alisha could see the mobiles on the ceiling faintly stirring in the heat rising from the radiators. She had yet to shower and change; time had passed and she'd been too absorbed in her fears, hopes and planning to move. As soon as Christmas and the New Year holidays were over, she'd telephone Emily and ask for her help. Emily would know who to contact to find her and Eva a safe place to stay. She'd talked about safe houses for women fleeing their husbands or partners. She was unlikely to be surprised when she asked for her help, Alisha thought, although she doubted that even Emily had any idea of what Amit was really up to.

Alisha instinctively tensed as she heard Amit's footsteps

coming upstairs. Not that he would come into this bedroom – he had no interest in his daughter or her as his wife. That had stopped years ago after the birth of Eva, and then she'd fallen ill herself. She and Eva were just burdens to him now that required feeding, and medical attention that he took care of. He would pass her door shortly on his way to his own room. She listened and waited for his footsteps to pass. Only once he was in his room could she relax. But his footsteps didn't come.

Alisha eased herself upright and looked at the small strip of light coming from under the door. She could see movement, a shadow. He was standing outside the door, but why? Hardly daring to breathe and her senses on full alert, she watched and waited, willing him to go. There was no lock fitted to the door, so she couldn't lock him out. She looked at Eva, still fast asleep. The door handle began to turn and she froze. Amit came in.

'What do you want?' she asked, her voice shaking.

There was no reply. She could make out his face in the half-light and saw the look of grim determination – anger fused with hatred. He came towards her.

'Amit, what is it?' Eva stirred in her sleep. 'What's the matter? What have I done?' Terror gripped her.

He grabbed her arm and pulled her roughly from the chair, then dragged her out of the room and downstairs, his fingers digging painfully into her flesh.

She cried out and tried to clutch the handrail to prevent herself from falling. 'Amit. Stop! You're hurting me.'

'Not as much as I'm going to,' he snarled.

Into the living room, he threw her on a chair and closed in, his face just in front of hers. She stared up at him, petrified.

'Why have you been phoning the bitch next door?' he demanded, his eyes blazing.

'I haven't,' she stammered, sick with fear.

'Really? So how do you account for all these calls?' He thrust a printed sheet at her.

She looked at the invoice and bile rose to her throat. It had never occurred to her that all telephone calls were listed somewhere. She thought the bill arrived as one figure and was paid automatically by direct debit.

'Recognize that mobile number?' he demanded, jabbing his finger at the paper.

'No,' she said, her voice slight.

'So you're stupid as well as a liar? Let me remind you. The bitch's name begins with E and she lives next door.'

Alisha shook with fear. There was no point in denying it. He knew. Thank goodness she'd been switching off the CCTV when Emily had visited. 'I get lonely sometimes and phone her,' she stammered.

'Lonely! You've got that idiot child to take care of. Have you been visiting her too?'

'Only that once when you told me to go so she would stop asking.'

His eyes narrowed. 'You'd better be telling me the truth.'

'I am.'

'Has she ever been here?'

'No.'

'So she doesn't know what we're hiding upstairs?'

Alisha shook her head and swallowed hard.

He paused, as if considering the likelihood of this being true. Then reached for the telephone and perched on the coffee table just in front of her. 'You're going to phone her now, and tell her everything is fine and that you misdialled her number.'

'But I haven't misdialled her number,' Alisha said, confused. 'I haven't telephoned her today.'

'Just do as I say!' He pressed the button to engage the speaker and handed it to Alisha. Her fingers shook as she keyed in Emily's mobile number. It rang. 'If it goes through to voicemail, leave a message saying you are OK.'

But Emily answered, heavy with sleep. 'Alisha?'

'Yes. It's me.'

'Are you all right? I was worried when you phoned earlier and hung up. Is something wrong?'

Amit glared at her. 'No. I misdialled. I'm sorry I troubled you. I'm fine.'

There was a small silence before Emily replied. 'OK. If you're sure. I thought you might need some help with Eva.'

The colour drained from Alisha's face. 'No. I'm fine, really,' she stammered.

'Have a good Christmas then, and we'll speak again in the new year.'

Amit thumped the speaker button to disconnect the call and grabbed Alisha by the neck. 'I thought you said she didn't know about Eva?' he hissed in her face and slapped her hard. She cried out. 'Well?' he demanded, and slapped her again.

'I might have mentioned Eva once over the phone,' Alisha whimpered. 'She hasn't seen her.'

'Once! You silly cow. Like she's going to forget!' His hands tightened around her neck until she began to choke. She was struggling to get him off and gasping for air. He was going to kill her. Then he abruptly let go and threw her backwards into the chair. 'Stay there, while I think what to do.'

He moved away and began pacing the room.

She rubbed her neck, tried to breathe and dared to raise her eyes. He was walking back and forth, agitated, and rubbing sweat from his forehead. He sweated a lot now. She kept still, trying not to draw attention to herself, and hoping Eva was still asleep and hadn't heard. Suddenly he stopped in front of her. She started.

'How much does the bitch know about what I'm doing?' he demanded, his face up close to hers.

She tried to keep her voice even. 'Nothing. Honestly.'

He slapped her cheek. 'I don't believe you. She's a nosy cow. She is sure to have asked you what I've been doing in my lab. I've seen her looking out of her bedroom window.'

'I told her you were trying to find a cure for my disease, which you are, aren't you?'

His eyes narrowed. 'And nothing else?'

'What else is there?' She forced herself to meet his gaze.

'And she accepted that?'

'Yes, of course.'

'And you're sure she's never seen the girl?'

'No. Never.'

'In that case you will be able to phone her and tell her there isn't a child, that she died, and you've never got over it, so you pretend she's still alive. Tell her hysterical hallucinations are part of your disease. That will make sure she doesn't tell anyone else. But before you phone her we'll just check you're telling me the truth and she hasn't been here while I've been at work, and neither has anyone else.'

Alisha watched, paralysed with fear, as Amit picked up the remote control for the television. He brought the menu for the CCTV onto the screen and began rewinding.

Calm down, she told herself. *He won't find any evidence of Emily's visits. You've deleted them all. But you need to think what you're going to tell Emily when he makes you call her. Clearly she knows Eva exists. She's seen her plenty of times and Robbie plays with her. He's sure to use the speaker phone again and will hear the astonishment in her voice if you tell her Eva is a hallucination.* How to warn her not to say something to betray her? She tried to think. It was nearly midnight now. Hopefully, Emily wouldn't answer or she could persuade Amit it was too late to phone, which would at least buy her some time until the morning, for she knew he wouldn't let it go.

Alisha watched Amit as he concentrated on the television screen, viewing the recording. His eyes were wide and staring, the green iris even more vivid now. Logic and reason had long since left him and so too had compassion, empathy or any other emotion she might have been able to appeal to. She and Eva were prisoners and at his mercy as surely as if they were bound and gagged.

She touched her neck again, sore from where he'd tried to throttle her. It was his worst attack yet. How easy it would be for him to make her and Eva disappear. So few people knew of their existence – or cared. Only Emily would worry if they went missing, and what could she do about it? Probably not much. Amit was devious and sly and would be sure to cover his tracks.

Alisha suddenly jolted from her thoughts. He had stopped the recording and was rewinding it again. He halted it and viewed a short section. Her blood ran cold. Had he spotted something she'd missed? Evidence that Emily had been here?

She looked at the screen but couldn't see anything wrong. There were just different views of their house from the CCTV cameras outside. She always deleted Emily's visit straight after she left and double-checked it had all been erased. She knew how much rested on it. So what was he so interested in?

He pressed play and continued viewing the recording. She allowed herself to breathe again. He hadn't found anything. He wouldn't. But then he stopped it again, rewound it a little and watched that section a second time. Again, she couldn't see anything untoward. Was he trying to scare her into losing her nerve and confessing to Emily's visits?

He moved the recording on and then stopped it again,

and scrutinized another short section. He was frowning hard now, his brow knotted as though trying to work out something. But what? She concentrated on the screen and tried to stay strong. There was no sign of Emily, Robbie or their visit. In fact, she couldn't remember if the days and times where he was stopping the recording were when Emily had visited. Perhaps there was another reason he was viewing these sections a second time.

A few moments later he stopped the recording and slowly turned to her. She met his gaze, the disparity in his eyes boring into her. When he spoke his voice was low, controlled and cold as ice. 'When did you learn how to use the CCTV?'

'I don't know how to use it,' Alisha blurted too quickly.

'Liar!' She saw his hand go up and ducked but not quickly enough. She took the full force of the blow on her cheek and cried out in pain. 'Someone's been tampering with the recording and it certainly isn't that idiot child.' He hit her again.

Alisha covered her head with her hands and tried to protect herself, but he grabbed her by the arm and jerked her from the chair like a rag doll. Throwing her to the floor, he forced her into a kneeling position, facing the television.

'Watch the right-hand corner of the screen,' he snarled and forced her head in that direction. 'Watch what happens.'

For a moment, she didn't understand what he meant, but then she saw the digital display clock in the lower right-hand corner of the screen that showed the date and time. He pressed play. Dread flooded through her. The minutes and seconds clicked up, then, to her horror, suddenly jumped forward. The section she'd deleted – the duration of Emily's visit – was obviously missing. She'd known the clock was there, but it had never occurred to her or Emily that it could be their undoing.

'See it?' Amit growled, without taking his eyes from the screen. 'Here's another example.' But Alisha didn't need another example, her tears were already falling. He moved the recording forward to another section and forced her head closer to the screen. She saw the display clock jump from 1.31 to 3.14. 'And here's another!' he cried with malevolent satisfaction. 'Someone's been visiting you regularly while I've been at work. Haven't they?' he shouted in her face. 'And I'd bet on the bitch next door. Am I right?'

She nodded.

'Pardon?' he yelled, pulling her hair to force her head back to look at him.

'Yes,' she whimpered.

'I thought so!' He let go, calmly returned the remote control to the table and turned to her again. His eyes bulged. 'You're not bright enough to have thought of that and worked out how to use the CCTV all by yourself. But no worries. You've done me a favour. That bitch is going to save me a lot of time and money. I won't need to fly in my next subject now. Stay there and don't move if you know what's good for Eva. You've just signed your friend's death warrant.'

Chapter Thirty-Three

Alisha stayed where she was on the floor, too scared to move. Amit had been in the study for over an hour now, working on his computer. She could hear the keys tapping. 'Death warrant,' he'd said. What was he planning? He'd hit her again and had then gone round the house locking all the outer doors. He had the keys with him. She was locked in. He'd shouted that if she moved he'd tie her up and Eva would starve to death. She hadn't dared to move, apart from straightening her legs when they went numb. There'd been no need to threaten her with being tied up. Years of being his victim meant she did as he'd told her; the one exception had been her friendship with Emily, and look where that had ended.

It was quiet upstairs. Eva was either asleep or lying there in petrified silence, too scared to call out. She and Emily were both in danger now – at the mercy of a madman –

and because of her. They were her responsibility. She needed to try to think of a way to help them. Amit would have to leave the house at some point – to go to work or his lab. Then she could seize the opportunity to phone Emily or even the police and ask for help. No. Not the police. Amit had told her many times that if the police or social services found out they'd been hiding Eva, they'd put her in an institution and both of them in prison. She couldn't bear the thought of being parted from Eva and her daughter would never survive without her. She'd phone Emily as she'd been planning to do before Amit had found out. But supposing Emily contacted the police or social services? Could they come to the safe house and take Eva away?

She started as the door to the study suddenly opened and Amit came out. He looked pleased with himself.

'Oh, you're still here?' he said as though he'd forgotten. 'All sorted and I've booked a week off work. You can go to your room now.'

A week off work. Her heart fell. She went to speak but decided better of it. Pulling herself to her feet, she silently left the living room and went upstairs. What had he 'sorted'? And why had he booked a week off work? He never just took time off and always worked over Christmas. Was it to guard her and make sure she didn't escape? He'd never bothered in the past. It must be something to do with Emily finding out.

Eva was asleep, thank goodness. Alisha sat on the edge of her own bed and in the semi-darkness gazed at her daughter as she slept. She felt an overwhelming need to protect her. Eva was helpless without her. She'd do whatever it took to keep her safe, but how? They were hostages to Amit's deluded ambition. Tomorrow was Christmas Eve, then it would be Christmas, a day like any other for them. Amit wasn't religious and forbade any of the trappings of Christmas or any other religious festival. He'd said he'd seen inside people on the operating table and knew there was no soul, only meat. The brain was a soulless lump of neurons and synapses – thinking meat, he'd called it. So no Christmas tree for them, no festive decorations or exchange of presents.

Alisha's thoughts drifted back to when she'd been well enough to go shopping and had secretly bought presents for her son and then her daughter, which they'd opened after Amit had left for work on Christmas Day. She'd also cooked them a Christmas dinner and they'd pulled crackers. But since she'd been ill, incarcerated in the house, and completely reliant on Amit, she hadn't been able to do any of that. She was sure Emily would have bought gifts and festive food for them if she'd asked, but asking her without admitting how Amit treated her would have been impossible. On Emily's last visit she'd expressed surprise that their decorations weren't up, and Alisha had told her they hung them on Christmas Eve and the presents were wrapped and hidden away. If only.

Eva began thrashing about in her sleep. Alisha immediately stood and went to her. 'Shh Shh. It's OK. Mummy's here,' she soothed. Not that she was much help, she thought bitterly. She stroked Eva's forehead until she settled again, then returned to her bed.

Lying down, she closed her eyes and tried to concentrate on the few good memories that remained from her past, and not the present or future. Eventually, exhausted, she fell into a fitful sleep, plagued by nightmares: Amit burying dead animals in dark woods, experimenting on live ones in his lab. Then he was dragging Eva from her bed to experiment on her. She could hear her screaming from his lab and see Emily at her bedroom window, but Emily couldn't see them.

Alisha woke with a start, the nightmare still vivid. But it wasn't the nightmare that had woken her. She was sure she'd heard a noise coming from the other side of their bedroom door. Yes, there it was again, a metallic sound. She sat upright. Amit's shadow was beneath their door again. She looked at Eva; the noise had woken her too. She put a finger to her lips to signal to her to keep quiet. It was dark outside and the bedside clock showed 4.09 a.m. What on earth was Amit doing out there?

Silence, then another noise, metal on metal. She kept still and listened, hardly daring to breathe. A second later, she heard it again, then the unmistakable sound of a bolt sliding into place. Too late, she realized they were locked in.

She ran to the door and tried to open it, but it was held fast. 'Amit!' she cried. 'Open the door! You can't lock us in.' But, of course, he could and had. She heard his footsteps receding downstairs.

Eva was crying now, small, stifled sobs that tore at Alisha's heart. She went over and lay beside her on the bed, held her close and soothed her. Eventually, she returned to sleep. Thankfully Eva had little understanding of the danger they were in, while Alisha's own thoughts see-sawed between despair and giving up, and a desperate bid to escape.

Time passed. The clock hands slowly moved. How long was Amit going to keep them here locked up? Then what would happen when he eventually let them out? What was his deluded brain planning now? There'd been no sound in the house since he'd fitted the bolt. Surely he hadn't gone to his lab now?

She slipped from Eva's bed and, parting the curtains, looked out of the window. It was 6.30 a.m. The lab was in darkness. She sat in the chair watching and waiting, although for what she couldn't have said.

Shortly after 8 a.m. the pitch-black darkness of the night reluctantly gave way to the grey of another winter's day. Eva slept on. No light was on in the lab, so Amit must still be somewhere in the house.

Alisha hadn't washed or changed her clothes since the day before and she now quietly crossed to the shower room. Closing the door behind her so she wouldn't wake Eva, she used the toilet and washed her face and hands. Eva would need a bath later when she woke. Would Amit let them out to go to the bathroom that had been adapted for Eva's needs? And what of their medicines? They both had to take tablets, which were stored in a cupboard in the kitchen. Was he going to let her go down to get them and make Eva something to eat? Or was he planning on letting them waste away up here without food or medicine?

Half an hour later, Eva awoke, apparently unaware they were locked in. It was better she didn't know before she had to, Alisha decided. This room had become her world; she only left it for a bath, so if she kept to her routine she wouldn't know for as long as possible. Forcing a smile, Alisha gave Eva a good-morning kiss, changed her on the bed as usual and then used the hoist over the bed to transfer her into her wheelchair. Eva normally watched children's television while Alisha made breakfast, so wheeling her over to the television, she switched it on. She placed the remote control within Eva's reach and waited by her side until she'd put on her headphones and was engrossed in the programme. Eva liked wearing her headphones and Alisha encouraged her to do so, so she didn't have to listen to children's television for large parts of the day. Now they would serve the purpose of blotting out the noise as Alisha banged on the door and tried to attract Amit's attention.

'Amit! We need our tablets. I have to make Eva breakfast. Amit, open the door!' she shouted.

She knocked on the door, rattled the handle and called his name for what seemed like ages without any effect. Then, suddenly, the door opened and Amit stood there, his face expressionless.

'Get what you need,' he said. 'But try anything and that will be it for both of you.'

He was still in the clothes he'd worn yesterday, and from the look of him hadn't slept either. Taking the handrail, she went carefully downstairs; he followed a step behind. As she crossed the hall to the kitchen, she saw the key was missing from the front door and the safety chain was in place. No chance of escape there. She continued into the kitchen and, trying to stay calm and focused, began preparing Eva's breakfast. Amit stood a couple of feet away, silent, menacing, and watching her every move. Any thoughts she'd had of taking a kitchen knife vanished. He'd see her and overpower her in an instant. She concentrated on making Eva's porridge. It was important the child ate. Perhaps she could try talking to him – appeal to his better nature. 'You don't need to do this,' she began, her voice slight.

'Shut up. Speak again and I'll put you straight back in your room.'

She did as he said and finished making the porridge in silence, then placed the bowl on a tray. She reached up to open the cupboard above.

He grabbed her arm. 'What the fuck are you doing?'

'Getting our tablets.'

He released her arm and she took the two dosette boxes from the cupboard, then removed the tablets she and Eva needed to take now. Amit replenished the boxes each week. She crumbled Eva's onto her porridge and stirred them in – it made them easier for her to swallow. She set her own tablets on the tray beside her glass of water to take upstairs. She didn't want anything to eat. Her stomach was knotted. Amit's eyes bored into her as she picked up the tray and began towards the kitchen door.

'I'll need to come down at 1 p.m. for our next tablets and make Eva lunch,' she said as if accepting her fate.

He didn't reply. She continued upstairs with him following close behind.

As soon as she was in the room, he bolted the door behind her. Eva was still watching television with her headphones on. Hiding her upset for Eva's sake, Alisha set the bowl of porridge in front of her and Eva began eating it while watching the television. Alisha took her tablets and drank the water, then sat beside her daughter. The children's programmes were full of Christmas images: Santa in his sleigh full of presents landing on a snow-covered rooftop; excited children hanging up their sacks on Christmas Eve; Christmas trees aglow with fairy lights. As far as Eva was concerned, these were just entertaining programmes, Alisha acknowledged bitterly. She didn't know what she was missing, and with no expectation of Christmas she wouldn't be disappointed.

The morning gradually passed. Alisha struggled with her thoughts but tried to appear calm in front of Eva. There'd been no sign of Amit since he'd let her out earlier and she hadn't heard him moving around the house. She'd looked out of the window from time to time, but there was nothing to be seen.

At one o'clock, when it was time to take their tablets again – when they usually also had lunch – Alisha sat Eva in front of the television once more with her headphones on. She then crossed to the door and began knocking, rattling the handle and calling Amit's name. Amit didn't appear. She tried again ten minutes later, then every ten minutes or so for the next hour, but he still didn't come. She checked the window and the light wasn't on in his lab, but given it was still daylight it might not mean he wasn't in there.

'I'm hungry,' Eva said eventually, taking off her headphones and looking to her mother.

'I know, love. But the door is stuck and I can't get out to make you lunch.' Eva looked confused. Alisha went to the door and rattled the handle to show her, at the same time shrugging as if to say it didn't matter. 'We'll have to wait for Daddy to open the door.' Eva seemed to accept this and, replacing her headphones, she continued watching the programme.

Alisha went to the window again – still no sign of Amit in his lab – then rattled and banged on the door. She kept doing so every few minutes. At three o'clock when she went to the window and the natural light was beginning to fade, she saw the light was on in the lab. He'd probably been in there all along and might be in there for hours yet. There was no way she could attract his attention and her anger flared, not for her but for Eva.

'I'm hungry,' Eva said again and began to cry.

Alisha went to her. 'I know, love. I'll get you something as soon as Daddy opens the door.' The word Daddy stuck in her throat. How she hated him. Abusing her was one thing, but abusing their disabled daughter by depriving her of food and medication was far, far worse. He'd reached a new level of depravity. Alisha comforted Eva as best she could and read her some stories to distract her.

Later, when Eva was watching television again, Alisha stood by the window looking at the lab, hating Amit more with each passing minute.

The last of the afternoon light faded, then shortly before seven o'clock she saw the door to the lab open and Amit come out. She banged on the window with all her might. He looked up, startled, surprised to see her, and quickened his pace towards the house. He'd forgotten they were there, she thought, so involved had he been in whatever he was doing in his lab. She heard him hurrying up the stairs, taking them two at a time. The bolt slid and the door was flung open. She glared at him and he had the decency to look abashed.

'You've missed your medication,' he said.

'Yes! And Eva hasn't had anything to eat since breakfast!' she replied.

Emboldened by her concern for Eva, she pushed past him, then hurried downstairs and into the kitchen, where she began hastily putting together a meal, seething with hatred and loathing. His cruel disregard of Eva fuelled her courage.

'If you are going to keep us locked up, then you need to remember to let me out so I can feed us and get our tablets,' she said. 'Every four hours we take our tablets: 9 a.m., 1 p.m., 5 p.m., and 9 p.m. when I get us a bedtime drink as well. And Eva needs a bath.'

'She can have a bath tomorrow,' he said. 'Take two lots of tablets now.'

She counted out the double dose of tablets, crushed

Eva's into her food and carried the tray past him, upstairs and into their room. As soon as she was inside, the bolt slid into place and his footsteps receded quickly downstairs. She heard him in the kitchen, trying to make himself something to eat. He wouldn't have a clue, and the small satisfaction added to her sense of power.

At nine o'clock exactly, the bolt slid and Amit opened the door. 'You can come down and get what you need,' he said.

Holding herself more upright – she had won this small battle – she carried the tray containing their empty dishes past him and downstairs. He hovered a little way off, waiting to escort her back to her room, as she made Eva a warm drink. On their return journey, as she passed the landing window, she saw a flurry of snowflakes. It was snowing on Christmas Eve, although she made no comment until she was safely in her room again.

'It's snowing,' she told Eva as soon as the bolt slid across. She pushed her daughter's wheelchair to the window so she could see out. Her face lit up in wonder; she'd never seen snow before. She tried to touch the snowflakes falling on the other side of the glass.

'They're outside,' Alisha told her, her eyes filling with tears. 'You can't touch them.' But, of course, 'outside' wasn't a word Eva knew or understood. She'd been far too young to remember the last time she'd gone outside, and it was unlikely she'd ever get the chance again.

Chapter Thirty-Four

'It all went very well,' Ben said as he undressed ready for bed on Christmas Day night. 'It's just a pity we couldn't persuade our parents to stay over rather than drive home in the snow.'

'They like their own beds at their age,' Emily said. 'I can understand that. When Dad phoned to say they were home safely, he said the main roads were clear. I'll take a picture of our garden with the snow from up here. It'll be a good view. We don't often get a white Christmas.'

Emily took her phone to their bedroom window and, parting the curtains, opened one window wide enough to take the photo.

'It's freezing,' Ben said, pretending to shiver, and jumped into bed. 'Be quick!'

Emily laughed and looked at their garden, the pure-white snow glistening magically in the light of the moon.

'It's perfect,' she said. 'Just like a Christmas-card scene.' She touched the camera icon on her phone to engage it and looked through the lens. It was only then she saw it. Without taking a photograph, she lowered her phone in amazement. 'You're not going to believe it, but Amit Burman is in that shed. And judging from all the footprints, he's been in and out all day. Poor Alisha.'

'Amit said they didn't celebrate Christmas,' Ben said. 'But hurry up and take the photo – you're letting in the cold air.'

Emily quickly took a few photos of their snow-covered garden and closed the window, but stayed where she was looking out. 'Even if they don't celebrate Christmas, you'd have thought he would have wanted to spend it with Alisha and . . .' She'd been about to say Eva and had stopped herself just in time.

'Each to his own,' Ben said easily. 'And mine is to end a perfect Christmas Day by making love to you.'

Emily smiled, closed the curtains and joined him in bed. 'I'll call on Alisha when you're back at work and see if I can tempt her to come here again, but for now I'm all yours,' she said, snuggling close.

'Good.' Raising himself on one elbow, Ben looked seductively into her eyes. 'And what can I tempt you with?'

Emily giggled and drew him closer still. 'Let's find out, shall we?'

Chapter Thirty-Five

At least Amit was letting her out every four hours to collect their tablets, and food for Eva, Alisha thought, trying to console herself. And she'd been able to give Eva a bath, have a shower herself and change their clothes. Amit must have set an alarm clock for 9 a.m., 1 p.m., 5 p.m. and 9 p.m., for at exactly those times he left whatever he was doing and came up to the room to let her out. He rarely spoke, unless it was to tell her to hurry up, and had spent most of the last two days in his lab. She'd watched him from the window as he'd gone in and out, head down and muttering distractedly to himself. She wondered if Emily had seen him too but had decided she'd probably be far too involved in enjoying Christmas to notice what was going on next door.

Alisha suspected it was in Amit's interest to make sure she and Eva took their medication regularly, presumably because he didn't want them falling ill yet – not until he was ready. She had little doubt now the cylinder was for her and she assumed he'd had another one delivered for Eva. It was madness to believe he could cure her, for although diseased organs could be replaced, reversing congenital abnormalities was clearly impossible. Another indication of just how deluded he'd become.

By early afternoon on 27 December, Alisha realized something had dramatically changed. It was four days since Amit had fitted the bolt and they'd become prisoners, but today his routine had altered. Instead of being in his lab all morning, he'd spent most of it going backwards and forwards between the house and the lab and appeared to be becoming increasingly nervous and agitated. Sometimes he was carrying printed papers and sometimes small objects, although Alisha couldn't see what they were. All the snow had melted now and a cold grey drizzle hung in the air and dripped from the bare branches of the trees.

Amit wasn't in his lab at all in the afternoon, and then at three o'clock, Alisha heard the low rumble of the garage doors as they were opened electronically, followed by the sound of his car being driven in. He hardly ever used the garage, preferring to leave his car on the drive. When he came to let her out at five o'clock, he was red in the face and very nervous. He kept pushing her to hurry up with the food she was making for Eva. Although she was existing on bread and cheese, Eva needed something more substantial. He was so agitated that Alisha was relieved when she could return to the safety of their room and the bolt slid into place. She wasn't expecting to see him again for another four hours, when their next tablets were due.

She sat by the window as Eva ate her meal and then watched a cartoon film. Usually she played with Eva and organized little activities, but now she was too preoccupied with whatever Amit was planning. There was no light on in the lab, so she assumed he was in the house, although she couldn't hear him moving around.

Just after eight o'clock, while she was reading to Eva before getting her ready for bed, she was startled by the sound of the bolt being drawn. She looked over at the door, so did Eva. It slowly opened and Amit stood framed in the doorway.

'Daddy?' Eva asked.

He moved out of her line of vision. 'Come here,' he said to Alisha. 'It's time.'

'Time? It's not nine o'clock yet.'

'Come here now or I'll drag you out if you want the child upset.'

'I'll be back soon,' she told Eva and, trembling, hurried out.

For a few moments, Alisha thought he was simply taking her down to the kitchen to fetch their tablets early, but at the foot of the stairs he pushed her into the living room and down onto a chair.

'You are going to telephone the bitch next door and tell her to come here now.'

'Why?' she asked, frightened. 'She won't come. It's late.'

'She will come if you make it convincing. And you will make it very convincing if you want to see Eva again. Tell her I'm at work and you've run out of milk and could you borrow some. That's what neighbours do.'

'That's ridiculous. She'll see your car on the driveway.' But as Alisha said it, she realized that Amit's car wasn't on the drive; he'd driven it into the garage earlier – so he'd been planning this all day. Her stomach churned. 'Why do you want Emily?' she asked, her voice quivering.

His lip curled into a humourless smile. 'She will be my last test subject before I set to work on you. If you'd agreed to sign up for ELECT, I wouldn't have had to go to all this trouble, so blame yourself. But I'm rather glad you didn't agree, as I shall go down in medical history for what I'm about to achieve.'

'You're mad,' Alisha said, without care for her safety. 'Emily will report you. She's not like me. She won't put up with your abuse.'

'She won't have the chance.' He grinned malevolently. 'I won't be bringing her back to continue her life. Just bringing her back to make sure I can, and have, perfected my technique before I freeze you.'

'You're mad,' she said again, her heart racing.

'Many great scientists were considered mad in their time,' he said haughtily. 'I shall be remembered as the first doctor to successfully bring a person back from the dead, and you will be remembered as my wife.'

'And Eva?' she asked, humouring him.

His eyes narrowed and the green iris glowed. 'She isn't worth preserving – nothing can be done to save her. I'll put her down painlessly, as one would a dog.'

Blind fury seized Alisha, eclipsing any fear for her own safety. She leapt at him and clawed his face. But her slight and emaciated frame was no match for Amit and he easily overpowered her and threw her to the floor.

'Do that again and I'll despatch Eva now,' he snarled.

Alisha knew he meant it. She watched, petrified, as he picked up the phone, pressed to engage the speaker and then keyed in Emily's mobile number. Surely his plan wouldn't work? If Emily was putting Robbie to bed she wouldn't answer her phone. And even if she did and agreed to bring some milk, she wouldn't leave the house without telling Ben where she was going. It was ridiculous. If she didn't return within a reasonable time, Ben would come looking for her. Amit's plan to entice her here was destined to fail.

'Hi Alisha, how are you?' Emily answered cheerfully.

'I'm all right,' she said, her voice flat. Amit pointed up to Eva's room as a warning for her to do better. 'I've run out of milk,' she said. 'Could you pop some round just to tide me over until tomorrow?'

'Oh, Alisha, I'm so sorry, I can't,' Emily said. 'Ben's working late tonight and Robbie's asleep in his cot.' But as Alisha breathed a sigh of relief, she saw the look of satisfaction on Amit's face and knew this was part of his plan. He had known Ben wouldn't be there! She was too stunned to say anything.

Amit looked pointedly up at Eva's room again for her to continue.

'It would only take a minute,' Alisha said. 'I'm sorry to be a pest, but Eva wants some warm milk. I feel awful running out.' She heard Emily's pause and willed her to say no.

'All right. It won't hurt to leave Robbie in his cot for a minute. Let me check he's still asleep and then I'll come round. How much milk do you want?'

Alisha hesitated and Amit snarled.

'Whatever you can spare,' she said, her voice slight and far-off. She wanted to shout, No! Don't come!

'OK. See you soon,' Emily said and cut the call.

'You see, it wasn't difficult,' Amit said with satisfaction. 'Now for the next part of my plan. Come with me and I'll show you what you're going to do.'

Chapter Thirty-Six

It was sod's law, Emily thought as she dropped her phone on the sofa beside her, that on one of the few nights Ben had to work late Alisha asked for help. Taking a quick gulp from the mug of tea she'd just made, she stood, and leaving the television on low – she wouldn't be long – went into the kitchen. Of course she didn't mind helping out Alisha. It wasn't as if she was always on the borrow. This was only the second time she'd asked for her help; the first had been when the hoist in the bathroom had broken and Eva had fallen. Alisha wasn't someone who took advantage of others, far from it. Indeed, Emily was a little surprised that she'd phoned at this time simply to borrow some milk. But then it was for Eva, and Alisha doted on her and would do anything to get her what she needed.

Opening the fridge, Emily took out an unopened carton

of milk. She had plenty, so Alisha could have the whole carton. She left it ready in the hall by the front door while she went upstairs to check on Robbie. He was fast asleep, flat on his back with his arms flung out either side of him like a little angel. She kissed his cheek and returned downstairs.

Slipping on her shoes and jacket, she tucked her house keys into her pocket and picked up the carton of milk. There was no need to take her phone; she'd only be gone for a minute. She let herself out of the front door and quietly closed it behind her so as not to disturb Robbie. The drizzle had stopped now, but the night air was cold and damp. Given the choice, she would have preferred the crisp snow of Christmas Day any time. A man walking his dog hurried by the end of the drive.

As Emily stepped onto the pavement, she automatically glanced back at her house. It looked welcoming even on a dismal night, with all their lights on. The Burmans only ever seemed to have the light on in the room they were in and even then it was gloomy because of the opaque film covering the window. She continued down their path and the light from the street lamp disappeared behind the trees. Emily pressed the bell on the entry system. She would remind Alisha to delete her visit from the CCTV footage before Amit returned, although she doubted she'd forget.

Emily had expected Alisha to be waiting at the door as she usually was when she and Robbie visited, even more so now as she knew Emily had left Robbie unattended.

She thought she'd be ready to take the milk and say a quick thank-you. Perhaps Eva had needed something at the last minute, for Alisha always answered her calls immediately as a priority. But as her eyes adjusted to the dark, she now saw the door had been left very slightly ajar. Alisha had done that once before when she knew she and Robbie were on their way and Eva had needed something.

Pushing open the door, Emily stepped into the hall. 'Alisha, it's me!' she called. The house was quiet. Alisha must be upstairs with Eva, but then her small voice came from the kitchen.

'I'm in here.'

Odd that she hadn't come out, Emily thought and opened the door to the kitchen. The light was no brighter in here, only a small glow from underneath the wall cabinets. Alisha was standing on the far side of the kitchen, leaning against the work surface and facing her.

'Hi,' Emily said. But something wasn't right. There was a haunted look about her and fear in her eyes. She seemed to be thinner and her shoulders were stooped. 'Are you all right?' Emily asked, concerned, going over to her. 'Are you ill?'

She didn't make it across the kitchen. She was aware of a small movement behind and then someone grabbed her. At the same time she felt a sharp pain as a needle plunged into her arm. She cried out, tried to fight him off, the carton of milk thrown to the floor. But the room was already tilting, swimming out of focus, then she was falling, down, down, a metallic taste in her mouth. A rushing noise filled her ears and the last sound she heard before she lost consciousness was Alisha screaming.

Robbie, Robbie in his cot. He was alone. She needed to get to him fast but couldn't see him in the dark. She'd left him alone! Panic set in. She needed to find him. She should never have left him. What had she been thinking? This was a nightmare, surely? She would never have left him. Where was he? She had to get to him.

Her eyes flickered but wouldn't open. Find Robbie, find him now, was her overriding thought. She tried to walk but nothing happened; it was like wading through mud. Then her eyes slowly opened and stayed open. It wasn't a nightmare. This was real. She was on her side on a cold hard floor and unable to move. She could make out a small light under some cabinets. Kitchen cabinets. She was in a kitchen, a familiar kitchen, but it wasn't hers. It was Alisha's.

Robbie! She screamed, but no sound came out. Her lips were stuck together. As she looked down at her body, she saw her wrists and ankles were bound together with tape. What had happened to her?

She struggled for all she was worth, managed to flip herself over onto her back. She stared in horror as Amit Burman came towards her, smiling venomously.

'So you're awake,' he said. 'Exactly ten minutes. The dose was perfect, but then that's my job, isn't it?'

Her eyes widened in terror. She pulled against the tape, tried to speak and free herself, but it was impossible.

What was she doing here? What did he want with her? Robbie was alone. She needed to get to him.

'It's no use thrashing around and squealing,' he said. 'When you have calmed down, I will explain why you're here. Then I will untie your hands so you can write a letter.'

She shook her head, struggled even harder and tried to cry out. He folded his arms loosely across his chest and waited, as though he had all the time in the world.

She pulled against the ties, tried to kick him, but he stepped out of the way and the tape held her legs fast.

He unfolded his arms. 'Suit yourself,' he said. 'I'll come back in an hour or so when you've calmed down. There's no hurry.'

She tried to shout out for him to stop, frantically shook her head, her eyes pleading with him to stay. She needed him to untie her so she could go to Robbie.

He paused and turned. 'So you are ready to cooperate?' Emily nodded furiously. 'Excellent. I knew you'd see sense in the end. But all that fuss. I thought you modern women were made of stronger stuff.' He grinned fiendishly.

Grabbing her roughly by the arm, he pulled her into a sitting position, dragged over a dining chair and sat in front of her.

'I'm going to tell you a story,' he said, his green eye gleaming. 'It may take a while, so you need to be patient, but at the end you will know why you are here. While I'm talking you will keep very still and quiet so I don't lose my concentration. I don't like a lot of noise or movement. Do you understand?'

She stared at him in terror.

'Do you understand?' he demanded, raising his hand and making her flinch.

She nodded.

'Good. That's better. If I ask you a question, I expect an answer. Do you understand?'

She nodded again.

'OK. I shall begin. In a village many miles from here, there lived a husband and wife who were very poor. They only had one son and they invested everything in him. All their money, hopes and ambitions. He would do well, make them proud and bring them prosperity. They hadn't been to school themselves and were illiterate and uneducated, but they made sure their son wanted for nothing and went to school. They planned from when he was a child that he would go to university and they told him this most days. They forced him to study every evening after school while his friends played outside. At weekends, he had to help his father sell fruit and vegetables from the roadside. It was their livelihood and Amit resented having to do this as much as he resented being made to study.

'If he complained, his parents beat him and said he was ungrateful. They had made their minds up that he was going to be a doctor, the best, a top surgeon or consultant, who would make them proud. However, Amit had no interest in medicine, but he couldn't object. Sons and daughters did what their parents told them; there was no room for argument. With regular beatings and being forced to study, he just about got the exams he needed to go to university, and a wealthy uncle paid for him to study in England. His parents were proud but indebted to the uncle.' Amit took a breath and licked his lips.

Emily watched him carefully. Once he'd told his story, surely he would let her go?

'Even at medical school, Amit had no desire to become a doctor and didn't do well. But there was no way he could leave; he was indebted to his uncle as much as his parents were, and they would all have to answer to him – a very influential man – if he failed. Amit only scraped passes in the exams and his internship was no better. His tutor wrote in his report that he showed little interest in hands-on medicine and making people better and that if he wanted to pursue a career in medicine then he should consider pharmaceuticals, or become an anaesthetist. His parents were bitterly disappointed in their son.

'"An anaesthetist! Putting people to sleep!" his father scoffed. "What sort of job is that? You have wasted your uncle's money." They didn't tell the people in the village, but his uncle had to know. After much discussion between the families, it was decided that Amit would remain in England and marry one of his uncle's daughters – Alisha.'

Amit paused and licked his lips again. Emily kept very still, hardly daring to breathe.

'Unfortunately this new wife was a modern woman, with ideas of her own and a job. To begin with, she wouldn't do as she was told, which made Amit very angry. He had to teach her. She soon learnt. When she was pregnant, he insisted she gave up her job to take care of the house and him. They had a baby boy and Amit's parents were delighted. He was partly forgiven for being a failure as a doctor. They announced it to their village and, for the first time, Amit seemed to have done something right.' He paused, his gaze drifting away. A small smile flickered across his lips but quickly vanished.

'The boy fell ill and tests showed he had a rare genetic condition, inherited from his mother. It was incurable and he would gradually deteriorate until he died. Amit's parents were angry that the uncle had not told them, but they couldn't do anything as they were still indebted to him for sending Amit to medical school. Nor did they tell anyone in the village, as it would bring shame on them. Some still thought that disabilities were the work of the devil, some still do. Alisha fell pregnant again and hopes were raised that it would be a healthy boy, but when it was born it was a girl and it was obvious she had the faulty gene too. It had begun its work in the womb, causing gross abnormalities.' He grimaced, clearly repulsed, and Emily hated him even more.

'Amit's parents said he should get rid of his wife so he could marry again and have healthy children. If she died, their debt to the uncle would be wiped out. They didn't understand that it wasn't that easy to kill someone in this country. But then Amit came up with an ingenious plan. He notified the authorities that he was taking his wife and children to live abroad and bought a house in another area where no one knew them or that they had a deformed child. He made the house very secure so people couldn't see in, installed CCTV and told his wife not to talk to anyone or the child would be taken away by the social services. He gave them the tablets they needed so no one else was involved.

'By chance, he read an article about a teenage boy who was going to die but was having his body preserved so he could be brought back to life later when a cure had been found. This gave Amit an idea and he started researching cryonics and visited ELECT, an organization that preserves people after death. He planned to have himself and Alisha frozen, and then once a cure was found they would be brought back to life, and finally his parents would be proud of him for this ground-breaking achievement. But Alisha didn't want to be preserved and ELECT insisted on seeing the person to gain their signature. Amit was very disappointed, but he didn't give up. He was used to disappointment. He struck upon an even better idea that would allow his plan to go ahead and make an even bigger name for himself. He, Amit, would carry out the work ELECT would not!

'Suddenly, for the first time in his life, he had a real interest in medicine and began researching and experimenting.' Amit laughed ghoulishly. 'Night after night, all weekend, he worked in his very own laboratory adapted from an outbuilding at the bottom of his garden, but you know that. I won't bore you with the technical details, but it took a while for him to perfect the process. Thankfully, cats and dogs are plentiful.

'Oh yes, and before I forget, thank you for donating Tibs. You will understand why I couldn't tell you where she'd gone, but console yourself – the cat's suffering was to advance medical science, just as yours will be.' He paused. 'In a minute, when you have calmed down again, I will explain your role and then remove the tape from your wrists so you can write a letter to Ben telling him why you have left him for good.'

Chapter Thirty-Seven

Emily fought against the tape binding her arms and legs and tried to cry out, but it was hopeless. The tape stuck fast. Amit was insane. All her suspicions about him were correct. He was a cruel, evil bastard who beat his wife and murdered defenceless animals for the sake of some hideous experiment. And now he was going to experiment on her. Robbie was in his cot alone at home and she was tied up and at the mercy of this madman.

Where was Alisha? Why hadn't she come to her rescue? She had been here at the start. She'd seen her. With a stab of horror, Emily realized Alisha must be working with him. She had lured Emily here on the pretence of needing milk for Eva. She must have been lying all along. What were the two of them planning to do with her? Amit had said that, like the animals, he would experiment on her, but how?

She thrashed around trying to free herself as he watched coldly from a short distance away.

Try to calm down, she told herself. *This isn't going to help. Calm down as he's told you to, and when he unties your hands look for an opportunity to overpower him and escape.*

He began to walk away.

'No!' she cried, but only a groan escaped her lips from behind the tape. 'No. Wait.'

He stopped, slowly turned, looked at her, detached and calculating. 'Yes? Did you want something?'

She wanted to lash out and strike him dead, but she told herself to stay calm, and nodded.

'Yes? What is it you want?' he asked, feigning ignorance.

She raised her bound hands, offering them up to him.

'You want me to release you?'

She nodded.

'But that's not possible until I can be sure you won't try anything silly.'

She forced herself to maintain eye contact and not react. He was playing with her, toying with her like a cat with a mouse, and enjoying it. She looked into his cold manic gaze, thought of Robbie and tried to convey that she would do as he said.

He took a step towards her and frowned, puzzled, pretending he hadn't understood her.

She held up her hands to show him, begging.

'You want to cooperate and do as I say?' he asked nonchalantly.

She nodded again.

'But how can I trust you? Women lie and can be very deceitful. For example, I know someone not too far from here who has been sneaking into my house while I've been at work. That person helped my wife to erase her visits from the CCTV. Know who I mean?'

Fear surged through her. Alisha must have told him, but why was she working with Amit? What was in this for her?

She thought of Robbie and forced herself to nod.

'So we agree on that point. Are you repentant?'

She nodded furiously.

'I doubt it,' he laughed, 'but it doesn't matter. I'll release your hands so you can write the letter to Ben. I had considered writing it myself or typing it, but it will look more authentic coming from you.' As he came towards her, he seemed to lose his footing and stumble, but righted himself before he hit the floor.

He crossed to a work surface and picked up a stainless-steel tray like the ones used in hospital operating theatres. Emily watched, terrified, as he carried it over and placed it on the floor just out of her reach. On the tray, laid out ready in a neat row like surgical instruments, were a pair of scissors, a pen, a notepad, a roll of parcel tape, her house keys and a hypodermic needle with a full syringe.

'I'll talk you through what I'm going to do so it's clear in your mind. We don't want any mistakes or accidents, do we?'

She looked at her house keys. *Stay calm*, she told herself, *keep your nerve and find an opportunity to overpower him and grab the keys.*

'So, these are surgical scissors,' he said, touching them. 'The same ones I used on Tibs, although I have sharpened them since. They go blunt very quickly cutting through flesh.'

Don't react, she told herself.

'If all goes well,' he continued, 'I shall only use them on you today for cutting the tape around your wrists, but we'll have to see. Next is the pen and paper for writing the note I will dictate.' He moved his hand along the items. 'Here is the parcel tape that hopefully I will only have to use for rebinding your wrists. It's not very effective for closing big wounds. Next are your house keys – I'm sure you recognize them. I took them from your jacket pocket while you were unconscious. I shall be using those to let myself into your house. And, last but not least is the syringe containing some of the sedative I gave you before, only more of it. There is enough there to knock out a horse, and it will put you to sleep for a lot longer than ten minutes and make you feel very unwell when you wake. I will not hesitate to use it if you don't do as I say. And remember, Robbie is in the house and I have your keys.' The green in his eye glowed darker still.

Emily swallowed the acrid taste of panic and forced herself to nod.

'Good.' He knelt beside the tray and, picking up the scissors, began cutting through the tape that bound her wrists. He ripped it off, making her flesh sting.

She rubbed her wrists, flexed her hands and glanced at the syringe. The sedative would work on him too if she could just get close enough to grab it and stab it into him.

He carefully returned the scissors to their place on the tray and passed her the writing pad and pen. 'Write exactly what I say, nothing more or less. Understood?'

She nodded.

'Dear Ben, I am very sorry, but I have left you for another man,' he dictated slowly, allowing her time to write. 'It's not your fault. You have done nothing wrong. It's me. I am not cut out for this life. I got bored and began an affair. I am sorry for the pain I have caused you. I know you will look after Robbie. Please don't come looking for me. I don't want to be found. Emily.'

He waited while she finished, then took the paper and checked it through.

It was ridiculous, Emily thought with a surge of hope. Ben would never believe that. He knew how much she loved him and Robbie and that never in a million years would she leave them. And she never signed herself Emily to him – all her text messages ended Em, his pet name for her. But Amit didn't know that. Ben would realize something was wrong and come looking for her. But how would he find her? He didn't even know she visited Alisha.

She watched Amit carefully, looking for any chance to escape, as he finished checking the letter. Satisfied, he folded it in half and half again, then tucked it into his pocket. He turned to the tray and picked up the roll of parcel tape and scissors. 'Time to tape your hands again,' he said.

Seizing the opportunity, Emily threw herself at him with all her force. The element of surprise unbalanced him. He fell onto his side, the tape and scissors flying from his grasp. She grabbed the syringe from the tray and brought it up to stab him, but not quickly enough. In a second, he had grabbed her arm and, forcing her fingers apart, took the syringe. She saw it plunge into her thigh, felt the needle's sharp sting and immediately, the room darkened.

The last thought she had before she passed out was that Robbie was alone and Amit had the keys to her house.

Chapter Thirty-Eight

Amit had assumed he'd have to use the second dose of sedative at some point. Women rarely did as they were told first time. He'd spent months beating Alisha into submission, and even now she couldn't be trusted to do – or not do – as he said. Emily would be out for at least a couple of hours and when she came to she'd have a blinding headache, shiver uncontrollably, vomit and be craving water. Serve her right. The bitch. He'd warned her of the consequences if she didn't cooperate.

But, on the positive side, he thought as he let himself into her house, she had written the letter to Ben without any problem. Had she refused, he would have had to send Ben a text message from her phone, but that would have meant a lot of unnecessary inconvenience for him. He would have had to have driven some distance away to send the message so it couldn't be tracked back to his house. Forcing her to write the note had been much easier, straightforward, and a more pleasant way to say goodbye to a loved one, he decided as an afterthought. Although he doubted Emily would see it that way.

Amit stood in the hall, listening. All the lights were on in the house and what sounded like a television with the sound on low could be heard coming from the living room. Was someone in? He didn't think so. The door to the living room was slightly ajar; he couldn't hear any movement. Ben wouldn't be back for at least an hour; he knew from the conversation they'd had that morning. He had got into the routine of going to his car at the same time as Ben and exchanging a few words so he was aware of his movements.

'First day back at work after Christmas?' Amit had asked him that morning, all neighbourly.

'Yes,' Ben had sighed. 'And a late one! A site visit, so I'm not likely to be back until after ten.' Excellent, Amit had thought.

He eased open the living room door and, as he'd thought, it was empty. Emily, believing she'd be back soon, had left the television on low. He'd switch that off now. Clearly, if she'd left Ben for good she wouldn't have left the television on. Picking up the remote control, he turned off the television and placed the control on the coffee table where he'd found it. A partially drunk mug of tea, again suggesting she'd been expecting to return, was on the table. That would need getting rid of. Now, where was her phone? He saw it on the sofa. Fantastic. He'd been slightly surprised it hadn't been on her, given that she seemed glued to it. But then again, she hadn't anticipated being out of the house for long. He tucked the phone into his trouser pocket and glanced around the living room for anything else that needed adjusting, but couldn't see anything.

Where to leave the letter for Ben? Where would she leave it? Somewhere he'd see it as soon as he walked in. Where would Ben expect to find Emily at this time in the evening? Most likely in here, relaxing in the living room, he decided. Amit propped the note on the coffee table and set her keys beside it. They added a nice touch. Leaving her house keys suggested a finality; that there was no chance of her coming back. He had thought about packing a bag of her clothes but decided it would take too much time and he'd no idea what she would take. A detail like that could be his downfall and arouse suspicion. She had her jacket with her, and he guessed Ben and the police – if Ben called them – would assume her new bloke would be providing for all her future needs.

Picking up the mug, Amit left the living room and went into the kitchen, where he poured the contents down the sink. He put the mug in the bowl for washing up later. Emily didn't seem the type of person to wash up a single mug when she was leaving Ben. He looked around the kitchen for anything else that seemed incongruous with her having left for good, but it all seemed OK. Satisfied, he returned to the hall.

'Mummy!' a child's voice came from upstairs.

Amit paused, his hand on the front door ready to let himself out. He'd forgotten about the child, he'd been so busy concentrating on making the house look as if Emily had left Ben. Oh well, it was nothing to do with him. He went to open the door, but the child called out again.

'Daddy!'

How old was he? More than one year, he thought, from having seen him on the CCTV. Too young to be able to tell about his mother's visits next door or point an accusing finger at him. Or was he? Amit wasn't clued up about children's developmental stages, as he'd had nothing to do with his own two. Could a child this age give him away or even raise suspicion? He didn't know, but he should find out. Better to be safe than sorry.

Turning from the door, he went upstairs as Robbie's voice called out again. 'Mummy? Daddy?'

Amit went along the landing to the second room on the right. The door was open and a night light was on. He could see the child standing at the bars of his cot, looking out hopefully, waiting for one of his parents to answer his call. Amit stood by the door and stared at the child. Robbie looked back, trusting and naïve.

He was an attractive-looking boy, and healthy. Normal, in fact. What right did they have to a healthy son when he had been denied one? It wasn't fair. Another injustice meted out at birth. A child like this should have been his. Amit's anger and frustration grew. A child like this would have made his parents proud. Emily and Ben had no right to the healthy child he had been denied.

Amit took a couple of steps into the room and saw the child's expression change, from trusting inquisitiveness to uncertainty and then fear. He continued up to the cot and reached in. Robbie cried loudly and tried to back away from the frightening stranger, but there was nowhere for him to go.

Chapter Thirty-Nine

Emily felt her stomach cramp and the nausea rise in her throat before she could open her eyes. She was cold, shivering, and her head pounded with the worst headache ever. Was she ill? She couldn't remember. It didn't feel as though she was in bed. She desperately needed a drink of water to stop her from being sick again. Too late. She vomited in a bowl.

A bowl. Being held. Someone was holding a bowl to her chin. Not Ben. She forced her eyes open.

'Alisha. What are you doing here?' she asked, groggy and confused. Alisha was holding the bowl and now offering her a glass of water. They were in Eva's room and the night light was on.

Emily gulped the water. She couldn't hold the glass; her wrists were bound with parcel tape. So were her ankles. Then she remembered. Panic and terror gripped her.

'Get away from me!' she cried, recoiling. 'You're evil. You lured me here. You and your evil husband. Robbie is alone. Untie me now. I have to go to Robbie.' But Alisha just looked at her. 'Now!' Emily screamed and pulled and twisted her wrists to try to free herself. The tape held fast. She was bound, just as she had been in the kitchen. Alisha and Amit were working together. 'Take it off now!' she screamed. 'I need to go to Robbie.' An excruciating pain shot through her head and she winced.

'I can't untie you,' Alisha said quietly. 'And you mustn't shout or Amit will come up and tape your mouth shut again. He said I could take it off to allow you to be sick so you didn't choke on your own vomit. But if you scream he will put it back on.'

'And I'm supposed to be grateful!' Emily cried. 'You're as evil and mad as he is. You tricked me into coming here. You didn't need milk for Eva. You made me leave Robbie alone.' She gagged and Alisha held the bowl to her chin again, then offered her more water.

'Amit forced me.'

'Why am I ill?' Emily asked.

'The injection he gave you. It will wear off soon. Drink plenty.' She held the glass to her lips and Emily drank.

She could see now that they were in the living area of Eva's bedsitting room and she was on the floor with her back against the wall. Alisha was kneeling beside her. 'Where's Eva?' Emily asked.

'In bed with her headphones on. I didn't want her to see or hear what he was doing.'

'Protect your own, but never mind Robbie,' Emily hissed, and tears sprung to her eyes. 'I need to get to him. Please help me. You have a child. Untie me so I can go to him. I won't tell anyone what you've done.'

'I can't, I daren't, and even if I did untie you, you couldn't escape. Amit has fitted a bolt to the outside of this door. We're prisoners in this room. He only lets me out to get tablets and food.'

Emily stopped struggling and, defeated, rested her head back on the wall and tried to think. 'You knew what he was planning and yet you went along with it. You've known all along.'

'No. Honestly. I haven't. He saw your mobile phone number on our telephone bill. I didn't realize all the numbers were listed. I had to admit I'd phoned you and said you'd been here once. But he checked the CCTV and saw the gaps in the date and time where I had deleted your visits. He beat me and threatened to kill Eva if I didn't phone you and bring you here.'

'But you must have known what he was doing in that lab?'

'Not until you showed me that video on your phone of the cylinder being delivered. That's when I became suspicious. You must believe me. Eva and I are in as much danger as you. He's insane. I should have told you about Tibs when I first found out.'

'You knew he killed Tibs?' Emily asked, horrified.

Alisha gave a small, regretful nod. 'Not at the time. But when I found out he'd lied to you about where and who had found Tibs' collar, I looked at the CCTV. I saw he'd accidentally dropped it in the dark outside our back door. He'd come from his lab carrying large dustbin bags that were clearly very heavy, together with cat and dog collars that he threw in the bin. That night, he put the dustbin bags into his car and was gone a long time. I realized later that he was responsible for the dead animals found in Coleshaw Woods. I'm so sorry, Emily, I should have told you sooner.'

Emily looked warily at Alisha. Her regret and sorrow seemed sincere. 'So why didn't you leave him, or tell me when you found out what he was doing?'

'I was too scared. I'd nowhere to go and Amit has always told me that if the police or social services found out we'd been keeping Eva here, they'd put her in an institution and us in prison. I couldn't bear the thought of Eva in an institution. She'd never survive without me.' Tears filled her eyes.

'He was lying to keep you silent,' Emily said. 'You wouldn't have gone to prison when the whole story became known. You were a victim. You would have been given help to look after Eva, not locked up.'

'Do you really think so?'

'Yes.'

'I'm so sorry, Emily. I never meant for any of this to happen.'

'You need to release me and we can plan our escape. Between us we can overpower him. You have to, Alisha. Robbie is all alone and Amit is planning to kill us for the sake of his monstrous experiment.'

But Emily saw the look in Alisha's eyes, the beaten, hunted animal, and knew that years of abuse had rendered her impotent to act, and even now she was incapable of saving them.

'Alisha, if you don't help me you will be in a lot of trouble. Ben will be home soon and he won't believe I've left him. He'll call the police and they'll go through the contacts on my phone. They'll see your telephone number and all the calls between us and will come here looking for me. Unless you help me to escape, you will be guilty – an accomplice to kidnapping me – and then what will happen to Eva?'

Alisha looked away. 'Amit has your mobile phone,' she said, her voice flat. 'He showed it to me when he brought you up here. He found it in your living room when he left your letter for Ben. He also switched off your television and poured away your tea so it would look like you had gone for good and not just popped out. I doubt the police will come looking for you here. Why should they?'

'Amit has my phone,' Emily repeated numbly. Were there any other clues to her being here? She didn't think so. 'Did Amit say anything about Robbie? Sometimes he wakes and calls out for me.'

'Yes, he heard him and went to his room. I don't know any more. But you don't have to worry about Robbie now. Ben has just returned.'

'How can you possibly know that?' Emily asked, astounded.

'I heard his car come down the road. Being shut up

inside a house for years sharpens your senses, a bit like being blind. I know the comings and goings of my neighbours from hearing them. I know when the carers arrive and leave at the elderly neighbours' on the other side, when you and Ben come and go or have visitors. It's like an eye to the outside world. You wouldn't notice those sounds because you have no need to, you are part of the world. Listen carefully. He's just pulled onto your drive.'

Emily concentrated and finally heard the sound Alisha referred to, the low throb of a car engine, then silence as he switched if off. Ben was home, but where was Robbie?

Please let him be asleep in his cot . . .

Chapter Forty

All the lights in the house were on, which meant that Em must have waited up for him, Ben thought as he took his briefcase from the passenger seat. If she went to bed, she usually just left the hall light on so he could see to let himself in. He appreciated it when she stayed up if he was very late back from work. It gave them a chance to talk and catch up on the day's news, although he understood why she would go to bed after the broken nights they were having from Robbie's teething. Em was always the one who saw to Robbie at night. She said it was only fair with her on maternity leave and him having to get up early for work. He was enjoying his new role, although it was proving challenging in some areas. Thank goodness he had Em's support.

The car locked behind him as he crossed the drive and he quietly let himself in so as not to disturb Robbie.

Setting his briefcase down in the hall, Ben took off his shoes and hung his jacket on the coatstand.

'Em?' he called softly, going into the living room. She wasn't there, and nor was she in the kitchen. She must be upstairs. Perhaps settling Robbie, or getting ready for bed herself.

He padded quietly up the carpeted stairs and along the landing, past the bathroom, which was empty, and to Robbie's room. He looked in, but Em wasn't in there. Just a mound under the duvet that was Robbie. The light was off in their bedroom and the door was slightly ajar. Perhaps she was in bed asleep, after all, or she would have heard him and called out by now.

Ben took a step into their bedroom. It was dark and it was a moment before his eyes adjusted, but he couldn't see a mound in the bed. He switched on the light. The bed was empty.

'Em?' he called quietly as he went out. He'd check the guest room, although what she'd be doing in there he'd no idea. It was empty. A slight feeling of unease ran through him, but he dismissed it. Of course she was here somewhere. She could be in the garage, although he wasn't sure why, or putting the rubbish in the bins down the sideway. Yes, that must be it; at the same time he'd let himself in the front door, she had gone out the back and was now putting out the rubbish so she hadn't heard him. She must still be there.

Hurrying downstairs, he opened the integral door to the garage and flicked on the light switch. He could see straight away she wasn't in there, and also that the door on the far side that led to the sideway was closed and locked. His pulse quickened. Where the hell was she?

'Em!' His voice echoed around the house, but there was no reply.

The garden? He hadn't checked the garden. There was absolutely no reason for her to be in the garden at this time of night in the middle of winter, but his mind was frantically searching for a plausible explanation for her not being in the house, and he was running out of options.

Going to the rear of their kitchen-diner, he unlocked the patio door and called into the darkness, 'Em!'

Nothing. Of course she wasn't in the garden, and the fact that the patio door had been locked confirmed that. His heart set up a queer little rhythm as he struggled to construct a rationale, an explanation for where she might be.

Robbie's room. He hadn't gone fully in. If Em had been sitting on the beanbag on the other side of Robbie's cot as she did sometimes while waiting for him to drop off to sleep, or had been standing by the window, he might not have seen her. It didn't make sense that she hadn't heard him and called out unless she'd fallen asleep on the beanbag or was listening to music with her earbuds in, or possibly she'd collapsed, ill.

He ran back upstairs, taking them two at a time, and went all the way into Robbie's room. He could see straight away she wasn't in here. He stood for a moment, listening for any sound that could be Em, his anxiety growing by the second. She wouldn't have gone out and left Robbie alone. That was impossible. The cover was over Robbie's face, he pulled it up sometimes, and Em always repositioned it, concerned he could overheat or not be able to breathe.

Ben went to the side of the cot and, expecting to find Robbie fast asleep, eased back the cover. To his surprise he saw Robbie was awake. He stared back unblinkingly, his eyes red from crying; he looked petrified.

'What's the matter, little fellow?' Ben said, reaching in and gently lifting him out. Robbie clung desperately to his father, his little body hot and wet from crying. 'What is it, son? Where's Mummy?'

'Mummy,' Robbie said and buried his head in his father's chest.

Em would never have left him to cry himself into this state, Ben thought. She always answered his calls straight away. Something was wrong. Badly wrong. Where was she?

'I'll take you down and fix you a cool drink,' he said, holding Robbie close.

As Ben passed their bedroom, he looked in again as if Emily might have suddenly materialized. It was irrational, he knew, but his brain was striving to create logic where there was none. Their bed was still empty, as was the floor around it. Still holding Robbie, he knelt down and looked under the bed, then checked the bathroom again before returning downstairs, his thoughts frantically searching for something that would explain Em not being here. He was certain now that she wasn't in the house. Was it possible they'd run out of an essential item like milk or bread and she'd popped to the local shop, and not wanting to disturb Robbie had left him sleeping in his cot? She'd never done it before. But why hadn't she taken her car? It was on the drive. The only shop open at this time was a mile away. She wouldn't have walked there, leaving Robbie alone. And if they had run out of something, surely she would have texted or phoned him and asked him to pick it up on his way home as she had done before? None of it made sense.

Her phone, of course. Why hadn't he thought of that sooner? She always had her phone with her. He wasn't thinking straight. He hurried downstairs and took his phone from his jacket on the hall stand and checked it for missed calls. There were none from Em. And no more text messages from her after the ones they'd exchanged at lunchtime when she'd sent him a video clip of Robbie waving and saying Daddy. He wasn't sure if that was a good sign or not.

He pressed her number. It rang three times and then went through to voicemail. He didn't leave a message but called again straight away. Perhaps she hadn't got to her phone in time. It rang and went through to voicemail again and this time he did leave a message.

'Em, where are you? I'm worried sick. I'm home. Robbie's here, but you're not. Phone me as soon as you get this, please. I can't think what's happened to you.' He stopped, and with no idea what else to say ended the call. Had he done the right thing leaving that message? He'd sounded a bit angry, but then he was – from worry. All this was outside any point of reference. There was nothing to tell him what to say or do in this situation. Em was missing and he hadn't a clue where she was.

Ben called once more to see if she would pick up and then jabbed the phone into his trouser pocket and carried Robbie into the kitchen to get him a drink. There was an empty mug in the sink but no other washing-up. He filled Robbie's trainer cup with water and took it into the living room. He sat on the sofa with Robbie on his lap and offered him his drink, but he wasn't interested. He was still clinging desperately to him, his little fists clutching handfuls of his shirt. Why was he so upset? Ben had never seen him like this before. How long had he been left alone to cry? What the hell was going on? What should he do? He hadn't a clue. It didn't make any sense at all.

As he placed Robbie's beaker on the coffee table, he saw Em's house keys beside a folded sheet of writing paper. His heart lurched. Why were her keys here? And what was this – a letter? He picked it up and unfolding it began to read.

Dear Ben, I am very sorry, but I have left you for another man. It's not your fault. You have done nothing wrong. It's me. The words blurred and jumped around the page. *I am not cut out for this life. I got bored and began an affair. I am sorry for the pain I have caused you. I know you will look after Robbie. Please don't come looking for me. I don't want to be found. Emily.*

The paper trembled in his hand as he stared at the words.

Nausea rose in his throat. It wasn't possible. This couldn't be happening, not to him and Em. They loved each other. All their friends and family said what a perfect couple they were. She loved him, she told him most days, and she loved Robbie – more than life itself. She'd sent him a video clip at lunchtime, signed *Em Luv you*. With a heart emoji. Why would she have done that if she was planning on leaving him? What had happened in the interim to make her pack and go? Pack. What had she taken?

Leaving Robbie on the sofa, Ben ran upstairs and into their bedroom. Throwing open her wardrobe door, he saw it was still full of her clothes. He pulled open the drawers; they were full too. She appeared to have taken nothing. It didn't add up.

Robbie cried from the living room and Ben ran back downstairs; picked him up and soothed him. There must be an explanation. Taking his phone from his pocket, he called Emily's number again. It went through to voicemail. He left another message, desperate and raw.

'Em, call me, please. I've read your note. We can sort this out. Call me as soon as you can. Robbie needs you. I need you. Please phone.' Tears stung his eyes and he swallowed hard. He'd beg her if necessary to come back. She and Robbie were his life. He knew he'd been working hard, but she hadn't seemed to mind. He'd cut back so he could spend more time with them. They could go on holiday, the three of them, have more days out. Whatever it took, whatever was needed to win her back.

Ben's gaze went to her house keys, left on the table as

if to say she would never return – but he couldn't accept that. Too much was at stake. When he finally spoke to Em, he'd persuade her there *was* a way forward. It was then he spotted her handbag beside the armchair. She always left it there when indoors. So she hadn't taken that either? But she never went out without her bag slung over her shoulder. He picked it up and began going through the contents. Her car keys were in there with all the other stuff she carried with her – hairbrush, tissues, cosmetics and so on, but not her phone. Her house keys were on the table, so she must have taken them from her bag and then left it behind. But why? It was as if she'd gone in a hurry, on the spur of the moment, without any forethought or planning. That could explain why she hadn't packed a bag and had sent a loving text at lunchtime. At the time she'd messaged, she'd had no intention of leaving him. Perhaps the guy she'd been seeing had suddenly turned up and pressurized her into going. Demanded she left now without giving her a chance to think about it and change her mind. That would make some sense, although Em was someone who usually planned ahead and thought things through. And he was still struggling to believe she was capable of having an affair at all. Not his Em.

Perhaps she wasn't, Ben thought after a moment. Perhaps she'd made that up. All this was so irrational and unlike Em; could it be she was having a nervous breakdown? It seemed more likely. There'd been no outward signs that he'd been aware of, but possibly she'd been suffering from postnatal depression and hadn't told him. Suffering in silence, until it became too much, and she'd just snapped and left. It was possible. He'd read an article about severe postnatal depression causing unpredictable and irrational behaviour. In which case, Em was out there on a cold dark night, alone, confused and in need of help. He picked up the phone and pressed 999.

'Police. It's an emergency.'

Chapter Forty-One

It tortured Emily to think of Ben, just a short distance away, reading the note she'd been forced to write. What was he thinking? He'd be shocked to find the note and Robbie alone, but she felt sure he'd see through it and realize something awful had happened. Thankfully, Robbie was unharmed. Alisha had said she'd heard him crying as Amit had left. Emily believed her as she now believed Alisha wasn't working with Amit. For the alternative – that they had conspired in this and had hurt her son – was too awful to contemplate.

Ben knew her too well to believe she would ever leave him for another man. But what would he do? She couldn't imagine and tried to put herself in his position. What would she have done if she'd come home and found Robbie alone and a note from Ben saying he'd left her? She would call the police and her parents, although not necessarily in that order. Ben would call the police for sure. But how long would it take before anyone came looking for her here without the list of contacts in her phone and no clue to say she was next door? Panic rose again and she tried to calm herself.

She couldn't just sit here waiting for help to arrive. She was tied up and at the mercy of a maniac. Now the effects of the sedative he'd given her had fully worn off, she was able to think more clearly. She had to escape, but to do so she would need Alisha's help. How to convince her?

In the small glow of the night light, she looked at Alisha, sitting beside her on the floor, with her back against the wall and her eyes closed. While she'd been ill, Alisha had wiped her mouth and given her sips of water, but thank goodness the vomiting had stopped now. The shivering, stomach cramps and headache were going too. Eva was asleep in her bed just out of sight around the corner in the L-shaped room so hadn't witnessed what had happened. Emily could hear her stirring sometimes in her sleep.

'Alisha,' Emily whispered into the semi-darkness. 'Are you awake?'

Her eyes immediately opened. 'Yes, what is it? Are you going to be sick?'

'No, but we can't just sit here and wait for Amit to come for us. We need to escape.'

'I can't release you, I've told you that. He will beat me and hurt Eva.'

'I have a plan. Come closer so we don't wake Eva and I'll explain.'

Alisha heaved herself closer. She seemed utterly exhausted and defeated.

'Listen to me,' Emily whispered. 'Amit won't ever be able to harm you or Eva again once we're out of here. He'll be in prison for a long time and you and Eva will be safe. But you need to trust me and do as I say.' She saw Alisha's doubt and willed her to make the necessary leap of faith.

'What is your plan?' Alisha asked, her voice low. 'All the doors and windows are locked, and this door is bolted.'

'You told me Amit unbolts this door to let you out to get your tablets and food.'

'Yes, but the last time was at nine o'clock. There is no more now until morning.'

'Supposing you needed something for Eva?'

'Then we'd have to wait.'

'Supposing Eva or you were ill. He would come in to see?'

'Maybe. I don't know.' Alisha shrugged despondently.

'I think he would,' Emily said. 'From what you've told me he doesn't want you dead yet.'

'It's possible, I suppose,' she conceded.

'So this is what we do. You will carefully cut the tape from my hands and legs so I can reuse it. Then, when I'm ready, you'll call out to Amit and say Eva is ill. She will still be in bed, and I'll be here as if I'm tied up. When he goes to Eva to examine her, I'll attack him – take him by surprise. I'll need something sharp or heavy to use as a weapon. We'll find something in this room. There are two of us, we can overpower him. It will work, Alisha, believe me, it will.' She held her gaze.

'I can't,' Alisha whispered, fear in her eyes. 'Supposing we fail?'

'We won't. Not if we plan this carefully, but I will need your help. I can't do it alone. Trust me.' Emily knew it was asking a lot of Alisha to be stronger than her tormentor and rise up against him after years of abuse. 'Alisha, how are you going to explain me being tied up to Eva when she wakes? You can't hide me here, the room is too small. You said yourself she likes me and would be upset to see me like this. She will blame you for not helping me.'

Alisha glanced in Eva's direction and then said, 'If I agree to your plan, she mustn't be hurt.'

'She won't, I promise. Do you have any scissors or a knife here to cut through the tape?'

Alisha hesitated, then, standing quietly, she crossed to a small set of drawers. Opening the top one, she took out a pair of children's scissors and returned to Emily. She knelt in front of her and carefully cut through the tape around her wrists, then handed the scissors to Emily to cut the tape on her ankles.

'Well done,' Emily whispered. She set the tape to one side to use later and stood; her limbs were stiff from being in one position. 'I'll need something heavy or sharp to use as a weapon.'

'There's nothing here,' Alisha replied anxiously.

'I'll find something,' Emily said and began quietly

searching the room for any object that could be used as a weapon. She'd only get one chance to attack Amit, so it needed to work first time. The children's scissors were no good as they had rounded ends – indeed, the whole room was child-safe. Perhaps Alisha was right and there was nothing here she could use. Then she spotted the coffee table and, going over, quietly turned it upside down. It was too cumbersome itself to use as a weapon, but if she could remove its metal legs they would make good weapons. She tested the legs – two moved slightly, some of their screws were already loose. 'You don't have a screwdriver up here, do you?' she asked Alisha.

Alisha shook her head.

'Let me have the scissors again.'

She gave Emily the scissors. Using the end as a screwdriver, Emily began undoing the already partially loose screws as Alisha watched, her hand pressed nervously to her mouth. She succeeded in removing one table leg and then a second. The other two were on too tightly to budge. She hid the rest of the table in the shower room so Amit wouldn't see it. She then placed one of the metal legs on the floor where she'd been sitting and tucked the other behind a cushion on the sofa.

'That one is for you to use,' she said quietly to Alisha. Emily looked around the room. 'Is everything in place as Amit would expect to find it?' she asked Alisha.

'I think so.'

'In a moment I am going to sit over there exactly as Amit left me and you're going to stick the tape back on my wrists. Then, when I tell you, you will start banging on the door and shouting that Eva is ill and you need him to come quickly. Make it convincing. As soon as he opens the door, draw him to Eva's bed. He will see me tied up and follow you over. If he doesn't come into the room, the door will be open so I should still have the chance to overpower him and for us to escape.'

Alisha stared back, wide-eyed and frightened.

'You can do it, Alisha,' Emily said, taking her hands. 'You must, for all our sakes, especially Eva's.'

She managed a small nod.

'Come on, let's do it now.'

Emily led Alisha over to where Amit had left her and sat on the floor, her back to the wall, tucking the metal bar beneath her. She picked up the tape that had bound her ankles and stuck it in place.

'Now, you do my wrists.'

Alisha's trembling hands resealed the tape around Emily's wrists.

'That's fine. It should hold long enough to fool him, especially in this light.' She drew a deep breath. 'Once you've lured him to Eva's bed, I'll strike. Understood?' Alisha nodded. 'OK. Let's do it. Make it good, Alisha. The performance of a lifetime. *Quick! Get help! Eva is ill. She's choking!*'

Incited by Emily, Alisha rushed to the door and banged on it with all her might. 'Amit! Come quickly! Eva is choking.' She stopped and listened.

'No, keep going, louder, more insistent,' Emily said.

'Amit! Come! Eva is choking, I need your help. She's

going blue in the face.' The noise had woken Eva and she began to cry, adding to the effect.

Emily felt the iron bar beneath her and concentrated on the door.

'Amit! Come quickly! Eva can't breathe! I need your help! Come before it's too late!'

Eva cried all the more and Emily knew Alisha must be hating herself for upsetting her child and not being able to comfort her.

Suddenly Amit's voice came from the other side of the door. 'What's the matter?' he demanded, without any trace of empathy. And for a moment Emily wondered if he would come in to save Eva after all.

'She's choking. Quick! I need your help,' Alisha cried. Emily felt her heart racing as adrenalin coursed through her.

There was silence from outside the door, then, 'Is that bitch still tied up?' he asked.

'Yes.'

'Where is she?'

'Where you left her.'

'If you're lying to me, you'll regret it.'

'I'm not lying,' Alisha replied, her voice faltering. Emily prayed Amit hadn't heard it.

Eva cried louder.

'Come! Eva is very ill,' Alisha said, now with slightly less conviction.

Another pause; Emily held her breath. Then Amit's voice again, 'Move away from the door and I'll come in.'

Emily nodded to Alisha.

The bolt slid and the door slowly opened.

'Put the main light on,' he ordered before coming in.

Emily hadn't reckoned on this, but the tape around her wrists and ankles was still in place. She kept very still.

Alisha switched on the main light and Emily blinked into the brightness. Amit was standing at the door, watching Alisha go to Eva's bed. She bit her lip, willed him to follow. He took a single, tentative step in, glanced at Emily and, satisfied, began across the room. Emily looked at the open door and the urge to run was almost irresistible, but she couldn't leave Alisha and Eva, and he'd come straight after her. Alisha had said all the doors were locked.

Emily watched and waited, her heart pounding as he approached Eva's bed.

Alisha was talking to Eva now in a small trembling voice, soothing her, and trying to stop her from crying. 'It's OK. You'll be all right soon.'

Wait until he's fully turned away and occupied with Eva, Emily told herself.

'She's not choking,' Amit said, leaning over the bed.

It was now or never. Emily quietly took the tape from her wrists, picked up the iron bar and hurtled herself across the room, the tape around her ankles falling away. But in that second Amit was instantly alerted to the movement behind him. He turned, and as Emily went to hit him, he grabbed the bar, deflecting it. It landed on his head, but its force was muted. He held onto it. Emily tried to raise it again, but it was impossible, he was holding it tightly.

'Alisha! The other bar!' Emily cried as she struggled with him. 'Hit him! Hard!'

But Alisha couldn't. Like a scared rabbit trapped in a car's headlights, she couldn't act to save herself or them.

Eva shrieked as Emily twisted and turned the bar, trying to reclaim it. Alisha watched impotently, her hands pressed to her face. A sudden hefty push from Amit caught Emily by surprise, and she lost her balance and went crashing to the floor. Alisha screamed.

Above her, Emily saw Amit raise the weapon, ready to bring it down. Only then did Alisha find the courage to act. She made a grab for the other weapon concealed behind the cushion on the sofa. But too late. Amit swung his bar down again. Emily cried out in pain and tried to roll away from him, but there was nowhere to go. Another blow across her back and she shrieked. He kicked her in the ribs and fled the room, the bolt crashing into place.

'You'll be sorry for this!' he shouted from outside.

Emily already was.

Chapter Forty-Two

Ben looked out of the window in Robbie's room. He couldn't believe it was taking the police so long to arrive. It was nearly an hour since he'd phoned and there was still no sign of them. The call handler had said they were very busy and were having to prioritize calls, and a missing adult who'd left home of her own free will wasn't a blue-light response. Ben had got angry and shouted his partner was fucking ill and didn't know what she was doing, but the call handler had replied that she wouldn't speak to him until he'd calmed down.

Leaving the window, Ben returned to Robbie's cot. At last he seemed to be asleep. Each time he'd tried to put him down, he'd screamed and cried uncontrollably, not wanting to be in his cot. Ben had never seen him so upset and frightened. He supposed it was because he'd been left alone to cry for so long, possibly for hours, for he'd no idea when Em had left. Now, finally, Robbie's eyes were closed and his little face was relaxing in sleep. A few more minutes and he'd go downstairs.

Ben returned to the window. Still no sign of the police car, and all this time Em was out there frightened and alone. It was a cold night and she only had her jacket with her, not her winter coat. He'd give the police another five minutes and then phone them again, and this time he'd threaten them with a complaint. It wasn't good enough. Em's health and welfare – indeed, her very life – was in danger, although the call handler had disagreed. It was the note that had done it and removed the urgency, but what did they know? He shouldn't have told them about the note and they would have reacted faster.

He'd telephoned both sets of parents straight after he'd called the police. He needed all the help and support he could get and they had a right to know. Distraught and struggling to get his words out and with Robbie crying on his shoulder, he'd explained he'd come home to find Em missing and thought she could be suffering from postnatal depression. He didn't tell them about the note after the reaction of the police. Em was ill and needed to be found. Why complicate it? They were shocked and horrified – none of them had seen any warning signs of Em's depression over Christmas. He said she must have hidden it well. They assured him they'd come straight over, but it would take them a couple of hours.

Finally, Ben saw a police car approaching. No flashing light or siren. It drew steadily up the road and parked across his driveway. He immediately left the window and went downstairs and opened the front door. He then waited with mounting irritation as the two officers sat in the car, talking for a few moments before getting out.

'DC Matt Davis and DC Beth Mayes,' the female officer said as they approached, flashing their ID cards.

'This way,' Ben said stiffly and led them into the living room. The Christmas garlands stirred obscenely in the air, now at odds with the atmosphere.

'Can we sit down?' Beth Mayes asked.

Ben motioned to the sofa as he took an armchair.

'Firstly,' Beth said, sitting down, 'we understand from your call there's a child here, Robbie? Is he safe?'

'Yes, of course. He's asleep in his cot upstairs.'

'We won't disturb him now, but we'll need to see him later.'

'Why?'

'Routine. To confirm he is safe. We'll begin by taking yours and your partner's full details, and anyone else who lives here. Then you can tell us exactly what happened while Matt takes some notes.'

Stemming his impatience, Ben gave his and Em's full names, dates of birth and said that they and Robbie were the only ones who lived here.

'And this is your only residence?' Beth asked.

'Yes, of course,' Ben said irritably.

Matt wrote.

'Please continue,' Beth said. 'What happened today?'

'It was my first day back at work after Christmas. I knew it was going to be a late one before I left.'

'What time did you leave the house?' Matt asked, glancing up from writing.

'I don't know exactly. Around seven-thirty this morning, I guess.'

'Did anyone see you leave?' Matt asked.

'I don't think so. Why?'

'Just a routine question,' Beth said.

'Oh yes, I remember now, my neighbour saw me leave, Dr Amit Burman.'

Matt made a note.

'So when was the last time you saw Emily?' Beth asked.

'Just before I left this morning. Around seven-fifteen. I took her a cup of tea in bed. She'd had a broken night with Robbie. That was the last time I actually saw her, but we swapped text messages around lunchtime. The last one from her was just after one o'clock and she seemed fine.'

'We'll need to take a look at your phone later,' Beth said. 'So when you left the house this morning, how were things between you and Emily?'

'Good,' Ben said sharply

'No post-Christmas tiff?' Beth asked. 'Christmas can put a strain on families; you know, being together all that time.'

'We were fine,' Ben returned curtly.

'So, as far as you were concerned, there was nothing going on between you two, and nothing in Emily's manner to suggest she was planning to leave?'

'She didn't plan to leave!' Ben snapped, his voice rising. 'I told that call handler already, Em's not well. She left on impulse. It must have suddenly become too much. She took her phone but nothing else. Em wouldn't leave Robbie and me if she was in her right mind.'

'Did she take any clothes?' Beth asked.

'No. Nothing. Only what she was wearing and her jacket from the hall.'

'What was she wearing? I'll need a description.'

'She was still in bed when I last saw her, but it would have been jeans and a jumper.'

'What colour jumper?'

'I don't know. I didn't see. Light blue or pink, I guess. She liked those colours.'

'And her jacket?'

'Dark-blue zip-up.'

'Can I see the note she left?'

Ben took it from his trouser pocket and passed it to DC Mayes. She read it, handed it to Matt to read and he gave it back to Ben.

'What about her passport?' Matt asked as he wrote. 'Did she take that?'

'No, of course not.'

'Have you checked?' Beth asked.

'No, but she wouldn't go abroad without us. We were planning on going on a family holiday next year when Robbie is a bit older.'

'Could you check to see if her passport is still here, please,' Beth said. 'It is important.'

Ben sighed and stood. 'It's upstairs.'

'We'll wait here,' Beth said.

He went quickly upstairs, into their bedroom and, opening the drawer where they kept important paperwork, took out Em's passport. Of course it was here. It was absurd suggesting she'd left the country without them. It was wasting valuable time.

He returned to the living room. 'Here you are,' he said brusquely, handing the passport to Beth.

He watched as she opened it, checked the details and handed it back.

'Her handbag with all her credit cards is still here too,' Ben said, pointing to it.

'Can I take a look?'

Ben passed her the bag and she looked through the contents.

'And you're sure there's nothing missing other than her phone?'

'Positive. I checked. She even left her car and house keys.'

'She's not planning on returning any time soon then,' Matt said.

Ben glared at him. 'Leaving us was an irrational act and completely out of character. She'd taken extra maternity leave to be with Robbie. She'd never leave him.'

'But clearly she has,' Matt said. 'Who is going to look after the child now?'

'Until Em is found, me of course, with the help of the grandparents. They're on their way.'

'Em?' Beth queried.

'It's my nickname for her, shortened from Emily.'

'Did she usually refer to herself as Em?' Beth asked.

'Yes, why?'

'I noticed she signed herself Emily on the note she left behind.'

'That proves she wasn't herself then,' Ben said. Taking the note from his pocket, he looked at it again. 'She would have signed Em if she'd been thinking straight.'

'Or possibly she felt the intimacy was no longer warranted – if she was leaving you for another man,' Matt said.

'Bullshit!' Ben snapped. The man was an insensitive moron. 'Why don't you understand that she wouldn't do that?' He ran his fingers distractedly through his hair. 'Her signature is more proof she was acting irrationally because she was depressed. She wasn't herself.'

'Ben, can you tell me why you think Emily was suffering from depression?' Beth asked gently. 'Did she tell you? Had she been to see her doctor? Called a helpline?'

'No. She didn't say anything to me. She must have covered it up. As far as I know, she hadn't seen a doctor or spoken to anyone about it. Her parents didn't know either.'

'We can check with her doctor,' Matt said, making a note. 'Which practice does she attend?'

'Dr Ross at the Coleshaw Health Centre.'

'Thank you,' Beth said. 'So, at present, it's just you who thinks she's depressed?'

Ben shrugged despondently. 'And my parents.'

Beth nodded. 'So the last time you heard from Emily was a little after one o'clock today, and you made the call to the emergency services at ten-fifty. Was that when you first got home?'

'No. About fifteen minutes after I got in. I searched the house first, then saw the note and realized she was missing.'

'So your child could have been alone from one o'clock in the afternoon until you arrived home, making a total of over nine hours?' Beth said.

Ben nodded sombrely. 'Yes, I know.'

'You realize it's illegal to leave an infant at home alone even for a short while. When Emily does return, the social services will need to be involved.'

'She's ill,' Ben said protectively. 'She wouldn't normally have left him.'

'Does Emily have a laptop, tablet or any other device apart from her phone that she uses to access email and the internet?' Beth asked.

'A laptop and tablet,' Ben said. 'They're still here.'

'We'll take those with us. What about banking and savings accounts? Do you have any joint accounts?'

'Two, a current account for paying bills and a savings account.'

'Has anything gone out of them today?'

'I haven't checked.' He stared at them, bemused.

'I would, and also put a stop on the joint accounts. Does she have a personal account?'

'Yes, but there's hardly anything in it. She's on extended unpaid maternity leave.'

'Do you know the login details to her personal account?' Beth asked.

Ben shook his head.

'If you give us her bank account details, we'll check to see if any money has been withdrawn. What about social networking, Facebook and so on?'

'She has a Facebook and LinkedIn account. Why?'

'When someone leaves in circumstances such as these, it's often with someone in their circle of friends whom their partner may know too.'

'Rubbish,' Ben said. 'She wouldn't.'

'I appreciate this is very difficult for you,' Beth said gently. 'But I suggest you think about her friends, see who she has been messaging a lot. We'll need to search your house and then we'll start a missing person investigation, but from what you've told us it seems very likely Emily left with another man of her own accord.'

'You're wrong,' Ben said angrily. 'She would never leave me for another man. Never.'

Chapter Forty-Three

The police car parked outside didn't immediately pull away. Beth was in the driver's seat gazing towards Ben and Emily's house, while Matt tapped at the police car's laptop.

'The poor bugger can't accept she's cleared off with another bloke,' Matt said.

'Maybe, although it's a lot to leave behind,' Beth said thoughtfully. 'Ben seems a decent bloke, and the child appears well looked after. Nice house and cars too. Perhaps she'll change her mind and come back.'

'Or maybe it's not what it seems,' Matt offered. 'He wouldn't be the first bloke to do his partner in after discovering she'd been having an affair and then try to make it look as if she'd run off.'

'True,' Beth agreed. 'Although you could have been more sensitive in there.'

'Point taken,' Matt said amicably.

Beth threw him a smile. She'd worked with Matt before and while they made a good team he often lacked subtlety, which was why she usually led the questioning on sensitive matters. 'Let's wait and see what her laptop and tablet reveal, then come back and talk to him again.' Her gaze shifted to the house next door, where the outline of a man could be seen standing behind the blinds at an upstairs window. 'Nothing like a police car to arouse the neighbours' interest, even in the middle of the night.'

Matt looked over. 'Might be worth asking him if he saw or heard anything when Emily left?'

'Yes, but not now, we're wanted elsewhere. We'll log this as a low-risk missing person and then, depending on what we learn from her doctor, raise its priority if necessary. My gut feeling is that Emily isn't ill and she's just gone off with this guy, possibly after an argument with Ben. She's taken her phone, so she'll probably text or phone him once she's calmed down to say she's all right.'

Beth started the engine and, as they pulled away, she saw the figure at the window in the neighbours' house disappear from view.

Ben heard the police car pull away. He was in Robbie's room trying to get him off to sleep, after the police search had woken him with a start and set him crying again. Despite Ben asking them to be quiet, they'd insisted on switching on all the lights, including the one in Robbie's room, and searching his built-in wardrobe. As if Em would be in there! They'd said it was standard procedure to search the house of any missing person – they'd even gone into the loft, garage and back garden. They'd wanted to take his laptop as well as Em's laptop and tablet, but he'd protested he needed his for work, and they'd agreed to leave it for now. Yet despite this, he'd felt there was no urgency in their approach, that they were going through the motions, and he knew they believed Em had left him for another man.

He looked down at Robbie, now asleep in his arms, and carefully laid him in his cot. The sooner the grandparents arrived, the better. He was struggling to cope with Robbie on top of Em's disappearance. It was all too much. If she wasn't found tonight, he'd have to phone work in the morning to say he wouldn't be in, but what exactly to tell them, he wasn't sure. He had a lot of responsibility now and couldn't just take time off. Hopefully she'd be back by then and he wouldn't have to tell them anything. When his and Em's parents arrived, perhaps they should go out looking for her themselves, he wondered as he returned downstairs. While he waited for them, he would check their joint bank accounts and Em's Facebook as the police had advised, although he was certain he wouldn't find anything untoward.

Collecting his laptop from where he'd left it in the hall, Ben went into the living room and sat on the sofa. As he lifted the lid, a report he'd been writing for work appeared. He had intended to finish it before going to bed. How far off and unreal his day at work seemed now with everything that had happened since. Closing the document, he logged into their joint bank account and saw it was exactly as it should be, with his salary going in and the standing orders for the household bills going out. He then logged on to their joint savings account; there were no withdrawals for the whole year. It was their savings and they tried not to touch it – the money was earmarked for a 'rainy day' or their holiday abroad.

Satisfied no money was missing, Ben logged out of their bank account and brought up the Facebook page. He no longer had a Facebook account, but Em used hers a lot, as did most of her friends. He entered her name and up came her profile picture but nothing more. He'd need her login details to gain further access: email address and password. She only had two email addresses, one for work and the other personal, but what was her password? He sat for a moment trying to think what she might have used and then remembered she kept a written list of all her passwords in case she forgot them upstairs with her other paperwork.

He went up, quickly found the sheet, then returned downstairs to the living room. The password was the name of their university and Robbie's date of birth. Logging in, he was surprised to see how many Facebook friends she had – 398. Although, as he looked, he saw they weren't all close friends; some were work colleagues and business associates. Her mother and sister were there, as was an aunt. He recognized some of her friends from school and university, many of whom she hadn't seen in years. They'd all had Facebook accounts at university, but when Ben had started work, on the advice of the company's human resources officer, he'd deleted his account so management and clients wouldn't have access to any information from his student days that could have been embarrassing.

Ben continued through her list of friends as the police had advised and saw pictures of couples they were both friends with and invited to dinner sometimes. Sue and Mike, Eddie and Josy. Indeed, many of the couples had been at their pre-Christmas drinks party Em had organized. There were photographs of that night shared and tagged between friends with captions: *A fantastic evening at Emily & Ben's. Great to see you all again, Max & Joe. Looking lovely as ever. Suzie & Simon.* Did he really believe any of these guys – friends of his too – could have been having an affair with Em? No. It was preposterous. Em wasn't a good liar and she'd appeared happy.

He stopped at a photograph of Em and Robbie in a park. It was recent, and they were standing beside a guy with a similar-aged child. A selfie taken by one of them, all four of them smiling into the lens. The caption beneath read: *Em and Robbie with Greg (proud house husband) and Jamie. Best buddies.* Who were best buddies? Ben wondered with a stab of jealousy. The children, or Em and Greg? Had she mentioned Greg? He couldn't remember, and when had she started using Em, her nickname, with Greg? He'd always thought it had been his and his alone, intimate and personal, just between the two of them.

Ben stared at the photograph, looking for any clue. Who was Greg? The more he thought about it, the more convinced he was that Em had never mentioned him. A bit more research on Facebook and he learnt that Greg was married to Amy, who had returned to work straight after the birth of their son. Greg had stayed at home to look after their child and did some freelance photographic work. Why hadn't Em mentioned him or invited him and his wife to dinner or their Christmas party if they were such good friends? Didn't she want them to meet? Or perhaps she had mentioned him and it hadn't registered. Sometimes when she talked about her day with Robbie he found his thoughts wandered to matters at work.

Ben enlarged the photograph. There was a warmth in Greg's smile that would appeal to Em. He moved the cursor to Messenger and saw the box contained messages between Em and Greg. The last was that morning and from Greg: *Survived Christmas? Amy back at work today. When does Ben return? Let me know when you are free to meet.*

Em had replied: *Ben back at work today. Had a good Christmas, but glad it's all over. Meet soon.* But no details about where or when, or running away together.

Ben scrolled further up to previous messages and saw that Greg had messaged on Christmas Eve: *Happy Christmas xx*

Em had replied: *And you xx*

Nothing suspicious in that except Greg's next message was: *Hope you've been a good girl and Father Christmas brings you whatever you want xx*

Suggestive, wink wink, nod nod, Ben thought, and began to feel uncomfortable. There were lots of messages stretching back to when they'd first met, which he now learnt was at the health clinic when they'd both taken their sons for their six-week check-ups. So they'd known each other a year. Where was Greg now? At home asleep with his wife and child, or had he left them and was now with Em? There was nothing in the messages to suggest this, but they were clearly close and shared similar interests and a sense of humour. Em liked a good sense of humour. She said she found it sexy in blokes.

Ben's fingers hovered over the keypad. There was a way to find out, he thought. He could message Greg from Em's account and see what his response was. If Ben messaged, *Hi, let's meet*, and Em was with him now, then they'd know they'd been rumbled. And if she wasn't with Greg, he could eliminate him.

Ben hesitated. Where was the trust they had? Until the police had arrived and taken the contents of the note at face value – believing she had left him for another man – he'd been convinced Em was suffering from postnatal depression. Yet here he was trying to catch her out instead of looking for her.

He snapped shut the laptop without sending the message, despising himself for doubting her. He needed to get a grip, try to think what to do for the best to help Em.

The doorbell rang and he rushed to answer it, hoping it was Em returning, but it was his parents.

'Hello, love, you poor dear,' his mother said and burst into tears.

Chapter Forty-Four

Amit paced the living room, seething with anger; his head hurt where the bitch had hit him with that metal bar. How could he have allowed himself to be tricked like that! He was annoyed with himself for being taken in, but she'd pay for it.

He paused to listen for any sound coming from Eva's room. Although he'd bolted the door, the bitch was untied and on the loose and still had another metal table leg she could use as a weapon. It was her fault things were going so badly wrong. Alisha would never have tried that on without her. He should have kept them separated, he now realized, but he hadn't prepared anywhere else safe enough to put Emily. He'd thought that threatening Alisha not to untie her would be enough, and it would have been had that bitch not influenced her.

He listened again. What were they doing up there?

Plotting their next move? Emily didn't seem the type to just accept her fate, but he was sure they couldn't escape. The door was bolted and he had the key to the window in the room – a double-glazed, sealed unit with toughened glass. His preparations in the lab weren't complete yet, but he'd had to seize the opportunity of Ben being late home to snatch Emily or he might not have had another chance for months. The old woman wouldn't have caused him all this trouble, he thought bitterly, nor would a bride from overseas.

But what to do with Emily until he was ready for her? He didn't want to keep injecting her with anaesthetic as it could compromise the outcome of his experiment. But he needed to contain her. It would be the end for him and his work if she escaped. One thing was for certain: she was going to regret the trouble she'd caused him when her time came. His lab was soundproof, so no one would hear her scream. He pictured her paralysed with muscle relaxant and fully conscious, lying naked in the ice bath as he drained her blood before he began the infusion process. When he'd tried this method on the animals, it had worked, although they'd writhed and squealed in agony as they'd bled out. He fully expected Emily to do the same. Serve her right for trying to escape.

Upstairs in the room above, Emily sat on the sofa in the gloom of the night light with a wad of tissues pressed to her cheek. She'd caught her face when she'd gone down and it was bleeding. Her ribs ached from where

Amit had kicked her, and she knew Alisha was in pain too. She was lying beside Eva on her bed, soothing her. Eva had become hysterical and had only just stopped crying. If only Alisha had found the courage to use the other metal bar, it would have given her the chance – the few seconds she needed – to get up from the floor and fight back. As it was, he'd got away and Alisha was blaming Emily for having persuaded her to try to escape. 'I should never have listened to you,' she'd said over and over again as she tried to pacify Eva. 'He'll kill us all now and it's your fault.'

Emily did feel responsible; not because she'd tried and failed but because she'd blown their one chance. She should have realized Alisha wasn't up to attacking Amit, even if it meant saving Eva. Now Amit would be on his guard, so there'd be no second chance to escape before he . . . She pushed the thought from her mind. How long before he came for her and dragged her to his lab? Alisha wouldn't stop him, she was far too scared.

And what the fuck was Ben doing? Emily thought with a stab of anger. She'd heard cars arrive and at least one leave. Had he called the police? There had been no siren. Surely the police would search their neighbours' houses and outbuildings? She'd seen news items of when children went missing and police and volunteers scoured the neighbourhood, and a police helicopter was sent up to help in the search. But, of course, she wasn't a child, and she'd left a note saying she'd gone off with another man and not to come looking for her. But Ben wouldn't believe that, would he? She turned the wad of tissues over and pressed the clean side to the wound.

How much did Ben trust her? she wondered, gazing into the semi-darkness. Did he appreciate the depth of her love for him and Robbie – enough to know she would never leave them? True, they'd had their disagreements, but then so did most couples. She knew from her friends that there were times when even the best-matched couples got on each other's nerves. Greg, who doted on his wife, said he felt hurt sometimes when Amy came home and insisted on talking non-stop about work and seemed to marginalize what he'd been doing. She could identify with that.

Christmas had put a strain on their relationship, Emily acknowledged, but then Christmas did. Although it had gone well, all the planning, upheaval, and high expectations, especially when Ben had wanted a quiet Christmas, had made them tetchy sometimes. He'd gone along with her wish to have a drinks party and both sets of parents to Christmas dinner when she'd said her life was quiet enough and she needed some fun. She hadn't meant it as a criticism, and she hoped Ben knew that. He'd said after that he'd enjoyed Christmas and was proud of her.

Her eyes filled at the thought of him and Robbie next door, and she willed them to feel her close. *Ben, Robbie, I'm here. I love you. I would never leave you. Believe me. Whatever happens, I'll always love you both with all my heart.*

Her gaze flew to the other metal table leg, still partially concealed behind the cushion on the sofa. One chance and she'd lost it, but she couldn't sit here doing nothing and risk never seeing Ben or Robbie again. Her anger and frustration flared. Jumping up, she grabbed the bar and running to the window struck the glass with all her force. Eva and Alisha screamed. She hit the glass again and again, all her anger and sorrow behind the force of the blows. Alisha clutched her daughter protectively, shielding her, expecting the window to burst and shower them with glass. But it was too tough and held firm. Emily raised the bar and hit it again and again and eventually a chip appeared in the centre of the window.

The door burst open and Amit was in the room. 'Stop that now,' he shouted. 'Or you'll all die. The child first.'

Alisha jumped from the bed and, with a force that surprised Emily, snatched the bar. 'He means it,' she screamed.

'Bring the weapon to me,' Amit demanded.

'No,' Emily said. 'Don't.' She tried to grab Alisha.

But Alisha pulled away, ran to Amit and gave him the bar. He quickly left the room.

'I'm sorry, I had to,' she said, tears in her eyes. 'For Eva's sake.'

Chapter Forty-Five

'Did you hear something?' Emily's mother, Pat, asked, putting her finger to her lips to silence the others. Both sets of parents had arrived and were now in the living room with Ben; their discussion had become heated. 'Perhaps it was Robbie. I'll go up and check.' Standing, Pat left the room, and the atmosphere shifted.

Ben's father, Richard, cleared his throat to speak. 'I don't want to upset anyone more than we already are, and I can understand why Pat won't have anything said against her daughter, but we have to be realistic. The note Emily left states clearly that she's left Ben for another man. I think we have to accept that, don't you, son?' He turned to Ben. 'It doesn't mean Emily won't come back, but it puts things in a different light.'

'Agreed,' Ben's mother, Mary, said. 'I don't know why you didn't tell us about the note when you telephoned.

I was worried sick all the way here, thinking Emily was ill and suicidal.'

Ben stared at them but didn't speak. He wished he'd come clean about the note sooner.

'I can appreciate why my son didn't want to tell us,' his father said. 'He's struggling to believe it himself. Pat is in denial too. It's understandable.'

'It's not denial,' Emily's father, David, said brusquely. 'Emily would never run off with another man unless she had a good reason. She's loyal and trustworthy.'

'Are you suggesting my son treated your daughter badly?' Ben's father said, rounding on him.

'No one knows what goes on behind closed doors,' David responded. 'Ben and Emily seemed to be happy, but who knows? Something must have made my daughter leave.'

'It wasn't my son!' Richard retaliated fiercely.

'Will you all stop it!' Ben shouted, exasperated. 'I didn't treat her badly, and I don't know why she's gone except . . .'

'Except what?' Ben's mother asked, her expression grim.

'Well, the police told me to check Em's Facebook account, and I found she'd been meeting a guy called Greg who I knew nothing about.'

'There, told you!' Ben's father said.

'It means nothing,' Emily's father retorted. 'Lots of young people have friends of the opposite sex. It doesn't mean she's run off with him.'

'Apart from the note,' Richard pointed out.

Ben sighed. 'I don't know what to believe any more, but I do wonder why Em never mentioned Greg to me.'

'Does Emily know all your friends and work colleagues?' Emily's father asked him.

'No.'

There was silence. Everyone avoided eye contact, then Emily's father spoke again. 'I think we should wait until the police have had a chance to speak to Emily's doctor.'

'Yes,' Ben agreed. 'That should be tomorrow. There's nothing missing from our bank accounts – the police told me to check and put stops on.'

'Have you put a stop on them?' his father asked.

Ben shook his head.

'I would do so, son, to be on the safe side.'

'So you're suggesting that not only would my daughter run off with another man but she'd clear out their money too!' David snapped.

The room fell quiet again as Pat returned; the Christmas decorations stirred in the air. 'Robbie is asleep,' she said, 'but keep your voices down or you'll wake him.'

'I think we should all try to get some sleep too,' Emily's father said, his tone flat.

'Yes, use the guest room,' Ben said. 'My parents can have my bed. I'll sleep down here.'

'Thanks, lad,' David said, getting to his feet. 'Hopefully we'll have some better news in the morning. Don't lose faith in her.'

'No, I wasn't.' Ben smiled wistfully.

No one spoke again until Emily's parents had left the room.

'That's all very well for him to say,' Mary said. 'But if Emily isn't coming back, we're going to have to make some practical arrangements for looking after Robbie. We can help out, but we're not young any more and couldn't do it permanently. You'll need to look at day care or employ a nanny.'

'I can't think about that now, Mum,' Ben said, dragging his fingers through his hair. 'I'm shattered.'

'I appreciate that, but the child is going to need looking after. I mean, who's going to get up tonight to change his nappy and give him a bottle?'

'Em,' Ben replied automatically without thinking, then stopped and swallowed hard. 'I will.'

Chapter Forty-Six

'He's doing it on purpose to punish me,' Alisha said, in tears again as she and Emily watched Amit from the window.

Emily banged on the glass with her fist to try to attract his attention, but he continued to his lab.

'You can't hear anything through that glass,' Alisha said. 'I tried knocking before when he forgot to let me out for our food and tablets. That film makes it worse.'

'Why do you keep it on?' Emily asked, picking at its edge.

'To stop anyone seeing us,' Alisha replied, surprised she didn't know. 'I told you what happened at our last house when people saw Eva at the window.'

'Yes, but we need someone to see us now!' Emily said. 'Not that there's likely to be anyone in their back garden in the middle of winter.' She looked as far as she could see left and right – to her own back garden and the other neighbours. 'Do the elderly couple next door ever go into their garden, maybe to feed the birds?'

'No, they're housebound. They have carers.'

'Even so, we have to try.' Emily began picking at the film, teasing the edges away with her nail.

'You mustn't do that,' Alisha exclaimed. 'Amit will be furious.'

'And what's he going to do that he hasn't done already?' Emily asked, annoyed. 'Get real, Alisha, we're trapped here. His prisoners. He's even stopped letting you out for food and your tablets, and he told me he's planning on killing us as part of his gruesome experiment. What have we got to lose?' She continued to work on the loose edges of the film.

'Mummy, I'm hungry,' Eva said.

'I know, love.' Alisha went to her. 'Have some more of your water, it will help.' She offered her the beaker. 'The door is stuck again, so I can't get out for food yet.' Alisha had washed and dressed Eva and put her in front of the television, where she was playing an interactive children's game.

'Daddy made the door stick,' Eva said.

'Yes, he did,' Alisha admitted.

Emily concentrated on picking the film from the window. It was stuck fast and came away in tiny pieces. Then a large strip running up the centre peeled off, allowing more light in and a better view. She continued picking at the film until most of it had gone. She could see out more clearly, but the trees and shrubs at the bottom of the garden blocked the view from the house behind. Realistically, it would need someone to stand on their roof, or to be in her or Alisha's other neighbours' garden to see them up here. Precious little chance of that, but she had to do something. Drawing up a chair, she positioned it in front of the window and kept watch as Alisha stayed with Eva. It was late afternoon now, the day after her capture. Slowly the dusk began to settle.

Since Amit had been depriving Eva of food and her medicine, Alisha had become angry and more assertive – but it was too late. They'd had their chance to escape and had blown it. What kind of man did this to his child? A mad, evil one who played God and believed he could bring people back from the dead. It defied reason and logic.

'Alisha,' Emily said, turning to look at her. 'What I don't understand is why you didn't leave Amit years ago, when he first started treating you badly?'

'I had nowhere to go.' She stood and came over so Eva couldn't hear. 'I am not in contact with my family. Amit saw to that. He was angry and wouldn't believe that none of us knew about the faulty gene. He thought we'd tricked him into marrying me and made me sever all ties with them.'

'Didn't they try to contact you?' Emily asked.

'They did to begin with; my parents phoned, but Amit refused to speak to them and wouldn't let me talk to them either. Then we moved and he didn't give them our new address. I haven't seen them in years.'

Emily's attention was suddenly drawn to the lab as the door opened and Amit came out again. He'd been in and out a few times during the day, head down and limping slightly, which Emily assumed was from their scuffle. Good. She was pleased he was hurt. She banged on the glass, but he didn't look up and continued into the house. He reappeared almost immediately with a coil of wire and returned to the lab.

'All those times I saw the light on in that outbuilding, and never in my wildest imagination did I have any idea what he was doing in there,' Emily said. 'But how did you not know – living with him?' She turned again to Alisha.

'I believed him when he said he was trying to find a cure for my condition. But you know, Emily, he's not the only one who believes it's possible to freeze people and bring them back to life when a cure is found. People pay to be preserved. He has.' Even now she found herself occasionally trying to excuse or defend him, such was his hold over her.

'But those people wanted to be preserved and gave their consent. You made it clear right at the start you didn't want to. He should have accepted that. You must see that none of this is right.'

'I do, although I feel responsible because I have given my children the disease. If it wasn't for my genetic condition, none of this would have happened and Amit wouldn't be like he is now.'

Emily stared at her. 'You can't possibly know that. It's not your fault. If Amit hadn't carried the faulty gene too, your children probably wouldn't have developed the disease. It was a million to one chance you were both carriers.'

Alisha looked at her, confused. 'No, it's me. I'm the one with the faulty gene, not Amit.'

Emily met her gaze. 'Amit has it too, although he's not obviously ill yet.'

'Whatever makes you say that?' she asked, astonished.

'His different-coloured eyes – heterochromia – it's a sign of your condition. I looked it up on the internet when he told me what it was. Heterochromia is very rare by itself but often appears in people with your genetic condition. It would be too much of a coincidence that Amit had heterochromia without the faulty gene, given that both your children have the disease.' Alisha continued to stare at her. 'Were you both tested?'

'Yes.'

'And the doctor showed you the test results?'

'No. I didn't go,' Alisha said. 'The tests were done at the hospital where Amit worked, so he went. It was difficult for me to leave the house by then – my son was ill, and I had Eva.'

'Alisha, I think there's a good chance Amit lied to you, and you are both carriers of the faulty gene.'

'No!' Alisha exclaimed, shocked. 'Why would he do that?'

'Because it suited him to have you feeling guilty and responsible, and possibly because he couldn't accept he's anything but perfect.'

Alisha looked away and it was a long time before she spoke. 'If you're right, then he must know he could become ill like me.'

'And that's what all this is about. It's not about saving you and Eva, but about saving himself.'

Chapter Forty-Seven

DC Beth Mayes put the phone down and looked at Matt over the top of her computer screen. 'That was Emily King's doctor returning my call,' she said. 'Emily has no history of depression and has never been to the doctor about injuries that could have been a result of domestic violence. She attended all her antenatal appointments, Ben went with her to most of them, and the birth of their child was normal. She has taken Robbie to the clinic for his injections and a cough that didn't need antibiotics.'

Matt nodded. 'So no mental health concerns and no reason to suspect Ben of being involved in her disappearance. That rather adds weight to her having run off with that guy she'd been chatting to on Facebook. The digital forensics report on her laptop and tablet is back. Are we going to apply for her phone records?'

'I don't think we have grounds to at present,' Beth replied.

'Her father, David King, phoned in earlier and wanted to know what we're doing to find his daughter. Shall I tell him nothing?'

Beth raised her eyebrows in mock censure. 'I'll phone Ben now and let him down gently.'

'Yes, gently is definitely your department.'

Beth smiled. 'Did the report say if there was anything on her LinkedIn account?'

'She just used it for work. No activity since she went on maternity leave.'

'OK. We'll leave it as low-priority missing persons for now then. There's nothing to warrant upgrading it.'

'I doubt her father's going to be happy.'

'I know, but we're not marriage guidance counsellors. Ben and Emily are going to have to sort out their own problems when she gets in touch,' Beth said and keyed in the number for Ben's mobile. It went through to voicemail. 'DC Beth Mayes speaking. Message for Ben Johnston. Can you give me a ring at Coleshaw police station when you pick up this message, please?'

'He's not exactly waiting by the phone then?' Matt said as she ended the call.

'Apparently not.'

Ben was at home by himself taking down, or rather pulling down, the Christmas decorations, any festive feelings having long since gone. He'd stood the decorations for as long as he could – two nights lying sleepless on the sofa watching the garlands stir overhead. Now, ripping them down and stripping the tree bare was an outlet for his frustration. His life was in turmoil, and he knew he wasn't coping, not at all.

Both sets of parents had gone out for a while, taking Robbie with them, which was a relief. Robbie was missing his mother dreadfully and kept crying and wanting to be held. His and Emily's parents were short-tempered from worry and kept sniping at each other, which wasn't helping. It was over forty-eight hours since Emily had vanished and not a single word from her. Even if she'd run off with Greg, why hadn't she phoned or texted to say she was safe and not to worry? The old Em would have done. They always let each other know where they were, especially if they were going to be late, so they wouldn't worry. But, of course, the old Em had gone, possibly for good.

Ben yanked another bauble from the Christmas tree and dry pine needles tinkled to the floor. He'd have to phone work before long and tell them. His father had phoned in and said he was ill, but that excuse couldn't continue indefinitely. And his mother had been right when she'd said they'd need to think about employing a nanny if Em wasn't coming back. Shit! What a mess. How quickly life could change. One day he was a happy family man, then he'd come home to find Em gone.

He took the note she'd left from his pocket. It was dog-eared now and he read it again with a mixture of anger and regret. The words jarred, as they had each time he read them. Not just their content – that she'd left him for another man – but the style of the sentences. They just didn't seem to be something Em would write, and, of course, she'd signed it Emily rather than Em, which was odd. But as the police officer had said, she'd probably felt that intimacy was no longer appropriate as she was leaving him for another man.

Yet there was other stuff bugging him, Ben thought as he returned the note to his pocket. He took the star from the top of the tree and threw it in the box. Things that didn't add up, were out of place, and suggested Em could have been depressed and was acting irrationally, although his parents didn't agree with him. They believed what the note said, while Em's parents didn't. However, one thing they all agreed on was that the police weren't doing anywhere near enough to find her.

Ben went into the kitchen where he'd left his phone charging and checked it. Shit. He'd missed a call and a voicemail message. He shouldn't have left the phone on silent, but he couldn't face speaking to friends or work yet. He played the voicemail message. It was Beth Mayes asking him to phone her. Had they found Em? He immediately returned the call, his heart racing. Not her body? Please no, not that.

'It's Ben Johnston,' he said, his voice quavering, as Beth answered. 'I just got your message. Have you found Em?'

'No. I take it you haven't heard from her either?'

'No. Nothing. I thought that's why you were calling.' He leant heavily against the kitchen cabinet.

'I do have some positive news though.'

'Oh yes?'

'I've spoken to her doctor and Emily hasn't been treated for depression, so that must be a relief for you.'

'OK,' Ben said. But was it a relief? No. Because if Em wasn't depressed the only other reason for her leaving was that she'd gone off with another man as she'd said in the letter. 'The note she left behind,' Ben said. 'I've been going through it. It really doesn't sound like Em. It's not how she would talk or write. Also, there's other things here that suggest she wasn't her normal self when she left. You know, not in her right mind.'

'Like what?' Beth asked.

'She left her mug in the sink. She always puts her dirty mugs and plates straight into the dishwasher. I was the one who left them lying around. She used to tell me off about it.'

'Perhaps the dishwasher was full?' Beth offered patiently.

'No, I checked. It was only half full. Also, she left the kettle switched on at the plug. She never does that. She always switches it off at night or if she is going out. It's a habit of hers, because when she was little her mum left a kettle on and it caught fire. She can still remember it. After that all her family began switching kettles off at the plug. And the television remote control was on the coffee table.'

'What's wrong with that?' Beth asked.

'We always leave it on the TV cabinet when it's not in

use. I know these are little things, but they are so out of character for Em.'

There was a pause before Beth replied. 'Ben, I appreciate what a shock Emily leaving must be for you. Doubtless, Emily would have been very emotional when she left. It can't have been easy for her making the decision to go. When people make these life-changing decisions, they are not themselves. They act out of character. But there is no evidence to suggest she was depressed or suicidal or that she didn't leave of her own free will. Have you contacted your mutual friends?'

'No.'

'I would do so. You can have her laptop and tablet back. We've finished with them. And if you haven't done so already, I would advise you to put a stop on your savings accounts. That's the best advice I can give you at present. I know it must be difficult for you with a young child too. Take all the support on offer. We will be in touch if we have any more information, but that's really all I can do for now. If Emily does contact you, please inform us so we can take her off our missing persons list.'

'So you're not going to put out an appeal for information?'

'No, not at this point. There's no grounds for doing so. Emily isn't a minor or vulnerable adult, and as far as we know she left of her own free will.'

Without saying goodbye, Ben cut the call, tears welling in his eyes. His father was right. He'd have to start accepting that Em had left him for someone else, as the police did, but his anger and resentment spilled out. Returning to the living room, he pulled down the last of the decorations and threw them into the bin. Taking the stairs two at a time, he went into their bedroom and began clearing out Em's belongings from their wardrobe and drawers. Her clothes, shoes, and personal items fell where they landed on the floor. He kept going until the cupboards were clear, then sat on the floor surrounded by her belongings and wept.

Why, Em? Why? I thought we were happy. Why leave us?

Chapter Forty-Eight

Amit settled on New Year's Eve. The noise of partying and fireworks would drown out any commotion the bitch might make when he dragged her from the house to his lab. It was 29 December now, so only two days to go. His excitement grew. There was something satisfying in choosing the milestone of New Year, he thought. A new year and a new life. He'd freeze the bitch on New Year's Eve then bring her back on New Year's Day. How neat and symmetrical that would be! He felt pleased with himself. Then, if everything went according to plan, which he was fully expecting it to, he'd be ready for Alisha. He doubted either of them would put up much resistance. By then they'd have been four days without food and heating.

His spirits soared with the promise of what was to come. Two more days, and by then hopefully the other set of grandparents would have gone from next door. He'd heard the kerfuffle, raised voices, and now there was only one of the grandparents' cars on the driveway. He'd caught glimpses of them moving around at the upstairs bedroom window while he'd been in his lab. One guy – he took to be Emily's father – kept looking out of the window. But the police hadn't been back. He guessed they wouldn't be very interested when they saw the note. Good move that, he congratulated himself again.

Satisfied all was ready in the lab, Amit came out, locked the door and began down the path towards the house. It was late afternoon and not quite dark yet. He'd make himself dinner and then write up his lab notes. This was ground-breaking stuff, and all good scientists kept meticulous notes. Glancing up as he walked, he saw the man he took to be Emily's father at the bedroom window, but then lost his footing and just managed to save himself before hitting the ground. Amit cursed. Nosy bugger watching him just like his daughter. He wiped the sweat from his forehead and continued into the house.

'I've put Emily's things away as best I could,' David King said, turning from the window. Ben had come into the bedroom. 'I wasn't sure where they went, but the room looks better than it did.'

'Thank you. I am sorry,' Ben said, embarrassed. 'I just lost it. I'm not thinking straight. I know this must be difficult for you too, and I'm sorry my parents went off like that.'

'There's no need to apologize, lad. We're all under huge

pressure. I don't know what happened between you and Emily, but blaming either of you isn't going to help.'

'I blame me,' Ben said dejectedly and sat on the edge of the bed. 'Yet I really can't see what I did wrong.'

'Maybe there was no single thing; sometimes situations develop and escalate.'

Ben nodded half-heartedly. 'I guess so.'

'Pat and I can stay for as long as we're needed, but I'm not good at sitting around doing nothing. I've just seen your neighbour coming up from his shed. How would you feel if I knocked on his door and a few others to see if anyone knows anything or saw Emily leave? It's not much, but it's more than the police are doing.'

'Yes, although Em didn't really have much to do with our neighbours. One side are out at work all day and she didn't like that guy, Amit, the one you've just seen. She tried to be friends with his wife, but she's not well and wasn't really interested.'

'OK. But it's worth a try. I'll go up and down the street, and while I'm doing that I suggest you message that bloke on Facebook you suspected of having a thing with Emily. I don't use Facebook, so I don't know how it works, but presumably you can send him a message asking if he knows where she is?'

'Yes, I can. I was going to message him just after the police were here, but I didn't in the end. I was hoping Em would return.'

'And she might yet. But message him. If she is with him, then at least we'll know she's safe.'

They returned downstairs and while Pat fed Robbie in the kitchen-diner, David put on his coat and shoes, ready to go out, and Ben went into the living room. Sitting on the sofa, he opened his laptop. The room was bare now the decorations were gone, but at least it was more in keeping with his mood. He would message Greg using Em's Facebook account.

Logging in, he saw she had unanswered messages and posts from friends, but nothing from Greg. Clearly she had better things to do now than chat on Facebook, he thought bitterly. The message he'd previously composed to Greg still sat in the *drafts* box – *Hi, let's meet.* He deleted it. No point in being subtle now. He needed to know.

Hi, it's Ben here, Em's partner. Is Em with you? he typed.

He read it back, but it seemed too casual and he tried again.

It's Ben, Emily's partner. If she is with you please get in touch asap. We are worried sick.

Then he felt vulnerable and exposed, admitting he was so worried. If she was with him, Ben doubted knowing how worried he was would make any difference. He tried again.

It's Ben, Emily's partner. Emily is missing and the police are involved. Please get in touch asap if you know anything.

Without analyzing the message further, he pressed send. He looked through the messages and posts from Em's friends, but there was nothing to be learned there. Photographs of children at Christmas and suggestions to meet for coffee or lunch but nothing confirmed.

Pat came into the living room with Robbie, and Ben closed the laptop and put it to one side.

'He knows quite a few words now,' Pat said with a small smile. 'Who or what is eve? He keeps saying it.'

Ben shrugged. 'Perhaps a friend of Em's or maybe he's trying to say Christmas Eve.'

'Yes, that would be it, Christmas Eve.'

Chapter Forty-Nine

Outside, a frost was starting to settle and David pulled up the collar on his coat as he went from house to house. He had approached the task systematically, as he did most things, beginning with the house on the left of Emily and Ben's and working his way up the street, then crossing over and continuing down the other side. Not everyone opened their doors now it was dark, but those who did were generally helpful. To begin with, he'd inwardly cringed and got choked up telling strangers that his daughter, Emily, was missing and asking if they knew anything, but he was hardening up to it now. It was taking time, as those who answered their doors wanted to know the circumstances of her disappearance and then expressed shock and sympathy. Some didn't know Emily at all, some knew her by sight, and a few remembered her from her calling round when her cat had gone missing. Now having to tell them the cat hadn't been found and Emily was missing too made him feel strange – desperate, pitiful and irresponsible.

Crossing the road again, David worked his way back towards Emily and Ben's house. The last house was their immediate neighbour, Amit Burman, whom he'd seen going in and out of his shed. It was nine o'clock now and as David opened their front gate and began down their path he could see why Emily hadn't taken to the couple. Their house was dark and inhospitable, creepy almost, compared to the others in the street where lights shone out and televisions could be seen glowing in front rooms. The opaque film covering the windows didn't help, nor did the tall shrubs and trees at the front that hid the street lamp. The CCTV gave him the feeling that he was being watched. Ben had said the man's wife was ill and virtually housebound, so he was hoping she might have seen or heard something.

He pressed the bell on the security grid and waited, expecting someone to speak into the intercom. The house remained in darkness, although he had the feeling someone was in. He pressed the bell again. No light came on, but suddenly the door opened and Amit Burman stood framed in the dark hall. 'Yes?' he demanded ungraciously.

'I'm sorry to disturb you. I'm David, Emily King's father. She lives next door.' He paused, expecting an acknowledgement, but there was nothing beyond a narrowing of his eyes, which he found unsettling. They were different colours. 'You may not be aware of this, but Emily is missing. She left some time during the afternoon or evening of the 27th of December and hasn't been seen since. The police are doing what they can, but obviously we're all very concerned for her safety. I've been knocking on neighbours' doors and asking if they saw or heard anything.'

'And have they?' Amit asked.

It wasn't the response David had been expecting and he struggled to hide his dislike of the man. 'No, but I was wondering if you or your wife saw Emily that day?'

'No. We didn't.'

'Would it be possible to ask your wife? I'm sorry to trouble you, but it's very important, and the police aren't doing an awful lot.'

His green eye seemed to shine. 'She's in bed, she's not well. I can't disturb her now.'

'Perhaps you could ask her when she wakes? It's possible Emily and she talked.'

'Why do you say that?' he demanded.

'Neighbours do. Sometimes they become friends. Emily was – *is* – a warm, caring person who reaches out to people. She has many friends.'

'Good. Well ask some of them where she is. She wasn't friends with my wife. Sorry I can't help you. Goodnight.' The door closed as abruptly as it had opened.

'Arsehole,' David muttered. No wonder Emily disliked him. What a shit!

As he returned down their path, he gave the middle

finger over his shoulder, hoping Amit Burman would see it on their CCTV.

'Your neighbour's an arrogant bastard,' David said as he entered the living room. Ben was there alone.

'Amit Burman? He's a doctor, an anaesthetist, I think,' Ben said.

'I wouldn't want him near me on the operating table. He was curt to the point of being rude. His eyes are different colours. It's very weird talking to him.'

'Em said that. I don't really know him. We just call hello on our way in or out. I told the police he saw me leaving on the 27th. I wonder if they spoke to him?'

'He didn't say. Probably not. Pity his poor wife. He doesn't seem like the type of person who'd have the patience to look after her.'

'That's what Em said too.' Ben sighed.

'She was always a good judge of character – I mean is.' David ran his hand over his eyes. 'Tomorrow, I'll knock on those doors where I didn't get a reply. I'm not sure what else I can do. Did you message that guy on Facebook?'

'Yes. I'll check later to see if he's replied. Em hasn't used her Facebook since the morning she went missing.'

'That's not good, is it? Do the police know?'

'I would think so. They've had her laptop and tablet. I can have them back now. There was nothing on them that could help.'

'Pity we don't have Emily's phone. It might have told us who she was last in contact with. Anyway, it's been a long day; I'm going to join Pat and have an early night. Are you going to sleep in your own bed now your parents have gone home?'

'No, I couldn't, not without Em. I'll stay down here on the sofa and listen for the front door.'

'OK, but try to get some rest.'

Chapter Fifty

'Dad!' Emily screamed. 'Dad, I'm here!'

'Don't, he's gone, honestly. I heard the front door close,' Alisha said, trying to calm her.

'And you're sure it was him?' Emily asked through her tears.

'Yes, I heard him say David, Emily King's father. My hearing is sharper than yours.'

'Please let him come back. Dad, please,' Emily begged, and wrapping her arms around herself, she shivered uncontrollably. Fear and no food or heating resulted in them all being cold most of the time. Eva was in bed fully clothed and had stopped asking for something to eat. Without meals and her medication, she seemed to be fading fast. 'Dad, please come back,' Emily said, more quietly, almost as a prayer, and wiped her eyes. 'They're so close, my parents, Ben and Robbie, yet so far away. What are we going to do?'

'There is nothing we can do,' Alisha said, defeated and too weak to think.

'I can't bear the thought of never seeing my family again,' Emily said and fresh tears formed.

'Perhaps your father will come back?' Alisha offered. But they both knew that was unlikely, for he had no reason to.

'Supposing we pretend *you're* very ill?' Emily suggested. 'Amit still seems to want to keep you alive for now.'

'I don't think he'd be worried if I was ill. That time has passed. This is about Amit achieving something others have not and taking care of himself. Once he's finished with us we'll end up in the woods just as those poor animals did.'

'I won't let him take me without a fight,' Emily said, trying to find her courage. 'At some point he's going to have to come in here and get me. I'll kick, bite and claw at his eyes. If you help me, we might stand a chance. It will be our last chance.'

Next door, Ben lay on the couch in the living room, unable to sleep or even doze. His laptop and phone were on the floor beside him, and despite the volume being on and alerts set, he was still checking his phone every ten minutes. There were no calls or texts from Em and no reply from Greg. Hardly surprising, it was 2.20 a.m. But Em had her phone with her. Why hadn't she called or texted just to say she was all right? She must know how worried they'd all be. All the years they'd spent together must count for something. They couldn't just disappear. She must have some good memories of that time. Of Robbie. But how she could have made the decision to leave if she'd been in her right mind was something Ben was still struggling to accept. It was what the police and his parents believed. Em's parents had doubts, but they were saying less about the reasons for her disappearance and were concentrating on practical matters. Pat was looking after Robbie, and David had been out knocking on neighbours' doors. Not that that had produced anything.

Ben checked his phone again. Still nothing. As David had said, it was a great pity they didn't have Em's phone – it would have shown them who'd she'd been in contact with before she'd gone missing, and possibly even led them to her. But Em was never separated from her phone, ever. As well as texting, making calls and accessing social media, she had news and weather alerts set up, and also did her banking on her phone. Banking. When he'd checked her bank account, he'd used her password. Ben sat bolt upright, senses alert. Of course! Why hadn't he thought of that sooner? Her login details for her mobile account would be on that list of passwords, so he should be able to check her phone account online to see the numbers she'd been calling.

Standing, he went swiftly and silently upstairs and into his bedroom. Everyone else was asleep. He took the folder containing Em's passwords from the drawer and returned downstairs. He closed the door to the living room so he wouldn't disturb anyone and switched on the lamp. Sitting on the sofa, he opened his laptop and brought up the website of Em's mobile phone provider, then entered her login details from the sheet. A page offered various options, including downloading her latest bill. That's what he needed.

He tapped the icon, his mouth dry and his heart drumming loudly. A long list of calls appeared. She was billed on the 30th of every month. He scrolled up to 1 December, the start of the current bill, and began going through the telephone numbers she'd called. Most were part of her call package, but a few had incurred additional charges. Somewhere in here was the answer, he felt sure; one of these numbers was Greg's, or the guy she'd gone off with – if that is what she'd done. But which one?

Scrolling up and down, he discounted those numbers he recognized: his mobile, their parents' landlines and mobiles, her work number and a few joint friends. It was impossible to know who the others were – a long list he'd have to work his way through. In the end it might turn out to be nothing, a waste of time, but somehow he didn't think so. Surely it made sense that Em would have phoned whoever she was planning to run off with?

Creating a blank Word document, he began copying and pasting those numbers he didn't recognize. There were dozens of them and by 3.30 a.m. he had filled the page. Now he needed to sort them into descending order, with those Emily had called most frequently at the top. They were the most likely, he thought. He logged out of the phone provider's website and studied the list. A few numbers stood out. It was too early to start calling them – or was it? He wouldn't be able to sleep, and presumably those who didn't take night calls would have their voice-mail or answerphones on. But first he'd check Facebook again – it was becoming obsessive – but there was still nothing from Greg or Em.

Returning to the list, he entered the first mobile number. He thought it was more likely that Em and the guy had been in touch through their mobiles than landlines as it would allow them privacy. It went straight through to voicemail. *Hi, this is Sophie Morgan, please leave me a message.* Sophie Morgan was a good friend of Em's. He didn't leave a message and crossed her off the list.

He keyed in the next mobile number. *You have reached the voicemail of Hana Gibbons. Leave a message and I'll call you back.* Another friend of Em's. Again, he didn't leave a message and crossed her off the list.

And so he continued down the list of mobile numbers. Some phones were switched off completely with no voice-mail service and he made a note to call them again in the morning. As he neared the bottom of the list – those Em had only called a few times – he got through to the voicemails of businesses, including British Gas and a parcel delivery firm, but no sign of Greg, unless his was one of the phones that was switched off.

Disappointed that his search hadn't revealed anything, Ben began on the list of landlines. The first went through to the council's answerphone. He remembered that Em had been calling them because they'd invoiced them twice for the same council tax bill and were now threatening legal action if they didn't pay. Ben felt a stab of regret that he hadn't been more supportive when Em had confided her frustration that no one at the council would take responsibility and sort it out.

He dialled the next most called landline number and listened to it ring; no answerphone cut in. He was about to cut the call, when an elderly woman answered in a fragile voice, 'Who is it?' Ben recognized Em's great-aunt and felt guilty for having woken her.

'I'm sorry, wrong number,' he said and cut the call. At some point she'd have to be told Em was missing, but not now.

He should really wait until morning before phoning the other landlines, he now decided. He didn't want to disturb anyone else. Doubly disappointed that nothing had come to light, he returned his phone and laptop to the floor, rested his head back on the sofa and closed his eyes. Thoughts came and went. Horrible thoughts, the product of stress, fear, no sleep and anger. Yes, he felt angry. How could Em do this to him? He imagined what he would do to Greg – or whoever it was – if he ever came face-to-face with him.

Em, get in touch please, even if it's just to say you have gone for good. I can't stand not knowing! It's driving me mad.

At some point, he must have dropped off, a fitful sleep fuelled by nightmares and macabre imaginings from which he was pleased to wake. He came to with a start. David was in the room.

'Sorry, lad, I didn't know you were still asleep. Pat's giving Robbie his breakfast, do you want anything to eat?'

'No.' Ben struggled upright.

'Coffee then? I'm making one for me.'

'Yes, please.'

Instinctively, he reached for his phone. There was nothing from Em, but there was a text message inviting them to a New Year's Eve party from joint friends. New Year's Eve was tomorrow, he realized; the days were merging. He checked Facebook, but there was still no reply from Greg. Was that suspicious? Ben didn't know any more.

It was 8.30 a.m. so he could continue calling the landline numbers on his list, then he'd return to the mobiles that had been off during the night. The next landline number had a local code. It was answered immediately with a brusque, 'Hello?' A male voice that sounded vaguely familiar.

'Hello, I'm sorry to trouble you, it's Ben Johnston, I—'

The line went dead. Strange, perhaps they'd been accidentally cut off. He pressed redial and after two rings it went through to answerphone with a generic message telling him his call couldn't be taken at present and to leave a message after the tone. He hung up and dialled again with the same result. Very odd. There'd definitely been someone there the first time, perhaps someone who'd recognized his name and didn't want to speak to him. But who? Greg? He lived locally. The voice had seemed slightly familiar. Had he ever spoken to Greg? Not as far as he knew, and with only a 'Hello' to go on he couldn't place it. He dialled a third time and, again, after two rings the answerphone cut in.

David returned carrying two mugs of coffee and set them down on the table. 'You OK?' he asked Ben, sitting beside him. 'I'm guessing you didn't get much sleep.'

'No, I've been working my way through this list of phone numbers.' He tilted the laptop so David could see. 'It was you who gave me the idea. I logged into Em's mobile phone account and these are the numbers she called this month. I've been going through them, so far without any success. But something odd just happened. I called this number here.' He pointed the cursor at the number he'd just called. 'A guy answered and when I gave my name he hung up. I've called twice more and it's going straight through to answerphone. I'm not sure whether to leave a message. His voice sounded slightly familiar, but I can't place it.'

'I'd leave a message; just give your name and ask him to phone. I can't see you've got anything to lose.'

'No, I guess you're right.' Ben took a sip of his coffee and was about to redial and leave a message, when he suddenly realized why the voice had sounded familiar. 'I think it was Dr Burman, our neighbour,' he said, turning to David. 'But why would Em be phoning their landline? She wasn't friends with his wife.'

David met his gaze. 'How many times did Emily phone them?'

Ben looked at the list. 'Since the beginning of December, seven; there may be more in the previous months. I'd have to log in to her account again to find out.'

'Have your coffee and then check. I'm planning on knocking on those doors where I didn't get an answer last night. I might call on your neighbour again and see if I can speak to his wife.'

'What will you say?' Ben asked, concerned. 'I'm not one hundred per cent sure it was him.'

'Don't you worry, I'll think of something.'

Chapter Fifty-One

'Shit! What the fuck?' Amit stared at the phone as the answerphone reset for a third time. Ben Johnston, his neighbour! What the hell did he want? He was sweating profusely now, despite the house being cold. Bile rose in his throat. Did Ben suspect him? Had the bitch's father said something? But what could he have said? He'd answered his questions, told him his wife wasn't friends with his daughter. He knew tact wasn't his strong point, but he'd been civil to him, and he was sure he hadn't given anything away. So why was Ben phoning him?

Perhaps he shouldn't have hung up like that. It had been a knee-jerk reaction. How the hell did he even get his number? It wasn't in the telephone directory, and Ben hadn't got the bitch's phone – he had. Surely she didn't use an old-style address book? No, young people didn't do that now, they kept all their contacts in their phone.

He was sure the bitch wouldn't have kept an address book, but Ben had his phone number from somewhere, and why was he calling?

Perhaps he should phone him back and ask him what he wanted? No, that was too risky. He might inadvertently say something, give himself away, and there was the chance Ben didn't know who he'd been phoning and hadn't recognized his voice. If he had, then wouldn't he have used his name? Wouldn't he have said, 'Hello, Amit, I'm sorry to trouble you, it's Ben Johnston' or similar?

He wiped the sweat from his forehead just as the phone rang again. He stared at it as the answerphone cut in. 'Hi, it's Ben Johnston, Emily's partner. Could you give me a ring, please? It's important.' There was a pause as if he might be about to add something and then the line went dead.

Amit felt sick. Ben still hadn't used his name, yet there was a casualness in his tone that suggested he knew him. If he came here, he couldn't risk him hearing the bitch shouting or screaming as she had when her father had come. He'd have to gag her and tie up her again, and quickly, and the only way he was going to be able to do that was to sedate her first. Not anaesthetic, he daren't risk any more. He'd use the muscle relaxant, which would paralyse her while he tied her up and gagged her. And, as a bonus, it would give her a taste of what was to come. Fully conscious but unable to save herself.

Wiping his forehead again, he stood and let himself out the back door, nearly tripping over as he went. It was happening too often, he thought, and the continual sweating suggested he could be sickening for something. Once he'd disposed of the bitch, he'd run some blood tests on himself and see if there was anything amiss.

Before entering his lab, he glanced up at the bedroom windows of his neighbour's house. There was no one there. Hopefully David King was getting ready to return to his own home now. He was too inquisitive for his own good, like his daughter, knocking on doors and asking questions.

Inside the lab, he worked quickly, and took a phial containing the muscle relaxant and a syringe from the cabinet and the roll of parcel tape from the drawer. The most difficult part was going to be getting the muscle relaxant into her. She would be desperate now, aware her end was close, and was certain to put up a fight. But Alisha wouldn't be helping her again, he was sure of that. He had her back where he wanted – too scared of him to act. He could see it in her eyes, and she and Emily would be feeling lethargic now without food, as their bodies used what little energy they had to keep them warm. A good move that, turning off the heating, he thought.

As Amit let himself out of the lab, he glanced up at the windows of his and his neighbours' houses, but there was no sign of anyone. Once inside, he tucked the parcel tape into his trouser pocket to leave his hands free and then filled the syringe from the phial. He crept silently upstairs; the element of surprise would give him the advantage. He listened at their door for a moment. It was quiet, not even the sound of the child's television or PlayStation. Perhaps they were asleep?

In one movement, he quietly slid back the bolt and burst into the room. Emily was sitting on the floor with her back to the wall and Alisha was by Eva's bed. With the syringe held like a dagger, he rushed at Emily. She tried to get up and Alisha made a move towards him.

'Stay there!' he yelled. Alisha froze and he plunged the needle into Emily's arm, emptying the syringe. She gave a small cry and grabbed his hand, but only for a second. The muscle relaxant took immediate effect. She crumpled to the floor like a rag doll and lay where she fell, eyes open and staring up at him, for even the muscles in her eyes were paralysed now. Just as he liked them.

Taking the tape from his pocket, he straightened Emily's limp legs and began binding her ankles, winding the tape round and round, working his way up to her knees. He was aware of Alisha out of the corner of his eye, watching him, petrified. 'Make one move and I'll do the same to you and Eva,' he snarled.

Having secured her legs, he bit through the tape, his face not far from her crotch. Her arms lay limp at her sides and she stared back impotently.

'Hope you don't want a piss – it might be difficult.' He smiled malevolently.

Picking up her lifeless arms, he laid them across her chest and began binding them together, starting with her hands and working up to her elbows.

'You don't say much now, do you?'

Her jaw hung open, slack and unresponsive, as if she'd had a stroke.

Eva began to cry. 'Silence her now or I'll tape her mouth shut,' Amit hissed.

Alisha went to her daughter.

As he bit through the tape at Emily's elbows, his head pressed against her breasts. 'Hmm, nice,' he said. 'Shame I haven't got time to linger.' Emily stared back mutely.

Arms and legs bound, he pressed the tape firmly over her sagging mouth, then wound it around the back of her head and over her mouth again. It gave him a thrill seeing her unresponsive but able to watch him. His patients on the operating table had their eyes closed when anaesthetized so they had no idea of the power he held, but Emily did. He could see the raw fear in her eyes.

Leaving her nose free so she could breathe, he cut the tape with his teeth again, his face close to hers. 'Intimate, or what?' he said. 'But not as intimate as we're going to be when I take off all your clothes ready for your ice bath.'

She stared back like a startled doll.

Leaving her on the floor, he straightened and looked at Alisha, cowering on the bed beside Eva. 'Don't you dare remove the tape this time or I'll come back and do the same to the both of you.'

'Can I just have some food for Eva and her tablets?' Alisha pleaded.

Amit was about to say no and that before long she wouldn't need either ever again, when he had an idea. He could use the idiot child as a bargaining tool, just to make sure Alisha did as she was told. 'I'll bring them up as long as you don't remove the tape. Any sign that it's been tampered with and I'll stop her food and tablets again.'

'I promise I won't touch her.' Alisha's voice trembled.

He knew she wouldn't, for any thoughts of saving her friend had now been erased by the opportunity to save her daughter, albeit for only a few more days.

Chapter Fifty-Two

David followed the same route he had the previous evening and knocked on those neighbours' doors who hadn't answered. There were six in all and three still didn't answer; perhaps they were at work. He made a mental note of their house numbers to return to later. He'd leave no stone unturned, although he was sure if anyone could help it would be Amit Burman's wife, Alisha. Not only because she was at home all day, but now he knew she and Emily had become friends – for why else would Emily have phoned her so often?

He opened their front gate with only marginally less foreboding than he had the previous night. Although it was daylight and dark shadows no longer fell across his path, there was still something inhospitable and menacing about the house. Something that told callers they weren't welcome and to stay away. He shrugged off the feeling.

He hadn't come here to make friends with the doctor but to find out if Alisha knew anything about Emily's disappearance. He pressed the button on the security grid. The intercom connected with a small crackle.

'Yes, who is it?' Amit's voice, but surely he would know who was at the door from the CCTV cameras?

'David King, Emily's father,' he said. 'I called round last night.'

'What do you want? I told you yesterday I didn't know anything about your daughter and I still don't.'

'But I think your wife might. I think they were friends.'

Silence, although the intercom remained open. 'What makes you think that?' he asked presently.

'Could you come to the door so we can talk? I would find it easier.' Didn't the man have any manners? David thought.

Silence again, then the intercom disconnected and a few moments later Amit opened the door.

'Thank you,' David said. 'Would it be possible to talk to your wife? I think there's a chance she might know something about Emily's disappearance.'

'She's not well enough,' he said bluntly. 'I'll tell her. What is it?'

'When I saw you yesterday you were under the impression that Emily didn't know your wife, but it seems they've been chatting on the phone and were probably friends.'

'Whatever makes you say that?' His green eye narrowed suspiciously.

'Emily called your landline from her mobile a number

of times in December. Ben has had access to her phone records. I'm guessing your wife phoned Emily too, and they probably saw each other. As they were friends, it's possible Emily might have confided in Alisha who she was seeing and where she was going.'

Amit smiled, unsettling David. 'I spoke to my wife after your visit last night, and it's true that Emily did call our landline a number of times, but they weren't friends. It seems your daughter was bored with being at home all day with a child and was lonely and looking for friends. To be honest, Mr King, Emily began pestering my wife and Alisha had to make it clear she wasn't interested in her friendship. She is busy and has plenty of friends. I'm sorry to disappoint you, but I can't be of any help and I need to tend to my wife now. She is very poorly.'

'Oh, I see, yes, of course, I'm sorry,' David stammered. 'Thank you for your time. Sorry to have troubled you.'

Bitterly disappointed, David returned down the path.

Upstairs in Eva's room at the rear of the house, Emily lay on her side and concentrated on not being sick. Her father had been here again, she was sure of it. She'd heard the front doorbell ring and then what sounded like his and Amit's voices, but she couldn't make out what they were saying. The drug he'd given her was starting to wear off, but with it came surges of nausea. If she was sick with her mouth taped over, she knew she'd choke on her own vomit. She breathed deeply through her nose and forced herself to calm down. In and out, in and out, just as her mother had told her to do when she'd suffered from car sickness as a child. In and out.

Alisha would know exactly what her father had said – her hearing had been sharpened by being incarcerated in this house. Emily waited until she was able and then struggled onto her back so she could see Alisha. She was slightly turned away, sitting on Eva's bed and stroking her forehead to stop her from whimpering. Emily tried to speak, but with the tape covering her mouth, only a low guttural noise came out. She tried again with the same result. Alisha must have heard her but refused to look in her direction.

Suddenly the bolt slid on the door and Amit came in. Emily froze. Had he come for her? Surely it wasn't time yet? She wouldn't stand any chance of fighting him off bound like this. Rigid with fear, she watched him go past her and to Alisha. He was carrying something. A plate. Yes, of course, she'd heard the trade-off, Eva's food and tablets as long as Alisha didn't untie her.

She saw Alisha accept the plate with a small, grateful nod, then Amit came towards her. Emily cowered as he loomed over her, grinning vindictively, and checked the tape. Straightening, he left and she breathed again. It wasn't her time yet.

Emily watched Alisha feeding Eva. The child was ravenous and ate without stopping, then Alisha gave her daughter the tablets, but there were none for her. She seemed not to care and had probably given up hope of saving herself.

The nausea was wearing off now, but what had passed

between Amit and her father? Emily needed to know. She needed that shred of hope, a small lifeline to cling to, so she wouldn't give up. Her family and the police were out looking for her. They must be. Why else had her father come here again? It was surely only a matter of time before they found her. But what had her father said to Amit? She tried to ask Alisha, but more unintelligible noises came out from behind the tape.

Alisha must have guessed what she wanted to know, for without looking at her, she said resignedly, 'Amit told your father we weren't friends. He won't come back again.' And that was all she said for a very long time.

David didn't feel able to go straight home and face Ben until he'd composed himself. He walked around the block, calling at those houses again where he hadn't got an answer before. A couple were in but didn't know anything.

With nothing more to prolong him, he returned home. As he let himself in the front door using Emily's key, Ben immediately appeared in the hall.

'You've been gone ages. How did you get on?' He was full of hope and expectation. 'I've checked Em's phone account and she called Alisha in previous months too. What did Alisha say?'

David avoided his gaze as he hung up his coat, steeling himself for what he had to tell him. 'Let's sit down, lad,' he said and touched Ben's arm to go into the living room. Pat was in there keeping Robbie amused and she too looked up expectantly.

David shook his head.

'I saw Amit Burman, not his wife,' he began, sitting on the sofa beside Ben. 'She was too ill to come to the door. Amit admitted Emily had been phoning Alisha but insisted they weren't friends.'

'That doesn't make sense,' Pat said. 'Why else would Emily phone her?'

'Hear me out, please,' David said a little sharply and turned to Ben. 'It seems Emily was lonely and bored with being at home all day and kept phoning Alisha, wanting to be her friend. Eventually Alisha had to make it clear she didn't want Emily's friendship.'

There was silence before Ben said, 'Em never told me.'

'No,' David said gently, 'perhaps she didn't like to admit that being a full-time mother wasn't enough for her.'

'But she was the one who wanted to extend her maternity leave. I asked her more than once if she was happy, and she said she loved being at home with Robbie. Why would she lie?'

'I don't think she was lying,' David said. 'But knowing Emily, she probably wouldn't want to worry you with her problems. You'd just got a big promotion and were working hard.'

'So it was my fault!' Ben snapped.

'No, he's not saying that,' Pat put in conciliatorily. 'I can see why Emily wouldn't want to burden you with her worries.'

'So she left me for another man instead!' Ben said bitterly. 'I bet she can tell him!'

The room fell silent. Robbie, sensing the atmosphere, left his toys and toddled to his father. 'Daddy, isha eve,' he babbled and tried to get his attention. Distracted and deep in thought, Ben ignored him.

'We've had Christmas Eve,' Pat said and brought him back to his toys.

'I'll phone the police again,' David offered, 'but I'm not sure what else I can do unless Emily gets in touch. Then I'll talk to her.'

'So will I,' Pat said.

'And say what?' Ben snapped harshly. Robbie moved closer to his grandmother.

'That she needs to come home,' David said.

'And what makes you think I'm going to take her back?' Ben asked, his eyes blazing. 'I couldn't trust her again after this.' Standing, he stormed out of the room.

Robbie watched him go. 'Daddy, isha eve.'

'No, love,' Pat said patiently. 'Christmas Eve has gone.'

'Isha eve,' he repeated agitatedly and began to cry.

Taking him on her lap, she cuddled him. 'I doubt the poor child will ever enjoy Christmas again,' she said quietly. 'It will be permanently scarred by the memory of his mother leaving.'

David nodded sadly in agreement.

Chapter Fifty-Three

Beth Mayes, Matt Davis and the rest of the team left the briefing from the DCI sombrely and with plenty to think about and work on.

'I hope that body they found in the quarry isn't Emily King,' Beth said as she and Matt returned to their desks.

'Ditto, but the DCI said first indications from forensics was that she was in her late seventies or eighties, so that would rule out Emily.'

'She also said they couldn't be one hundred per cent certain yet because the pike had got to her. I didn't realize fish could be that vicious.'

'Pike eat anything,' Matt said. 'My father used to be an angler and he said they could take off your fingers if you caught one. They can grow to three feet long.'

'Nasty critters,' Beth said with a grimace. 'Well, whoever she is, she certainly didn't fall into the quarry by accident, not with all those stones in her pockets. It was either suicide or someone threw her in. Forensics will be able to tell if she was dead before she went in the water.'

'And if it was murder, then whoever put her there didn't know the quarry was used by divers to practise.'

'But then neither do most people,' Beth said, tapping her computer keyboard. She paused. 'I thought so. All our missing persons logged in the last three months – apart from Emily King – have been accounted for now. The runaway teenagers are back with their parents or in care, and the two missing husbands have been in touch.'

'Which could suggest the woman wasn't from around here,' Matt said.

'Or she hasn't been reported missing yet. Either way, I think I'll call in on Emily's partner on my way home. He's sure to see it on the news and Emily's father has phoned in again.'

'You're good,' Matt said. 'You're already signed up for the New Year's Eve shift tonight as well, aren't you?'

'Yes, but I'm off now though. I'll call in on Ben on my way home, get some sleep and be back on duty for tonight. Don't you just love New Year's Eve?'

'Not a lot.'

Half an hour later, Beth pulled up outside Ben's house. She knew David and Pat King were staying there; she also knew that no one at this address would be celebrating New Year, although they were likely to be up and unable to sleep from worry. For anyone with a loved one missing,

New Year was just another painful landmark, another night of agony to get through while trying to remain positive. Thankfully, most missing persons turned up or got in contact within forty-eight hours, but that clearly hadn't been true of Emily.

As Beth got out of the car, she wondered now, as she had before, about the attraction of the guy who had persuaded Emily to walk out on her child, apparently decent partner and nice home. Ben had no recorded history of violence. She'd checked.

A man she assumed to be David King answered the front door and she showed him her ID. 'Has she been found?' he asked, his face immediately creasing into anxiety lines. 'I'm Emily's father.'

'No. But I need to talk to you and Ben. Can I come in?'

He showed her into the living room and called upstairs to Ben.

'Where's the little boy, Robbie?' Beth asked as she sat down.

'My wife has taken him out for a breath of fresh air. The poor kid.'

Beth nodded sympathetically. 'It must be very difficult for you all.'

'That's an understatement,' David said. 'What are you doing to find my daughter?'

Ben appeared in the living room, unshaven and with dark circles under his eyes. He'd visibly aged and lost weight since the last time she'd seen him. 'You've got news?' he asked straight away.

'Not exactly, but I wanted to speak to you in case you saw the bulletin that will be going out later on the news.' Ben frowned. 'The body of a woman has been recovered from the quarry in Coleshaw Woods, but we are almost certain it isn't Emily.'

'Almost?' Ben said, immediately anxious.

'First indications from forensics are that she was in her late seventies or eighties, but we'll be able to confirm this once we have the autopsy report.'

'How long will that take?' David asked.

'Allowing for New Year, two to three days,' Beth said. David sighed. 'But we're not expecting it to be Emily,' Beth reiterated. 'I'll contact you again as soon as we have any further news.'

'Is that all you have?' David asked bluntly.

'For now, yes. I thought you should know.'

'Thank you,' Ben said.

'I've been knocking on neighbours' doors asking if they know anything,' David said. He looked as tired and unkempt as Ben, Beth thought. The strain a missing loved one placed on the whole family was enormous and far-reaching.

'And did you find out anything?' Beth prompted.

'No, but I've been thinking,' David said. 'The neighbour on that side.' He pointed. 'Amit Burman, he has a lot of CCTV cameras. It's possible one of their cameras might have captured Emily leaving or a car pulling up outside. Can you ask to look at their recording?'

Beth hesitated. It was a big ask.

'He's the one who saw me leave for work the morning Emily went missing,' Ben added.

'If you're too busy to view all the recording, perhaps we can have a copy to view here?' David suggested.

'You'd need your neighbour's consent to do that because of data protection.'

David sighed. 'But you could ask to see it?'

'Yes, I could,' Beth agreed. His desperation was palpable. 'I'll go there now when I leave.'

'Thank you.'

Beth stood. 'I'll phone when I have anything further. Take care.'

As Beth walked from their drive, she saw Robbie with a woman she assumed to be his grandmother coming towards her. The child stopped outside the neighbour's house and was peering through the gate as if he wanted to go in.

'DC Beth Mayes,' she said, going up to them. 'Are you Pat King?'

'Yes.'

'I've just spoken to David and Ben. There's no news yet, I'm afraid.'

Pat gave a small resigned nod, her sadness and despair obvious. 'If Emily would just get in touch to say she's OK. We won't be angry with her. We just need to know she's all right.'

'I know,' Beth sympathized. 'I'm going in here to see if the neighbours' CCTV picked up anything on the day Emily left.'

'Thank you,' Pat said. Taking Robbie's hand, she tried to draw him away from the gate so Beth could get in, but he clung to it. 'That's not our house,' she said and gently tried to move him again. He let out a sharp cry of protest. 'He can be very strong-willed sometimes,' Pat said apologetically.

'I'm going in there,' Beth tried, smiling at the child.

Pat picked him up and Beth opened the gate. Robbie shrieked again.

'Come on, your house is next door,' Pat said and carried him off crying.

Beth pressed the button on the security grid and waited. There were three CCTV cameras at the front of the house. David was right, there was a chance they would cover the pavement and some of the road outside the house. They appeared to be good-quality cameras, giving a wide-angled view and clear definition. Whether they had recorded Emily leaving remained to be seen. If she had turned left when coming out of her house instead of right then she would be outside the range of the cameras.

Beth pressed the bell again, waited some more, then, satisfied no one was in, took a business card and pen from her pocket, and wrote, *Please phone.* She signed it *DC Mayes* and posted it through the letter box. Most people responded to the card if only from curiosity. It was the best she could do for now.

Chapter Fifty-Four

Amit watched the police officer leave on the CCTV before he went into the hall to retrieve her business card. What the hell did she want with him? He was almost certain she was one of the two investigating officers who'd visited next door when the bitch had first gone missing. *Please phone*, she'd written on the card below the police station's contact details. He might, but not for a few days. Once he'd finished with Emily; he was far too busy right now. New Year's Eve had finally arrived and everything was back on course and going to plan. The bitch was tied up, ready to be taken to his lab after dark. He was certain Alisha wouldn't help her or get in his way this time as she knew food and medicine for Eva would be stopped for good. Once he'd disposed of the bitch – he was thinking of the quarry again – he'd phone DC Mayes and see what she wanted. Always good to know what you were dealing with so you could stay one step ahead. Tucking her business card into his pocket, Amit returned to his study.

Sunset was at 4 p.m. today, but he'd wait until closer to midnight before he moved her. It was his good luck, he thought, that there was no moon tonight, and the weather forecast was that the heavy cloud cover would continue overnight. He took another painkiller – the pains in his legs were getting worse – then set about checking his calculations one last time before going to his lab.

When he came out, it was pitch-black and the neighbours' curtains were all closed. In the distance he could hear some early revellers, already drunk and singing football songs. Amit carefully made his way up the path – he didn't want to trip and fall again – and let himself in the back door, another syringe, phial of muscle relaxant and large black plastic dustbin liners at the ready. If any of his neighbours did by chance look out of their bedroom window when he was moving her – and it was a big if – all they would see was him dragging a big bag of rubbish to his shed. Nothing unusual in that.

Inside the house, he went upstairs and then stopped outside Eva's bedroom door, wiping his sweating palms down his trousers. It was all quiet inside the room and he filled the syringe. He noticed his hands were trembling – hardly surprising, he thought, considering the excitement he was feeling at what lay ahead. Sliding the bolt, he carefully opened the door and gingerly looked in to make sure there wasn't another trap set. Everything was as it should be. On the far side of the room, Alisha was huddled with Eva on her bed, expecting more food and tablets, and the bitch was where he'd left her on the floor. He went over, checked the tape hadn't been tampered with and raised the syringe.

'Don't!' Alisha cried.

'Shut up and stay where you are,' he shouted.

She buried her head in Eva's shoulder so neither of them could see. Amit plunged the needle into Emily's thigh and watched as the paralysis crept through her body. A final blink of her eyes and that was it. She was all his.

Imprisoned in her paralysed body, Emily could only watch in horror as Amit spread two large heavy-duty dustbin liners on the floor. She tried to kick him but her legs wouldn't move. Even her tongue was limp. Suddenly she was encased in darkness as he roughly pulled one of the bags over her head. Panic set in and she tried to cry out, but no sound came. He pulled the other bag up over her feet and legs. In her mind, she was kicking out, struggling to break loose, fighting for her life, but not a single muscle moved. She lay helpless and immobile and felt him winding the parcel tape around her middle, sticking the two bags together. She'd suffocate in here for sure. Would he realize? Perhaps it was part of his plan now. Why hadn't her father or the police returned to find her? Dear God, this was it. Utter hopelessness engulfed her.

She could hear Eva crying. Amit shouted at her to shut the fuck up, then he was picking Emily up by her feet and dragging her out of the room. He paused on the landing and she heard him bolt the door. Then downstairs, thud, thud, thud, her spine bounced painfully off each step. Across another floor, she thought it was the hall, and into the garage. A door opened and she was dragged over a small sharp step and then they were outside. The freezing night air seeped through the plastic bags. Down the garden path, she supposed towards his lab, the rough hard concrete chafing her back. *Dad! Ben!* she cried out in her mind, but no sound escaped her lips. *I'm here, please find me before it's too late!* He dropped her feet and she heard him unlock the padlock on the lab door, then he had her by the feet again. He dragged her over the step and locked the door behind them.

Silence. Her heart raced and nausea rose to her throat. She couldn't swallow because of the paralysis caused by the drug he'd given her. Breathing was difficult too. What was he doing? Suddenly a small slit appeared in the bag close to her face and slowly grew larger. He was cutting her out. She could breathe again through her nose but still couldn't swallow or move. Her head lolled to one side, and in her line of vision she could see a spotlight, a monitor, wires, an oxygen mask and what looked like an operating table. Terror gripped her.

His hands slid under her. She could smell and feel the heat of his body as he jerked her into a sitting position, then up and onto the operating table. Terrified and helpless, she could do nothing but watch as he laid her flat. Then he tore open a sterile package and roughly inserted a cannula into her arm. She felt the pain but no cry came. He tore open another sterile package and attached a drip. 'This will allow me to control the level of muscle relaxant just as I do at work,' he said. 'Although, of course, there my patients are unconscious, but you will be awake. Not too much that you won't be able to breathe and swallow, but enough to stop you from calling out.'

She watched, petrified, as he cut through the tape and roughly pulled it off. Pain shot through her as hair stuck to the tape came away at the roots. He threw it in the bin and then removed hospital scrubs from a sterile plastic bag and put them on. Her eyes widened in terror. He was really going to operate on her as he'd threatened, and without any anaesthetic.

'Not so cocky now, are you?' he said, leering over her; she smelt his foul breath. 'But console yourself that you will be making medical history.' He grinned. 'I always like to explain to my patients what will happen to them during their operation. Shortly, I will start the process to drain off your blood, then I will lower your body temperature and replace most of your blood with preservation fluid. That will be rather uncomfortable, but don't worry – if you can't bear the pain you will pass out. Then, as part of my experiment, I shall remove one of your kidneys and pop it into preserving fluid, here.' He tapped a large glass bottle. 'You will go in that aluminium tank there.' He picked up her head and forced it round so she could see. 'Yes, it's the one you filmed being delivered. Then, after twenty-four hours – during which time you will be technically dead – I will return your kidney and bring you back to life. Just long enough to make sure the process works, then you will join Mrs Jones in her watery grave. Any questions? No? So let's begin. First I need to get rid of your clothes. I can't operate on a fully clothed woman.' He laughed manically.

Emily watched, paralysed and terror-stricken as he began cutting off her jumper, then her bra, jeans and finally her pants. He threw them into the bin, then returned to stand beside her. His gaze travelled up and down her naked body. Was he going to rape her first? He touched her breasts, her pubic hair; she inwardly cringed and braced herself for what was to come. Parting her legs, he ran a hand slowly up the inside of her thigh. She stared at the ceiling, petrified. But, suddenly, he seemed to change his mind and stopped and turned away.

He began moving in and out of her line of vision as he opened sealed sterile packages – a Petri dish, swabs, and gauze. He was getting ready to operate. There was no saving her now. She tried to struggle and cry out, silently pleading for her life. She watched as he put on a surgical mask and tilted the light so its beam fell directly onto her torso. A sharp stab of pain as he inserted a second cannula into her arm; it ran down to a large bottle on the floor. He switched on a machine – she heard its low hum and steady bleep. Her blood filled the plastic tube and then dripped into the bottle. Dragging over the stool from the workbench, he sat down and watched the monitor.

Gradually the room began to swim in and out of focus, then a pain like she'd never felt before ran through her as if her insides were being torn apart. Every part of her throbbed, raw and relentless – death would be a release. She saw Amit sway and her last thought before she passed out was that she hoped Robbie and Ben knew how much she loved them. Then nothing.

Chapter Fifty-Five

'Robbie's tired, he got woken by the fireworks,' Pat said to Ben. 'He might have a sleep while we're gone.'

'OK.' Ben helped Robbie climb onto his lap and held him close.

'Are you sure you don't want us to take him with us?' Pat asked, concerned. 'It would give you a chance to have a rest.'

'No. I feel I need to keep him close with Em gone.'

'I understand.' She touched Ben's shoulder. 'Take care then, we'll be back as soon as we can. We just need to collect some more clothes and check the house is OK.'

Ben nodded.

David appeared in the living room with his coat on. 'See you later then, lad.'

The front door closed and the house fell silent, so very quiet, like the grave, Ben thought. Quieter than it had been since he'd arrived home to find Em gone. And the trouble with silence was that it allowed him space to think, thoughts that he was trying to block out and not deal with. Tomorrow, when everyone was back at work after the New Year, he'd have to call his boss and tell him the truth: that Em had left him and he needed time off work. A week at least, to try to sort out his head – he'd be useless at work like this – and arrange childcare for Robbie. Em's parents couldn't stay forever. But in doing that he'd be admitting Em had left them for good.

Robbie rested his head against his chest and began sucking his thumb. He'd be asleep soon, their precious son, now without a mother. How could she? He would never understand it, not in a million years.

Careful not to disturb Robbie, he reached out and checked his phone again. There were more Happy New Year messages but nothing from Em. He'd virtually given up hope of hearing from her, but he'd wondered if there was a chance she might use the New Year to get in touch. He'd already checked her Facebook account twice that morning. Nothing. Greg hadn't replied either. He thought it a little strange that Em hadn't used her Facebook account to wish her friends a Happy New Year, nor had she responded to any of their wishes. The old Em would have done – but of course that person had gone. She appeared to be cutting ties with her friends as well as her family. A new year, a new start. Unless the body in the quarry was hers, after all. And for a second

Ben almost welcomed the thought as it would allow him closure.

Robbie's gentle rhythmic breathing fell lightly against Ben's chest. He was fast asleep now, his warm little body completely relaxed. After a few minutes, Ben reached out and checked his phone again. It was now 1.33 p.m. He was knackered too; he should probably take Pat's advice and try to get some sleep while he had the chance. Resting his head back and with Robbie snuggled close, he allowed his eyes to shut. Thoughts came and went as they did when he wasn't occupied – of him with Em when they had been happy, but then of Em and Greg.

He came to with a start and immediately checked his phone: 2.30 p.m. He didn't remember dropping off, but he'd been asleep for an hour. There were no missed calls, yet something had woken him. He thought he'd heard a ring. The doorbell? Unless he'd been dreaming. He often dreamt that Emily had come back and was at the door. But there it was again. No dream. Someone *was* at the door. Not Em's parents, they weren't due back for ages, and they had Em's key. Robbie was still asleep. Ben carefully laid him on the sofa and went to answer the door, retaining the faintest hope it might actually be Em. But no, a man in his early thirties stood before him. Slightly familiar. Was he one of the police officers who'd visited them? He didn't think so.

'Ben?' the guy asked. At that moment, Ben placed him from the photograph he'd seen.

'You're Greg!'

'Yes, I'm sorry. I only just got your message.'

Ben's anger erupted and, taking a step forward, he squared up to him. 'Jesus! You've got a nerve coming here. Where is she? Where's Em?'

'I don't know, that's why I'm here. You sent me a message saying she was missing, and the police were looking for her.'

'She's not with you?' Ben asked, confused, and backing down.

'No, of course not. Why would she be with me? I read your Facebook message and came straight here. My phone's being repaired, and I used my wife's today to log in to Facebook. I haven't heard from Emily since before Christmas. I tried calling her, but her phone's off. It's never off. I'm as worried as you are.'

'So you're not having an affair with her?'

'No. Why would you think that?' he asked incredulously. 'We're friends. Our kids are the same age. I'm happily married. I thought you and Emily were too.'

'We were. Are. At least, I thought so,' Ben said helplessly. 'You'd better come in.'

Out of his depth and not knowing what he should be thinking or feeling, Ben showed Greg into the living room where Robbie was just waking.

'Hi,' Greg said to him.

'Jamie?' Robbie asked clearly.

'No, mate, he's at home with his mum.' Then to Ben, 'Jamie is my son.'

'So you were just friends with Em?' Ben asked, still struggling to accept what he'd been told.

'Yes. Good friends. Why would you think anything different?' He sat in the other armchair.

'Em left a note saying she'd left me for someone else and I assumed it was you.'

'Shit! Well, it's not, and that doesn't sound like Em – having an affair.'

'She didn't say anything to you about it then, or about leaving me?'

'No. She was always talking about you and Robbie. She was so proud of you both. Why did you think it was me?'

'The photograph of the two of you together on Facebook and all your messages and phone calls.'

Greg sighed. 'I can see why you might think that, but trust me, we're just friends. Good friends, and as far as I know she wasn't seeing anyone else. She loved you.'

'So where the hell is she?' Ben demanded angrily, all the days and nights of worry taking their toll.

'I don't know. But not using her phone or social media isn't a good sign. What do the police say?'

'They've listed her as missing, but they're treating it as if she's run off with someone because of her note. A body has been found in the quarry at Coleshaw Woods, but they're almost certain it's not Em.'

'Thank God. And you can't think of anywhere she might be?'

'No. I was convinced she was with you.'

Greg shook his head in disbelief. 'Come and check my

house; she's not there, and I've no idea where she could be. Seriously.'

Robbie climbed onto his father's lap and babbled something. Ben looked at him questioningly.

'He wants his beaker,' Greg said, nodding to the trainer cup on the table. 'You get used to baby talk when you hear it all day.'

Ben passed the beaker to Robbie.

'Did you and Em have an argument?' Greg asked after a moment. 'I mean, all couples have fallouts sometimes.'

'No, we had a really good Christmas. When I left for work on that last morning, she seemed fine.'

'And she's not said anything to her parents?'

'No, they've been here helping out. They're due back later.'

'And there are no other relatives she could have gone to for a cooling-off period?'

'No, I've contacted all the family, and all the friends I know of. And why would she go anyway?'

'I really don't know. It doesn't make sense. I saw Em a couple of weeks before Christmas – we met up with the kids in the park. Then Amy and I were supposed to come to your Christmas party but our babysitter let us down at the last minute. I swapped Merry Christmas messages with Em then my phone went down. The last time I heard from her would have been Christmas Eve.'

'Isha eve,' Robbie babbled from his father's lap.

'No, Christmas Eve has gone,' Ben replied absently as he had been doing each time he said it.

'I'm so sorry. I don't know what to suggest,' Greg said

with a heartfelt sigh. 'Em was the last person I'd have thought would ever clear off.'

'And there are no other friends you know of who she might be with?' Ben asked helplessly.

'No. We didn't really have mutual friends. We met by chance at the health centre when we were having our babies checked.'

'Isha eve,' Robbie said again.

'No, son, Christmas Eve has gone,' Ben replied with less patience.

Greg threw Robbie a knowing smile. 'I don't think he's saying Christmas Eve. I think he's trying to say Alisha and Eva. Is that right, mate?'

Robbie grinned while Ben frowned, puzzled.

'Alisha and Eva are your neighbours, right?' Greg said to Ben.

'Alisha is, but I don't know who Eva is.'

'Their daughter.'

'They don't have any children,' Ben said, confused.

'Yes, they have one. A badly disabled daughter, but they hide her away because of stuff that happened before.'

Ben stared at him dumbfounded. 'Are you sure?'

'Yes. Em wasn't supposed to tell me, but one day it just tumbled out. She was so worried.'

'I'd no idea.'

'She wanted to tell you, but worried you might let something slip to the husband. Em's been visiting Alisha and Eva regularly, with Robbie. He likes playing with Eva. I know Em was worried that Alisha's husband was abusing her. She tried to persuade her to leave him, but she was too frightened. He's a doctor and seems to have a hold over her.'

Ben held his gaze and his brow creased. 'Em did try talking to me about them, but looking back I don't think I showed much interest. It just seemed like gossip to me.' He paused. 'But Em's father went next door after Em disappeared to see if Alisha knew anything. Amit, her husband, denied she and Em were friends. He said Em was bored and had kept phoning Alisha, so eventually she had to tell her straight not to contact her any more.'

'Bullshit!' Greg blurted. 'Alisha was the one who kept phoning, but Em didn't mind. She felt sorry for her. The woman is ill, has a badly disabled daughter and a brute of a husband. Have you asked Alisha if she knows where Em could be?'

'No, but the police went there. I assume they saw her. They've asked for a copy of their CCTV to see if it showed Em leaving here. Why would Amit lie?'

'He probably didn't know,' Greg said. 'Alisha kept her friendship with Emily a secret from him. He's a control freak and didn't let her have friends. I understand they used to wipe Em's visits from their CCTV so he wouldn't know.'

'Really? That's a bit drastic.'

'Yes, but that's the sort of person he is.'

'Eva,' Robbie said clearly.

'Your friend, right?' Greg asked.

Robbie nodded.

'Will you tell the police she's not with me?'

Ben nodded, deep in thought.

'If they want to speak to me, that's fine, but I best be getting back now. Amy's at home and she doesn't get much time off. Tell me as soon as you have any news. I'm as worried as you are. I'll let myself out.'

Chapter Fifty-Six

'It's not Greg, the guy on Facebook,' Ben said as soon as David and Pat returned that evening.

'What?' David exclaimed.

'Greg came here. He and Em were friends, nothing more, and he hasn't heard from her since before Christmas.'

'And you believe him?' David asked sceptically, setting down their suitcase in the hall.

'Yes, I think I do. He seems a decent guy. I'm sure he's telling the truth. Otherwise he wouldn't have chanced coming here, would he? And what's more, according to him, Em and Alisha Burman were friends. Greg said Em took Robbie next door to play with their daughter, Eva. She's badly disabled and never goes out. I didn't even know they had a child. That's what Robbie has been trying to tell us – Alisha and Eva, not Christmas Eve.'

'So Amit Burman lied to me,' David said, pausing from taking off his coat.

'Greg said he probably didn't know, because Alisha wouldn't have told him. He's a control freak and didn't allow her to have friends or visitors.'

'Have you told the police all of this?' Pat asked.

'I left a message,' Ben said. 'Beth Mayes wasn't there. She's not working New Year's Day.'

'So you don't know if she was able to view the Burmans' CCTV?'

Ben shook his head.

'I think I'll knock on his door again,' David said.

'What will you say?' Pat asked, worried. 'He doesn't sound like a nice person.'

'I'll try to speak to his wife as it seems she and Emily were friends, and I'll ask if I can view their CCTV. I'm not convinced the police will follow it up.'

'I'll come with you,' Ben said, pushing his feet into his shoes. 'I would have gone before but for Robbie.' Then to Pat, 'He's asleep in his cot.'

'I'll listen for him,' Pat said. 'But be careful, you two.'

Ben followed David out and into a sharp north-easterly wind.

'I never believed Emily was having an affair,' David said. 'She loves you too much.'

'But where is she?' Ben asked in despair.

'I don't know, lad, but hopefully Alisha will be able to point us in the right direction.'

The Burmans' house was in darkness as usual.

'Doesn't the guy believe in electric lights?' David said as he pressed the doorbell.

They stood side by side and waited.

'Come on, answer,' David said impatiently and pressed the bell again. 'Someone must be in if they have a daughter who never goes out.' He moved away from the door and looked down both the side alleyways, testing the gates. 'Padlocked,' he said, returning to Ben. 'The guy's obsessed with security. It's almost as if he's got something to hide.'

Bending down, David opened the letter box and tried to look in but a letter box protector blocked his view. 'Hello!' he called. 'Anyone there? Alisha, it's Emily's father with Ben from next door. We'd like to talk to you.' He paused and listened. Nothing. Not a sound and no light. 'Dr Burman?'

'He might be in his workshop,' Ben said. 'He's often down there in the evening, sometimes until very late.'

'Alisha, Mrs Burman?' David called once more, and then allowed the letter box to snap shut. He tried the bell again and, disappointed, reluctantly gave up. 'We'll come back tomorrow.'

They walked home in silence. Once indoors, Ben went straight upstairs and into his bedroom, where he parted the curtains. He looked over to the outbuilding in their neighbour's garden just as Em had done many times before. A faint glimmer of light could be seen escaping from around the edges of the blinds, suggesting Burman was in there. Ben remembered Em wondering what he found to do in that shed every evening and most weekends. He also remembered he'd never shown any interest, and the last time she'd commented on Burman was on Christmas Day night when she said he'd been in there most of Christmas and she felt sorry for Alisha. Em's concern made more sense now. She'd been aware they had a daughter. But why hadn't Em confided in him about Eva and her friendship with Alisha? There was so much he didn't know. Partly because Em hadn't told him and partly because he hadn't been listening or asked the right questions, he acknowledged with regret. Em was kind and he could see why she'd befriended Alisha and her daughter, and from what Greg had said she was Alisha's only friend. Wasn't Alisha worried about Emily's disappearance? Unless she knew where she was.

Ben continued to gaze through the window, but there was nothing to be seen beyond the faint light escaping around the edges of the blinds. Tomorrow, he and David would return and try to speak to Alisha if they could get past Amit. All those polite good mornings and neighbourly chats he'd had with the man, with no idea he had a daughter or treated his wife badly. But Em had spotted something, which was why she'd never liked him. If only he'd listened to her and had shown more empathy.

Chapter Fifty-Seven

'I'll return Ben Johnston's phone call now we know for certain the body in the quarry isn't Emily King,' Beth said to Matt as she read the summary of the autopsy report. 'Late seventies; she'd had a stroke within the last year, and died from natural causes – very likely a cardiac arrest. She was dead before she went in the water.' Beth looked at Matt over their computer monitors. 'So how the hell did she get in there?'

'That's what the DCI told us to find out,' Matt said.

'Someone obviously put her there, but why, if she was old and died of natural causes? It doesn't make any sense.'

'That's what the DCI said,' Matt replied.

'I know. Will you stop saying that. I'm thinking aloud. So who was she?'

'Wonder no longer,' Matt said, concentrating on his

monitor. 'It looks like they've found a match on the national database of missing persons.'

Beth opened the file on her screen and began reading the report. 'Mrs Lynda Jones, seventy-eight, stroke victim, wheelchair user, reported missing by her nephew, her only relative, from St James' Hospital. There seems to have been a mix-up at the hospital and she was discharged into the care of someone else. What!' Beth exclaimed. 'How on earth did they manage that? Whoever took her must have known they had the wrong person, surely?'

'Unless he was short-sighted,' Matt quipped.

Beth threw him a look. She read on and then looked up again. 'So they discharge a vulnerable patient into the care of the wrong person and then she turns up dead over fifty miles away. Presumably whoever took her put her in the quarry. But why would anyone want to take her in the first place?'

'Perhaps it was the nephew wanting to get his inheritance and he's made up this story?'

'Possible, I suppose,' Beth said. 'He *is* her only relative. The local team are speaking to the hospital staff, checking their CCTV and taking a statement from the nephew. Someone should remember something. At least I can tell Ben the body in the quarry definitely isn't Emily.'

Beth picked up the phone but, as she did, their boss, DCI Aileen Peters, came over. 'I know you're up to your eyes in it, but this needs handling sensitively,' she said to Beth and passed her a printed sheet.

'Can't understand why you're not asking me, ma'am,' Matt said with a smile.

DCI Peters ignored him. 'As you can see, drugs have been going missing from the operating rooms at St Mary's Hospital for some time,' she said as Beth read. 'A nurse has come forward and accused one of the doctors of taking them. He's off work at present. It's given management a chance to check his records with the stock. There's a big discrepancy going back at least six months. I want you to pay him a visit and see what he has to say for himself. Diplomatically. If they're right, this is a serious charge.'

Beth looked up with a mixture of confusion and astonishment. 'Ma'am, the doctor accused, Amit Burman, lives next door to Emily King, our missing person.'

'Coincidence, I suppose,' the DCI said. 'How could there be a connection?'

'I don't know. I've been trying to see Dr Burman to view his CCTV for the day Emily King went missing. I pushed a business card through his door but he hasn't got back to me.'

'So now's your opportunity. Two birds with one stone,' the DCI said.

'Yes, ma'am, I'll go there now.'

'Update me as soon as you return, please.'

DCI Aileen Peters went to speak to another officer as Beth stood and slipped on her jacket. 'Can you do me a favour, Matt? Check to see who is living at the Burmans' house. According to the message Ben left yesterday, a friend of Emily's told him there was a disabled child living there that no one knows about. I might need social services.'

'Will do. Do you want me to call Ben and tell him the findings of the autopsy report?'

'No, I'll go there after I've seen Dr Burman.'

Coincidence, Beth thought as she drove. As the DCI had said, it couldn't be anything else, could it? Emily goes missing, she and Alisha are good friends, although no one knows because – according to the message Ben left – Dr Burman is a control freak and doesn't let his wife have friends. Now he's accused of stealing drugs. Could there be a connection? But how? Was it possible Emily was part of a drug cartel, peddling the stolen drugs? From what she knew of Emily King and her family it didn't seem likely, but it could explain her disappearance. Drug barons were ruthless and she wouldn't be the first person to vanish after crossing one of them. When she'd finished interviewing Dr Burman, she'd go next door and talk to Ben. Ask him about Emily's movements in the weeks and months leading up to her disappearance. Was there extra cash lying around the house or in her bank that he couldn't account for? She'd better go see this Greg, too, and find out exactly what he knew about Emily. Handle it sensitively, the DCI had said. Diplomatically. But if her suspicions were correct about a drug cartel, she'd need search warrants for both houses and backup too.

Parking outside the Burmans' house, Beth cut the engine

and checked her phone. A message from Matt read: *No child registered at the Burman address. Do you want me to notify social services?*

She thought for a moment and then replied: *Not yet. It's possible Greg got it wrong.* She would establish there was a child living there first.

Getting out of the police car, Beth crossed the pavement and opened the gate to the Burmans' front garden. The house looked just as shut up and deserted as it had before. No car on the drive, curtains and blinds closed although it was daytime. She pressed the bell and looked up at the CCTV so she was easily recognizable. No one answered. She pressed the bell again, then tried to look in the downstairs window, but it was impossible to see beyond the opaque film and blind. The DCI had been sure Dr Burman was at home on leave.

Beth pressed the bell for a third time, knocked on the door and then opened the letter box. 'Dr Burman! Mrs Burman!' she called. 'It's DC Beth Mayes.' But her voice didn't carry past the letter box protector. Taking a step back, she looked up at the house. No sign of life upstairs. Then she looked down both side alleyways and tried the gates.

'They're padlocked.' A man she recognized as Emily's father called from next door.

'Yes, I know.'

'Ben and I have already been here twice this morning,' David said, now coming down the front path.

'Perhaps they've gone away,' Beth suggested.

'But his car is in the garage. You can just about see it through the gap in the garage doors.'

Beth went over to the doors and peered through the slit between them. She could make out the dark outline of a car. 'When was the last time you saw the family?' she asked.

'I've never seen Mrs Burman, only him, and that would be on the evening of the 30th December. I went knocking on neighbours' doors to see if anyone had seen Emily, but no one had. I understand there's a child there too.'

'Have you seen the child?' Beth asked.

'No. Nor has Ben. But it seems Emily used to visit her and her mother. Did you get the message Ben left for you?'

'I did, thank you.'

'Have you seen their CCTV?'

'Not yet. That's one of the reasons I need to speak to Dr Burman.'

Beth tried the bell again, but there was no response. David was looking at her expectantly. 'We're sure they're in,' he said. 'Burman is in his shed. Has been all night.'

'How do you know that?' she asked, surprised.

'There's a light on.'

'He might have left it on by accident.'

'And they've all gone out without their car?' David asked sceptically.

'It's possible. They might have walked.'

'Mrs Burman is terminally ill and they have a disabled daughter. Ben told you all that in his message. They never leave the house.'

'All right, David, I'm going to make a phone call from my car. It would be helpful if you went back inside your house for now. Once I've finished here I'll come in and bring you up to date. I'll need to speak to Ben too.'

'Why don't you force the front door?' he asked, testing it.

'There's no justification for that yet,' Beth said and waited for him to move away and leave the property. He was clearly anxious, understandably, but being arrested for criminal damage wouldn't help.

She watched David return indoors before she got into the police car and phoned Matt. 'Is the DCI still in the office?'

'Yes. Do you want to speak to her?'

'Please.'

She heard Matt say, 'Ma'am, Beth Mayes.'

DCI Aileen Peters came on the line. 'Yes, Beth?'

'Ma'am, I'm outside Dr Burman's house. No one is answering and the place looks shut up, but Emily's father who is staying next door with Ben thinks they are in. Their car is in the garage and there's a light on in an outbuilding at the bottom of the garden. There's a possibility there could be a child in the house, although no child is registered as living at this address.'

There was a short pause before DCI Aileen Peters replied, 'Drugs and children don't mix. Go in, but wait for backup. I'll authorize it now.'

'Yes, ma'am.'

David King and Ben Johnston appeared on the driveway next door. Beth got out of the car and went over.

'I'm waiting for assistance and then I'll go in. But you will need to stay here. You won't have any right to enter their property and you could be done for trespassing, apart from the danger involved. Understood?'

'Yes,' Ben said. David gave a half-hearted nod and followed Ben back inside their house. Beth had little doubt that as soon as the backup arrived they'd be out again.

Beth returned to the car to wait. It could all turn out to be nothing, she thought as she looked at the Burmans' house, in which case the police would be billed for a new front door. She'd seen the drug squad in action before and they didn't hang around. There was still no sign of any movement in the house. The blacked-out windows, high security and secrecy surrounding those living there was in keeping with a drug den. *We'd no idea. They were polite but kept themselves to themselves,* was the usual reaction from neighbours in a nice street like this when a house was busted for drugs. Yet Emily appeared to have forged a friendship with Mrs Burman. Could that be why she'd disappeared? Was it possible that Emily wasn't part of the actual drug running, as Beth had first thought, but had stumbled upon it while visiting Alisha? It would make more sense, fit in with what she knew of Emily. In which case it was highly likely she was dead.

Fifteen minutes later, Beth saw the police van enter the road in her rear-view mirror. It parked further back, out of sight of the Burmans' house. Beth got out and walked towards it, adrenalin kicking in. She knew her role and what to do; she'd been part of similar raids before. Often, the squad raided a suspect's home in the early morning when they were still in bed, the element of surprise giving them the advantage, but because a child could be in the house, the DCI had wasted no time. Four helmeted officers jumped out of the van, one holding the battering ram they'd use to break down the door.

Beth quickly introduced herself to the lead officer.

'How many inside the house?' he asked.

'We think at least two adults and possibly a child.'

'Ready, lads,' he said, addressing the other officers. 'We all know what we're doing.'

A murmur of agreement and they snapped shut their visors. They went swiftly along the pavement two abreast, with Beth following close behind. Up to the front door, then the cry of, 'Police! This is a raid!' The battering ram hit the door once, twice and it sprang open.

They poured in ahead of her, immediately dispersing to check the rooms, two straight ahead into the living room, one to the right into the kitchen and one upstairs. All the while shouting, 'Police! Get on the ground now! Do it now! Down now!' Then as they checked each room and found that nobody was there they shouted, 'Clear!'

Beth felt her heart thumping wildly; she knew to stay in the hall until the house was made safe, when she'd be asked to search any females present. Upstairs, she could hear doors being flung open to the shout of, 'Police. Get down!' Then, 'Clear.'

'Clear,' 'clear,' 'clear,' was shouted three times then a pause and another shout from the landing. 'Bolted door! Up here! Going in!'

Beth stood back as the officers downstairs rushed past her, their heavily booted feet thumping up the stairs and onto the landing.

'Police! Get down. Now!' They burst into the room. 'Down now! Do it!'

Then complete and utter silence, and Beth knew that whatever they'd found was shocking.

Chapter Fifty-Eight

Senses tingling, on full alert, and fearing the worst, Beth waited at the foot of the stairs for one of the officers to call down that the room was safe and she should go up. Sometimes, thankfully not often, rooms were booby-trapped in drug dens. She could hear the officers moving around and then one appeared at the top of the stairs.

'You'd better come up now,' he said sombrely. 'There's a woman and child in here and they're in a bad way. We've called for an ambulance.'

Beth went steadily upstairs. So Ben and David had been right when they'd said someone was in and that there could be a child. She'd phone social services just as soon as she'd searched them to make sure they weren't concealing any drugs or weapons. Dealers sometimes hid drugs and weapons on the children or in their bedroom, in the belief that the police wouldn't search them.

As Beth entered the room, she noted the bolt was on the outside of the door. The smell of vomit, faeces and urine was overpowering and she instinctively breathed through her mouth. The room was large and with a sofa, television and two single beds. She took in the broken furniture – possible signs of a fight – the dark stain on the wall that could be old blood and the brighter red stain on the floor that was almost certainly fresh blood.

The lead officer was standing on the far side of the room keeping watch over a woman and child. They were huddled together on the edge of the bed, a duvet around their shoulders. The room was freezing, just like the rest of the house. Why wasn't the heating on in winter? Other officers were searching the room.

Beth went over and exchanged a look with the lead officer.

'I'm DC Beth Mayes,' she said gently to the woman, who was trembling violently. She looked emaciated, with hollow cheeks and dark circles under her eyes. Old and new cuts and bruises were clearly visible on her face and neck. The child was close beside her and partly concealed, but it was still obvious she was severely disabled, just as Ben had said. Surely this couldn't be Dr Burman's wife and child? How did they get in this state when he was a doctor? 'Medical help is on its way,' she said. 'But first I need to check neither of you are concealing any drugs or weapons. Can you stand up for me, please?'

The woman shook as Beth helped her ease the duvet from her shoulders and then drew her to her feet. She could barely stand, she was so weak. The child began to cry. Quickly patting Mrs Burman down, Beth helped her sit again.

'I need to check the child too,' she said.

'She can't stand unaided,' the woman said and drew her protectively to her, like a mother guarding its cub.

'Let me check her over where she is then,' Beth said. It had to be done. She eased the child into a more upright position, away from her mother, and removed the duvet from around her. The smell of stale urine hit her.

'I've run out of pads,' the woman said almost apologetically. 'And I'm not well enough now to clean her up.'

Beth nodded. She could see that the child's pad was overflowing and her pyjamas and the bed were soaked. As Beth lightly patted her down, another officer checked that the duvet and pillows weren't concealing any drugs or weapons and gave them the all-clear. Satisfied the woman and child were both clear too, Beth draped the duvet around their shoulders, but it was no match for the icy cold in the room. It was the middle of winter and they'd been left in this state, locked in a room and with no heating. Beth was quickly forming the opinion this wasn't a straightforward drug cartel but something far worse.

'Are you Alisha Burman?' she asked as the lead officer stood beside her.

The woman stared back, petrified, but managed a small nod.

'Is this your daughter, Eva?'

Another small nod and she drew the child closer.

'You both appear ill and neglected, an ambulance is on its way and I'll phone social services.'

'No.' Alisha clung desperately to her daughter.

'You need help, Alisha,' Beth said, touching her arm reassuringly. 'How long have you been in this room?'

She shook her head, either not knowing or not able to say. Officers could be heard in other rooms as they now searched the house more thoroughly.

'Why was the door to this room bolted on the outside?' the lead officer asked her.

Alisha shook her head again and clung to her daughter.

'Has someone been keeping you here against your will?' Beth tried.

Alisha's eyes widened in terror, saying what she could not.

'Where is your husband, Amit Burman?' Beth asked.

Alisha continued to stare at her, panic-stricken.

'OK,' Beth said and patted her arm again. She wasn't going to get anything out of her now. She was too frightened. They'd try once she was away from here and in hospital.

Straightening, she took the few steps to the window and looked out. There were signs there'd been film covering the glass here too, as with all the other windows in the house, but most of it had been removed. She could see the outbuilding David had spoken of and the light was still on, just visible around the edges of the blinds.

'Have you searched that building?' she asked the lead officer.

'Not yet.'

'Can we do so now? There's a chance Amit Burman might be in there.'

The lead officer called to the other officers working upstairs. 'Search the building at the bottom of the garden now and take the ram.'

But as Beth turned from the window, she saw David and Ben appear in the Burmans' garden. 'How the hell did they get in?'

Leaving the room, she hurried downstairs with the two officers assigned to search the building and ran out of the back door.

'Leave it, David!' she cried, rushing down the path. He was pulling on the door to the outbuilding, trying to force it open. Apart from causing criminal damage, he could be contaminating what might be a crime scene if drugs were found there.

David stopped.

'Stand further back,' the officer carrying the battering ram told him. David and Ben moved away and waited beside Beth.

The door to the outbuilding sprung open on the second blow and the officers burst in and stopped dead.

'Stay there,' Beth told David and Ben and took a step in. For a second she couldn't understand what she was seeing, then the horror hit her. They were in what looked like a laboratory and there were two bodies, both apparently dead. The clothed body of a man on the floor and the naked body of a woman strapped to what looked like an operating table.

'What the fuck?' one of the officers said. Kneeling beside the man, he searched for a pulse.

'That could be Dr Amit Burman,' Beth said.

Her gaze shifted to the deathly white corpse of the woman on the table. Emily King? Please no. A tube ran from her arm to a bottle containing what looked like blood. Electrodes were attached to her head and chest with wires running to a monitor.

'Stay outside,' she ordered Ben and David and made her way carefully around the equipment to the table. The woman's eyes were closed, her lips were blue, and her face was swollen from what could have been a beating. She was just about recognizable from the photograph Ben had given her. 'I'm almost certain this is Emily King,' Beth said. 'Our missing person.'

'I've found a pulse,' the officer kneeling beside the man said. 'But it's very weak. I'll phone for another ambulance.'

Beth picked up Emily's lifeless wrist; her skin was cold. She felt for a pulse. Nothing. She hadn't expected to find one. Emily looked as though she'd been dead for a while. Laying her arm beside her on the table, Beth took a step back. She needed air. 'I'll go outside and phone forensics,' she said.

But as she passed the heart monitor something caught her eye. She stopped and looked at it, concentrated on the continuous black line that showed Emily's heart was no longer beating and she was dead. Then suddenly there it was again – a tiny spike in the line as she thought she'd seen before. It disappeared and was followed by another long continuous black line. It must be the machine malfunctioning. It couldn't be a heartbeat, not with the two spikes that far apart. But there it was again.

'Come here and look at this,' she said to the other officer. 'Is it me?' She pointed to the continuous black line on the screen and it remained flat. Twenty seconds or more passed, then suddenly another small spike appeared.

'Jesus!' the officer exclaimed. 'Is she still alive?'

Beth looked at Emily's body. It was impossible. The woman was icy cold and there was no sign she was breathing, yet there was the spike again. She took off her jacket and laid it over her. 'Update the ambulance crew, please.'

'Em!' Ben suddenly screamed, appearing at the door. The officer closest grabbed him. 'Let me come in! Em!' His cries continued as he was removed.

'Take them indoors,' Beth said. It was better Ben and David didn't see this. It would haunt them forever, just as it would her.

Beth remained standing beside Emily's cold, lifeless body and waited for the ambulance. Her eyes remained closed and her body corpse-still. Only the occasional tiny spike on the heart monitor showed any different. Perhaps it was an unusual cadaveric spasm, but not like any she'd ever seen before and not this long after death. It would surely stop any moment now. She watched the monitor and another spike appeared.

What was this place? She glanced around but didn't touch anything. It was a crime scene now. It looked like a cross between Frankenstein's laboratory and an operating room. Rows of shelves lined two walls on which stood dozens of glass bottles containing organs suspended in formaldehyde. Were they human organs? They certainly could be. What the hell had Burman been doing here? It wasn't just drugs. The place was full of medical equipment and they hadn't even searched the cabinets yet.

She looked again at Emily's swollen lifeless face. The poor woman. What had he done to her? Was it possible she'd been here – next door – since she'd gone missing on 27 December, only yards from Ben and her father frantically searching for her? If she'd listed Emily's disappearance as high priority or had returned to the Burmans' to view their CCTV, she might have prevented this. But there'd been no reason to raise the priority. If the monster lived, she'd make sure he paid for all his crimes for the sake of Emily's family.

Sirens sounded in the distance. The line on the heart monitor showed another small spike, then went completely flat. Beth began CPR. Never had a body felt so cold.

Chapter Fifty-Nine

A week later, Beth made her way to Interview Room 3, feeling she was as prepared as she was going to be. Burman had been discharged from hospital and was now in custody. Matt was with her, but they'd agreed she would lead the questioning. She'd been up most of the night running through the evidence against Burman, preparing her questions and imagining his responses and her replies. It was possible he might give a 'no comment' interview, which was his right, but she doubted it. Arrogant and cocksure, he'd want to be heard. She knew she was going to have to be sharp and on her wits if she was going to obtain a confession. Amit Burman was intelligent and unrepentant. The worst kind of criminal. He was probably also delusional, a sociopath and psychotic, but that was for the psychiatrist to decide.

Beth opened the door and Matt followed her into the

interview room. Burman was already there, sitting beside his solicitor. Dressed smartly, he looked every bit the doctor; someone you could trust and rely on. She nodded stiffly to them and sat in the chair on the opposite side of the table to Burman. Matt took the chair beside her. First, the formalities that preceded every police interview.

'Dr Amit Burman,' she began, 'this interview is being recorded and may be given in evidence if your case is brought to trial. We are in an interview room at Coleshaw police station. The date is the tenth of January two thousand and nineteen and the time by my watch is 11.15 a.m. I am Detective Constable Beth Mayes and the other police officer present is Detective Constable Mathew Davis. Please state your full name and date of birth.'

His solicitor, writing pad open on his lap, glanced at him to answer. Amit sighed as if answering was an imposition. 'Dr Amit Burman, my date of birth is the thirty-first of October nineteen seventy-eight.'

'Also present is Mr Joshua Smith, Dr Burman's solicitor,' Beth continued for the recording. 'Do you agree that there are no other persons present?'

'Yes,' Amit said disparagingly.

'So let's start. Amit . . .'

'Dr Burman to you,' he snapped contemptuously.

'Dr Burman,' Beth said, 'what can you tell me about Mrs Lynda Jones?'

'Nothing. I don't know her. No comment.'

'Let me remind you. Mrs Lynda Jones was the elderly widow you kidnapped from St James' Hospital on the twenty-second of December last year, while posing as her nephew.'

'Rubbish,' he snapped.

'You put her in your car, where she subsequently died, probably from shock. You then drove towards Coleshaw – we can map the route you took from the CCTV cameras you passed. You didn't go straight home though, because you had to dispose of Mrs Jones' body, so you went to Coleshaw Woods, where you weighted down her body with stones and the jack from your car and dumped her in the quarry.'

'Preposterous!' Amit exclaimed. 'I don't have to listen to this nonsense.'

'I'm afraid you do,' Beth said. 'The charges are very serious and there is a lot of evidence against you.'

'Like what?' he demanded. His solicitor threw him a warning glance.

'Forensics have found traces of Mrs Jones' DNA on the rear seat of your car despite you cleaning it with disinfectant. And your fingerprints are on the jack we recovered from the quarry. Someone matching your description can be seen on the hospital's CCTV making two visits to St Anne's Ward, where Mrs Jones was a patient. A nurse remembers taking a phone call from you when – posing as Mrs Jones' nephew – you made arrangements to collect her.'

'It must have been someone else,' Burman said arrogantly.

'I don't think so, because on the day you took Mrs Jones, you forgot her bag and left it under her bed. The lady in the bed opposite noticed and sent her son, who was visiting at the time, after you with the bag. He caught up with you as you were about to leave the ward. Both he and his mother remember you, and he has described you accurately. He says you seemed agitated and were sweating a lot. He has also described your eyes exactly. It's very unusual to have completely different-coloured irises, Dr Burman. It's a wonder you didn't buy yourself a pair of matching contact lenses before you began your crimes.' Beth saw his fists tighten in anger as his forehead glistened with sweat. She knew he was only just keeping control.

'Not me,' he said stiffly. 'I wasn't even in the area.'

'Really?' Beth asked. 'That's odd, because the curator of the History of Surgery Museum distinctly remembers you going there on the morning you took Mrs Jones. The museum is only a short drive to the hospital.'

'He must be mistaken.'

'No, he's not. Because we found an entry ticket to the museum for that day in one of your jacket pockets. Together with a receipt from the hotel you stayed in the night before. You really didn't cover your tracks very well, did you? Probably because you are so arrogant you thought no one could touch you.'

'Bitch,' he snarled, leaning forward.

'Careful,' Matt warned him. His solicitor glanced at his client.

'Let's move on,' Beth said, 'to the charges of stealing drugs and body parts from St Mary's Hospital.'

'Ridiculous!' Burman sneered. 'No comment.'

'Dr Burman, you worked at St Mary's Hospital as an anaesthetist. Drugs on your shift have been going missing. You were responsible for signing out the drugs before an operation and then returning any that weren't used after. There are big discrepancies going back nearly a year, always when you were on duty.'

'If you had any knowledge of the workings of hospitals you'd know you can't return drugs that have been opened, even though a fraction might have been used,' Burman said.

'I do know that,' Beth replied. 'It's the same at any pharmacy. But these drugs hadn't been opened. Here is a printout of the drugs that went missing on your shift compared to average wastage.'

'I'll need a copy of that,' his solicitor said and Matt nodded.

Burman shrugged dismissively. 'So I made a couple of recording mistakes.'

The arrogance of the man was unbelievable. 'Too many mistakes to be human error,' Beth said. 'And why did we find drugs labelled St Mary's Hospital in your garden shed?'

'It's a lab,' he growled.

'A nurse has come forward and made a statement saying she saw you slipping unopened drugs into your scrubs in the operating room on a number of occasions.'

'She's lying,' he snapped.

'I doubt it. It took a lot of courage for her to speak out and accuse a doctor. But not only did you steal drugs, you took away body parts without permission. Human organs that we found stored in your so-called lab. Apart from it being illegal, some of those organs were going to be examined for signs of cancer. Those tests haven't been done, so it's likely people will die because they don't know they have the disease. And you call yourself a doctor!'

'They would have died anyway,' he spat defiantly.

There was silence. His solicitor wrote something down. Then Matt asked, 'Why would you want diseased organs?'

Burman sneered at him as if his question didn't deserve a reply. 'No comment,' he said contemptuously.

'For experimenting on?' Matt prompted. 'That's what it seems you were doing from the evidence we took from your lab and office.'

'One day those organs can be cured of the disease and used in spare-part surgery,' Burman said. 'I was advancing medical science, making history, until you heathens stopped me.'

'So you don't deny you took those body parts?' Beth said.

Burman shrugged and wiped the sweat from his forehead.

'There's water there if you want it,' Beth said, referring to the polystyrene cups of water.

Burman ignored her.

'Let's move on, then,' Beth said. 'Unlawful imprisonment of your wife, daughter and Emily King, first in your house, and then later Emily was kept in your so-called lab.'

'No comment.'

'You will also be charged with child abuse, causing grievous bodily harm to your wife, Alisha, and Emily King, and cruelty to animals.'

'Child abuse! That idiot had everything she needed and more than she deserved,' he said.

'Really?' Beth said. 'So Eva deserved to be kept a prisoner, confined to one room, denied an education, social interaction or medical and dental treatment, did she?'

'I'm a doctor, I knew what she needed, and she had her mother for social interaction!' His voice had risen. 'As for using animals, scientists have been experimenting on animals for hundreds of years. How else is medicine to progress?'

'Experiments on animals are carefully monitored,' Matt said. 'You need a licence and checks are made to make sure the animals don't suffer. The ones you took very likely did suffer, and when you'd finished with them you dumped them in Coleshaw Woods.'

'Nonsense,' Amit said.

'Preserving fluid was found in the animals,' Beth said, 'the same solution that was found in the bottles in your lab. And the same solution you'd begun infusing into Emily King before you passed out, which ironically saved her life.'

'That solution is common,' he said agitatedly. 'Taxidermists use it. I'm not taking the blame for those animals.'

'I think you might have to,' Beth said. 'We've found a connection to Emily King. One of the dismembered animals found in Coleshaw Woods belonged to Emily

King: her cat, Tibs. You had its collar and returned it to her, pushing it through her letter box with a note. I think it was at that time you decided to make Emily your subject so she too would suffer. But why pick on her? Because she was friends with your wife?'

'That's nonsense,' Burman said. 'Emily wanted to be part of my experiment.'

Matt stifled a laugh and Burman's solicitor wrote in his notepad.

Beth continued. 'At approximately seven-thirty on the morning of the day Emily disappeared, you saw Ben Johnston, Emily's partner, leave for work. He told you he wouldn't be home until late and you spotted your opportunity to kidnap Emily. You spent all day hatching your plan and getting everything ready, then that night at nine o'clock, threatening to harm Eva if Alisha didn't cooperate, you made your wife phone Emily and ask for her help. Of course Emily would come, she was a nice person and liked to help people. She hesitated because her son, Robbie, was in his cot, but she was just popping next door for a minute and Eva needed milk. She told herself she wouldn't be gone long. Once she arrived, you injected her with a sedative – stolen from St Mary's Hospital – tied her up and forced her to write a letter to Ben, telling him she had left him. Then you took her keys and let yourself in her house, placed the note where Ben would see it and took her phone.'

'All conjecture,' Burman said haughtily. 'You have no evidence for any of this nonsense.'

'No?' Beth said, savouring the moment. Now to bring him down. 'When you forced Emily to write that note it left a perfect impression of all the words on the sheet beneath. We found the writing pad you used in your office. Also, your call history shows your landline was used to phone Emily at nine o'clock that evening. It was only a very short call – Alisha doing what you told her to and asking Emily for help, unlike her other calls to Emily when they chatted for some time. And if all of this wasn't enough to convince a judge and jury of your guilt, Dr Burman, we also have Alisha's statement confirming it.'

Burman couldn't contain himself any longer. 'You're lying!' He thumped the table. The water in the cups jumped. 'Alisha wouldn't dare betray me. She knows what would happen to her and Eva if she did.'

Silence, then Beth said evenly, 'Alisha has betrayed you, Dr Burman. Her statement includes your abuse of her and Eva and the events that led to Emily being taken: you dropping the cat collar, your obsession with preserving life, how you lured Emily to your home, tied her up, injected her and kept all three of them prisoner. I dread to think what went through Emily's mind as she faced being experimented on and certain death. You will be charged with manslaughter, kidnapping, causing grievous bodily harm, unlawfully disposing of a body, false imprisonment, stealing drugs and animal cruelty, all of which will result in a very long sentence. Dr Burman, you will be going to prison for many years, possibly for the rest of your life.'

Unbelievably, Burman began to smile. Beth, Matt, and his solicitor stared at him in amazement. 'It won't matter,' he said. 'Locking me up may slow research, but you will not stop me. I have signed up with ELECT. When I die, my body will be preserved until science discovers a way of giving me immortality, when I shall be woken up and continue where I left off.'

'Wake up dead, more like it,' Matt quipped.

'You can sneer now,' Burman said, his green eye glowing. 'But science is nearly there. I shall have the last laugh when I am living and you two are rotting in your graves.'

Chapter Sixty

'Life, with a minimum of twenty years in prison,' Emily repeated. 'I am pleased. Not just because of what he did to me, Alisha and Eva, but to that poor woman he took from the hospital, and Tibs and the other pets. He's a monster and deserves to be locked up.'

Ben nodded. 'The jury decided he was bad not mad, but I'm not so sure. He left the court shouting that he'd come back from the dead and get his revenge. Sounds pretty mad to me.'

Emily squeezed his hand. 'Thanks for going to court every day. I know it was difficult for you and Dad, but I needed to know what happened to me. I try to remember, but it's a blank after you left for work that morning.'

'The doctor said that wasn't unusual following a trauma. In some ways it's probably best you can't remember.' Ben kissed her cheek. 'Anyway, I'm glad the trial's over and Burman got what he deserved. We can start to rebuild our lives now.'

Emily shifted position on the mound of pillows and tried to get more comfortable. She should be used to hospital beds by now: intensive care, then the high dependency-unit and now this side room attached to the general ward, where she would stay until she was discharged. She couldn't wait to get home and back to the comfort of her own bed.

'The pathologist was good in court,' Ben said reflect-ively, helping himself to another grape from the bowl of fruit on her bedside cabinet. 'He explained everything very clearly to the jury. Some of them had never heard of cryonic preservation before. He said that the only reason you were alive was because Burman had lowered your body temperature to the point where you were in a state of suspended animation. Your heart was only beating once every twenty seconds. We came so close to losing you, Em. If Burman hadn't fallen ill himself and passed out, you wouldn't be here now.' Ben's eyes filled as they did whenever he talked or thought about what had happened. 'I'm pleased he's succumbed to that disease too, bad though that sounds.'

'Alisha wasn't in court to hear the verdict then?' Emily asked, taking his hand.

'No. As far as I know, she hasn't been there since she gave her evidence by video link. I haven't seen her next door either. The house is empty and up for sale. There are some estate agent pictures online.'

Emily shivered. 'Who'd want to buy that house with its history? And that lab.'

'The police took away most of the contents of the lab for evidence. But I was wondering if we should move? Will we ever feel OK about living there, Em, with all those reminders next door?'

'I don't know. Let's see how it goes. Once we have new neighbours we might feel differently.' She gave his hand a gentle squeeze. 'I wonder how Alisha and Eva are doing?'

'I phoned Beth Mayes like you suggested, but all she would say was that they were safe.'

'Poor Alisha. She had such a sad life. She won't have long to live now, with that cruel disease. Her biggest fear was that Eva would end up in an institution. Burman used to threaten her with it.'

'I know, Em, but there's nothing we can do, and the social services will be involved now. You concentrate on getting well so you can come home. Robbie and I miss you dreadfully.'

Emily's phone vibrated with an incoming text message and she picked it up from the bed and read the message. 'It's Greg. He's just heard the verdict and is pleased.' She turned the phone so Ben could see, then she laughed. 'I still can't believe you really thought I'd run off with Greg. He's a good friend but hardly my type.'

Ben laughed too. 'I thought that when I met him, but at the time anything seemed possible. We'll have to invite him and his wife to dinner when you're fully recovered.'

'Yes, that would be nice.'

The door burst open and Robbie flew into the room crying, 'Mummy! Mummy!' excitedly. Ben helped him onto the bed and he snuggled beside his mother.

'Thanks,' Emily said to Ben's parents as they drew up a couple of chairs.

'It's our pleasure. It's the least we can do. So, now the trial's over you'll return to work?' Richard asked his son.

'Yes. I'll go back tomorrow.'

'Your mother and I, together with Emily's parents, will continue to look after Robbie for as long as we're needed.'

'Thank you, Dad.'

'So the jury saw through Burman's lies and the bastard has been found guilty on all counts. I hope he rots in hell,' Richard said vehemently.

'He won't have an easy time of it in prison for sure,' Ben said. 'A doctor convicted of all those crimes, including manslaughter and child abuse, when he's supposed to make people better.'

'He deserves it,' Mary agreed, while Emily nodded and held Robbie closer still.

Chapter Sixty-One

Sleaseford prison, like many prisons in the UK, was overcrowded and short-staffed. Processing new arrivals was a slow job and occupied staff whose time could have been better spent elsewhere in the prison. Burman's arrival at Sleaseford was expected, but processing him took much longer than most new arrivals, which didn't endear him to the staff, not at all. He came across as arrogant, clearly thought the prison officers were beneath him and believed he knew his rights and they did not – not an attractive combination. He complained continuously, refused to cooperate and objected to everything: being placed in a holding cell with others, the intimate body search and having his photograph taken for the ID card he was supposed to carry at all times. So the whole process was tedious and prolonged for all involved. Even when he got to see the medical staff, which he'd been demanding from the moment he'd arrived, he was rude and threatening.

'You're just nurses,' he spat disparagingly. 'I want to see a doctor!'

'You will be able to see a doctor later if necessary,' the senior nurse said. 'Our job is to address any immediate health concerns you may have.'

'I told that idiot at the desk, I have a rare genetic condition. If I suddenly die it's important you contact an organization called ELECT straight away. That stands for Eternal Life Education Cryonics Trust. Have you got that? They will send a practitioner to prepare my body so my organs don't deteriorate.'

'Is this for organ donation?' the younger nurse asked.

'No, you silly cow!' he fumed. 'Just the opposite. It's to prepare me for being transported to the ELECT facility, where I shall be preserved.'

'Don't speak to the staff like that,' the lead nurse said. 'But you don't have to worry about transport. If you do have to leave the prison for any reason we will arrange it for you.'

'Idiots!' Burman shouted, and the prison officer positioned outside the medical room came in. 'I want to see a doctor!' he demanded.

The officer escorted him out and to another holding cell, where he was left to calm down.

Two hours later, he was taken to see the prison doctor.

'You seem to be limping,' the doctor remarked as Burman walked in.

'You noticed,' Burman sneered sarcastically and sat down. 'It's part of my condition, genetic and very rare. They confirmed it while I was in hospital. I'm also sweating a lot. But, more importantly, you need to know what has to happen to my body when I die. An organization called ELECT – it stands for Eternal Life Education Cryonics Trust – must be phoned straight away, the minute I die – before if you know I'm dying.'

'ELECT, you say,' the doctor said and made a note. 'I haven't heard of them, but I will look into it.'

'Look into it! You have to do it now! Supposing I drop dead tomorrow? No one here will have a clue what to do.'

'I'm sure that's not likely to happen, Dr Burman, and the medical staff here are very good if you are unwell. I will look up the organization you mention, but you have to understand that things take time in prison. Resources are stretched to the limit and I have nearly a thousand patients, many of whom have complex needs, so I have to prioritize my time.'

'Fuck you!' Burman shouted. Which brought in the prison officer, ended the consultation and did nothing to persuade the doctor to look into ELECT.

Prisoners like Burman were held on the high-security wing in solitary confinement for their own protection, as child abusers tended to get their faces slashed open if they mixed with other prisoners. Sleaseford prison remained short-staffed, so prisoners were only allowed to exercise in the yard once a day. Sometimes they didn't get let out at all and tensions ran high. Those in the high-security wing passed most of the day lying on their beds watching television, reading or writing letters to loved ones. They hardly stirred when an officer checked on them through the viewing hatch. A quick look to make sure they were behaving themselves and on to the next. So it was 6 p.m., towards the end of the day shift, before anyone suspected Burman might not be just asleep – and by that time it was too late.

'Stone-cold dead,' the officer who found him said. It was six months after his arrival.

A sudden death required an autopsy, so Amit Burman's body was removed to the morgue, where it was kept cold until the autopsy could be done and his organs were removed and examined. The conclusion was that he'd died from natural causes – his heart had just stopped as a result of the condition he'd inherited. No one was to blame, the coroner said, and while short-staffing at the prison resulted in his body not being found for some hours, it was unlikely that anyone could have saved him, even if an officer had been present at the time he'd collapsed. His body was released to his next of kin.

Chapter Sixty-Two

Was she really doing the right thing? Emily asked herself for the umpteenth time that morning. Wouldn't it bring back horrific memories, open doors that had remained locked for good reason? Reveal secrets? Show her things she'd be better off not seeing? Ben had thought so. 'Don't go,' he'd said. 'It will be too upsetting. You can't help her. You don't have to go.' But in a way she did. She was hoping it might give her some closure, for Alisha and Eva remained the missing pieces in a jigsaw. She remembered them from before – when they were friends – but couldn't see them in the room where she'd been held captive. She saw snapshots, glimpses of scenes, experienced smells and sensations, but could never picture them there in the room, and it gnawed at her. Her therapist said it was unlikely she'd remember any more now, not after all this time, unless there was a trigger. Could seeing

Alisha and Eva be that trigger? She wouldn't know unless she tried.

Arriving at the block of flats where Alisha and Eva now lived, Emily parked her car in one of the bays at the side of the building and took her handbag and the bunch of flowers from the passenger seat. Taking a deep breath to calm herself, she got out. A chill had settled in the air, suggesting autumn wasn't far away. It was two years since she'd first got to know Alisha and it was incredible she was still alive given how ill she'd been the last time she'd seen her.

She opened the rear car door, unfastened Robbie's safety harness and helped him out.

'Good boy, hold my hand while we're in the car park.' He tucked his hand into hers.

Emily glanced at him as they walked to the front of the building. Would he remember Alisha and Eva? She doubted it. He'd been very young when they'd all been friends and he'd stopped saying their names during her stay in hospital.

Flat four was on the ground floor, through the main doors and turn right, Alisha had told her on the phone. Her telephone call last week had come as a complete shock. A mobile number Emily hadn't recognized; she nearly hadn't answered. Then the female voice, slight, tentative, as if unsure she had the right to call. 'Emily? Is that Emily King?'

It had taken Emily a moment to place the voice and realize it was Alisha, although she'd thought about her many times and wondered how she was. She'd assumed the disease had progressed and she might even be dead. Alisha had said very little on the phone – only that she needed to see her. Emily had hesitated. 'It's just me and Eva,' she'd said. 'If you could come, it would help us a lot. We're struggling to come to terms with what happened.'

You and me too, Emily had thought, but agreed to go. They set a date and Alisha had texted her address; but it was an hour's drive away. Now she was here her doubts returned and her anxiety grew. She held Robbie's hand tightly and pressed Alisha's doorbell. Was she doing the right thing? There was still time to turn and run. But the decision was made as the door opened and there stood Alisha. Her face rounder, fuller, her hair shining, healthier than Emily ever remembered her being. She handed Alisha the flowers.

'Thank you so much for coming,' Alisha gushed, her voice full of emotion. She hugged Emily and then Robbie. 'It's good to see you again. Come in. Eva can't wait to see you.'

'She remembers Robbie?' Emily asked as they went in.

'Oh yes. And you, and everything she saw in that . . .' She stopped, leaving the sentence unfinished.

They were now in a large open-plan living room adapted for a wheelchair. Eva came towards them, working the controls on a new motorized wheelchair. She looked different, Emily thought. Her forehead seemed less pronounced, perhaps because she'd grown. Then she was smiling.

'Robbie and Emily, thank you for coming.'

'You see!' Alisha cried to her daughter. 'I told you they were OK.' Then looking at Emily, 'One of the reasons I needed you to come was to prove to Eva you were still alive. She wouldn't believe me after everything.'

Robbie hesitated and then ran to her. 'Eva.'

'He remembers me,' Eva said. 'You want to play?' she asked him.

'Yes.'

'Come with me.' Turning her wheelchair, she led the way into a recess off the room that was a large play area. Emily could see shelves full of books, games and toys, all at wheelchair height. 'You choose,' Eva told Robbie.

'Can I make you tea?' Alisha offered.

'Please,' Emily said and tried to relax. Seeing them both again had stirred up many uncomfortable feelings, as Ben had warned it might.

'Sit down and make yourself comfortable,' Alisha said.

Emily did as she said. Alisha not only looked different, but she was behaving differently too – far more confident and self-assured. She was like a different person, not at all what Emily had expected. She could hear her moving around in the kitchen, preparing tea as she had done at the start of their friendship in her old house, but that was the only similarity. Through the patio windows there was a clear view of the open countryside beyond, very different from the views they'd had before. Emily experienced a flashback of her picking dark film from a window, but as usual with these snatches of memory, it vanished as quickly as it had begun.

Alisha returned, carrying a tray laid with tea and home-made pastries, and set it on the coffee table. 'You read about Amit's death?' she said almost casually as she passed Emily tea and a plate.

'Yes,' Emily said, a familiar chill creeping up her spine at the mention of his name.

'He can't harm you now,' Alisha said, seeming to know.

'No, I suppose not,' Emily said. She accepted a pastry and changed the subject. 'You and Eva are doing all right then?'

'Oh yes.' Alisha sat on the sofa beside her. 'I've received a lot of help from social services – this flat, the wheelchair, in fact everything Eva needs. She attends a day centre for children with disabilities. She fits in there, she's normal. She's had an operation on her head to relieve the pressure and will have another one next month.'

'I thought she looked different,' Emily said, finally taking a sip of her tea.

'There is no cure for her condition, but the doctors can help alleviate some of her symptoms and make her more comfortable. They can extend her life.'

'That's good,' Emily said and returned her cup carefully to its saucer.

'I'll never forgive Amit for denying her medical treatment,' Alisha said. 'She should have had proper care.'

'Yes,' Emily said and looked over towards Robbie and Eva playing quietly together.

'Just like old times,' Alisha laughed.

'Not quite,' Emily said and placed her half-drunk tea and untouched pastry on the table. It had been a mistake to come here after all. It didn't feel right, although Alisha seemed very at ease.

'I used to love it when you visited me,' Alisha said brightly. 'You were my only contact with the outside world. I'm sorry for the part I played in you being hurt.'

'What part did you play?' Emily asked, turning to her and dreading what she might say.

Alisha met her gaze. 'I lured you into Amit's trap and didn't help you escape.'

'I know. Ben told me; it came out in court.'

'But what didn't come out was that I discovered what he was planning to do and I did nothing. I couldn't admit that in court in case I was sent to prison as an accessory. I couldn't bear the thought of Eva having to live in an institution.'

'That was always a worry of yours, but you were a victim of Amit's and in his power,' Emily said, her voice flat.

'That's what the judge said in his summing-up.'

Emily felt a shudder of unease as she experienced another flashback; this one was of Alisha watching her as she fought with Amit. She dragged her thoughts back to the present. She didn't want to go there now. 'You look very well,' she said. 'Better than I expected.'

'That's probably because I'm not ill,' Alisha said and gave a low, humourless laugh almost as Amit had that unsettled Emily further. 'I never was ill. I don't have the faulty gene.' Emily stared at her incredulously. 'Only Amit has the faulty gene. He lied to me about the test results and then fed me tablets to mimic the symptoms and make me ill. Eva's tablets were placebos; they did her no good and might have worsened her condition. She is on the correct medication now. Amit played God and lost. I'm in charge now.'

Emily continued to stare at Alisha, her unease building. She wished she could feel as confident as Alisha did that Amit couldn't harm her. 'Where is his body?' she asked; it was one of the questions that had tormented her.

'You needn't worry. When it was released by the coroner, I had him cremated. I hope that gives you the closure you need.'

'Yes, it does,' Emily said. She still had plenty of questions, unresolved issues, but not now. Amit had been cremated, so there was no chance of him coming back from the dead – now or ever. Did she really need to know more? She'd think about it. She could always phone Alisha, for she doubted she'd visit again.

Her phone vibrated with a text message and she took it from her bag. It was Ben. He knew she was coming. *Are you OK?*

'Who's that?' Alisha asked, trying to see her phone screen.

'Ben,' she said and texted back: *Yes. Just about to leave* xx

'Well, thanks for the tea,' she said, making a move to go.

'You're leaving already? You didn't eat the pastry I made.'

'Sorry, I'm not hungry,' Emily said and stood, an overriding need to get away.

Robbie seemed ready to leave too and came to her without being asked.

Alisha was clearly put out they were leaving so soon. 'Make sure you stay in touch,' she said as she reluctantly saw them to the door.

'Of course,' Emily lied.

Alisha waited by her front door and watched Emily and Robbie go. Just before they left the path and disappeared from view, Emily turned and gave a little wave. Alisha waved back and closed the door.

Alisha was so different from the vulnerable victim Emily remembered, and her need to know more was lessening. Ben was right that some things were better left alone. She would accept this visit as closure and move on.

Robbie was very quiet; perhaps seeing them had stirred up bad memories for him too. Who knew what a small child could remember?

'Are you OK, little man?' Emily asked him.

He nodded but didn't say anything. She'd talk to him later about their visit. She opened the car door and Robbie clambered in and fastened his own safety harness. She checked it and then went round to the driver's door and got in. Setting the satnav for home, she started the engine, relieved she'd been brave enough to come here and confront her fears but glad it was over. She'd be home well before Ben and would make a nice meal and open a bottle of wine. They could toast their future, one without the ghosts of the past. She'd seen Alisha and that was enough. The family who'd moved in next door were lovely and she and Ben were getting to know them. They'd got the house cheap at auction because a quick sale was needed and were making big changes. The small dark windows had been replaced by bigger, lighter picture windows, and the overgrown gardens – back and front – were now trimmed and neat. Amit's lab, which had formed so many of her nightmares, had been completely demolished and in its place was a raised flower bed, alive with flowers throughout the year. The owners knew what had happened to Emily but were sensitive enough not to want to discuss it.

Halfway home Robbie fell asleep and Emily switched on the radio for company: an easy-listening channel, the music interrupted every fifteen minutes for news updates. The usual items: the stock exchange, a bomb going off in a war-torn country, a state visit, a lottery win, then, 'Scientists have had a major breakthrough in extending life indefinitely through a process called cryonics.' Emily slowed the car and turned up the volume. 'Scientists working in the research unit of ELECT, a life-extension foundation, have taken a huge step towards allowing us to live forever. They have successfully brought back a chimpanzee from the dead. It had died from organ failure and was preserved in liquid nitrogen until a suitable donor organ became available. A spokesperson from ELECT said,

“Humans share ninety-nine per cent of their DNA with chimpanzees, making them our closest living relatives. It’s only a matter of time before we carry out the same procedure on humans.”’

Emily’s heart raced and she felt clammy with a familiar panic attack. She tried to calm herself and breathe deeply. Of course this research would continue. Why shouldn’t it? But there was no chance of Amit being brought back, he’d been cremated. There was nothing of him left to work on, just a heap of ash. Or was there?

She braked, her stomach contracted and she went cold with fear. Pulling to the side of the road, she stopped the car. Something hadn’t been right with her visit to Alisha. She’d felt it as soon as she’d walked in. It was as if it had been staged and Alisha had been putting on an act, but why? What for? She’d made a point of telling her that Amit couldn’t ever harm her again as she’d had him cremated. But was that true? She’d lied to her before. And something else was bothering her. Alisha had said – *I don’t have the faulty gene. Only Amit does,* in the present tense as if he was still alive. Her hands shook as she took her phone from her bag, googled the number for ELECT and then pressed to connect.

‘Good afternoon. Eternal Life Education Cryonics Trust. How can I help you?’ a female voice asked.

Emily tried to hold her voice steady. ‘I’ve just heard your news on the radio.’

‘Yes, isn’t it fantastic? We’re all very excited. Would you like some literature?’

'No, I'm aware of your work.' She paused and steeled herself. 'I just wanted to make sure my husband is being well looked after. I'm Dr Burman's widow.'

'Yes, of course. Everything is fine. As you know, Dr Burman's body wasn't preserved as quickly as we would have liked at the time of his death, but we're confident his damaged organs can be replaced when the time comes. And your registration is complete, so we'll let you know as soon as we have any more news.' Emily cut the call and stared straight ahead, sick and cold with fear. 'Amit played God and lost,' Alisha had said. 'I'm in charge now.' And it seemed she was just as evil as he was, maybe worse.

Author's note

While this story is fiction, human embryos are routinely frozen for later use and cryonic preservation is very real. At the time of writing this book, 1,000 people have signed up to have their bodies or just their heads stored in liquid nitrogen, in the belief they will be brought back to life, cured and continue living. The numbers are growing year on year, and who knows? They may be right. Time will tell.

Suggested topics for reading group discussion

The Doctor begins with the words: 'We all want to live forever, don't we?' Would you?

Dr Burman takes his research to the extreme. What do you think fuels his misplaced ambition?

How would you describe the main characters: Emily, Ben, Alisha, Amit, Greg and Eva?

When Emily is kidnapped, she and her partner, Ben, have a lot of time to reflect. What do we learn about their relationship?

Given that Alisha loves and protects her daughter, Eva, couldn't she have done more for her? What stopped her?

Why do you think Emily and Greg became good friends? Did their partners, Ben and Amy, have anything to worry about in respect of them becoming more than just friends?

Bearing in mind the evidence at the time, were DC Beth Mayes and DC Matt Davis right in grading Emily as a low-priority missing person?

Near the end of the book, Alisha apologizes to Emily for the role she played. What choices could she have made?

The book ends on a cliff-hanger. How do you see the story progressing after we leave it?

His death was just the beginning. . .

The first spellbinding crime thriller from
bestseller Lisa Stone.

FORBIDDEN SUNS

BY D. NOLAN CLARK

The Silence

Forsaken Skies
Forgotten Worlds
Forbidden Suns